CROSSING A LINE

A John Deacon Action Adventure

Mike Boshier

VIP Reader's Mailing List

To join our VIP Readers Mailing List and receive updates about new books and freebies, please go to the end section of this book.

Copyright © 2018 Mike Boshier
All rights reserved.
ISBN: 978-0-473-42622-4
www.mikeboshier.com

Acknowledgements

I would like to thank the following people for their assistance and support in completing this book. Sandra van Eekeren for her proofreading and editing skills, Peter Cook for proofreading, and the Pilot Readers Team for their support and enthusiasm. Eternal thanks to my wife and daughters who support me in my dreams.

If you liked reading this book, please leave feedback on whatever system you purchased this from.

Check out the rear pages of this book for details of other releases, information and free stuff.

Author's Other Books

High Seas Hijack - Short Story

The Jaws of Revenge

Terror of the Innocent

Chapter 1

He was running for his life. But he knew he wouldn't make it!

They'd beaten him. Hard. And used water torture. But he hadn't admitted anything. After six hours they'd left him unconscious, half hanging off the chair. Three teeth had come out - he'd swallowed one - and his lips were bloodied and bruised. Two fingers were broken - bent outwards at unnatural angles, and two had been cut-off with shears. He'd screamed and passed out when they'd done that, but they'd kept waking him back up by dowsing him in icy cold water. They'd also sliced off an ear before partly bandaging his head to quell the bleeding. He'd passed out then as well. Then they had needed a break and left him tied while they went and for their evening meal.

Slowly at first, he'd managed to slide one bruised and twisted arm up towards the knots. His first and second fingers of his right hand were missing and crudely bandaged, but with a supreme effort, he managed to gently grip the rope between his thumb and third finger. With vomit rising in his throat from the pain, he gently began pulling on the knots until at last one began to ease free.

As the ropes holding him relaxed their grip, he fell heavily to the floor into a drying pool of his own blood and urine. The barn was dark and stank of animals, the concrete floor covered with straw, soil and animal waste. He vomited as it splashed into his face and mouth, but he slowly recovered and tried to stand. They hadn't damaged his feet yet. One of the last things they'd said laughingly before leaving for their meal was his toes would be next when they returned, but for now, he could still walk, albeit shakily.

He moved cautiously towards the doorway. The only faint lighting was coming from the main building showing dimly from behind the shutters. Feeling a little strength coming back he hobbled towards the gates. He unlatched the first, closing it behind him to try to mask his escape, before moving on to the outer exit. His mind, still foggy from the beating, assumed the gate guards had also left for their meal.

Finally, he was free. The single track would be easy for them to catch him on when they found him missing, so he headed into the forest. There was no moon and although the stars were incredibly bright, very little light managed to break through the dense forest canopy. He was cold. His muscles were slowly warming and loosening, but a cold thin, misty rain had started falling. Moving as fast as he could over the wet slippery leaves he could feel sharp branches and thorns swiping at his face and snagging at his clothes. The ground was covered with pine needles, fallen dead branches, dead and decaying leaves as well as new vegetation trying hard to grow in the constant shade. Some parts were almost bare allowing him faster movement over the hard terrain, others denser, slowing him down. It was only early August, but this year the summer had been miserable, and it was as warm as it got here. Soon the icy fingers of winter would crawl south over this land freezing it solid as the days grew shorter.

The faster he tried to run the more he stumbled. Twice he fell and bumped straight into trees, the second time his damaged hand hitting the trunk with a rush of pain making him dry-vomit yet again. He knew the compound was near the center of the private land and that the nearest perimeter fence was almost nine miles away, with any other property at least a mile or two further, but he estimated if he could make maybe two miles an hour he would be clear before first light.

After an hour he stopped for a five-minute breather, leaning his back onto a wide tree trunk for support. Although his body was battered and damaged, his brain was still sharp, and as his mind cleared he began to question why the gates had been unmanned? They were always guarded. Even at mealtimes, he thought. Why had it been empty now? Had someone arranged this to allow him to escape? Did he have a friend there? They'd left his feet alone. Why?

Then it came to him, and he vomited again. They were going to send out a hunting party, and he was the prey!

The fear renewed his energy and he lunged on. Keeping to a straight line through the forest was impossible. There were no tracks or paths to follow and the trees and vegetation varied from sparse to impenetrably dense. Twice he got tangled so badly he had to backtrack, wasting valuable minutes. He estimated he'd gone almost another four miles when he thought he heard the horn. He stopped; pulse racing. Could he be sure? Had he imagined it? Then he heard it again. Very faintly. The soft breeze gently bringing the sound to him through the trees. Pulse racing he ran as fast as he could, although in practice it was little more than a quick hobble through the undergrowth.

Over the next half hour, the horn sounded louder and clearer. The pursuers were gaining, but the thickness of the forest made it impossible to estimate how close they were. Pushing on, he stumbled into a clearing. He could make fast time across this area, but so could his pursuers. Looking up briefly he was amazed at the vastness of the sky. The rain had stopped, and the cloud had dispersed while he had been under the tree canopy. It seemed to him to be the biggest sky he'd ever seen, stretching infinitely into the distance. With the cloud gone and with the chilled air so clear the hundred billion stars were so bright he could almost have read a book by the light of them. Truly, he thought, some of God's better work.

Hurrying on towards the darkened edge of the clearing, he made rapid progress, but as he passed into the arms of the thick foliage, he glanced back and saw the loom of torches where he had been just minutes before. Panicked now and with an extra surge of adrenaline he rushed on as fast as he could manage, not caring about making noise. He'd made another three hundred yards progress when a sound so demonic, so terrifying, made his skin crawl and his bowels open. Shaking with fear he saw the glint of moonlight reflecting off the dark brown eyes of the General's two Rottweilers. They were standing facing him almost fifteen feet away, lips drawn back and uttering soft growls.

Terrified, he froze. Minutes later four men came up from behind him, two of them carrying shovels. As they approached, he couldn't hold back the tears. It was all over. This had been a game to them. He'd never see his wife or son and daughter again. Even worse, they'd never know what happened to him or where his body lay, to visit his grave. His only solace was if his body was going to lie somewhere then amongst the trees and under the stars was as good a place as any.

The General looked at him and said, "You made better time than we thought. Another mile and you'd have been free. It was a good chase. Now tell me, who do you work for?"

He considered his options and thought about the outcome. Then, looking the General straight in the eye, he said, "Go fuck yourself!"

The General's face filled with rage and he screamed, "Attack!" and both growling dogs leapt at the injured man. One clamped his enormous mouth tightly over the man's groin crushing his testicles before shaking his head from side-to-side, while the other latched onto the man's wrist chewing the bones to a pulp. As he collapsed, the dog let go of his wrist, jumped over his leg and sank its teeth into the man's left calf muscle before beginning to tear at it.

"Hold!" and the dogs stopped twisting, merely pulled and kept their jaws clamped.

Playing with his hunting horn, the General said, "We know you're with the FBI. You're from the Buffalo, New York office. You're married with two rug rats. We've known all along. You never had a chance. One of your colleagues betrayed you. You and your sort will never stop us. We're stronger than ever, and more are joining us every day. How does it feel to know you've lost?"

As he began to pass out through pain and loss of blood, he could see the other two men were trying to dig a shallow grave. The matting of pine needles and vegetation were making it hard for their shovels to penetrate the hard ground and he smiled a little. He thought he could hear the sound of cloth tearing. Suddenly the pressure on his leg relaxed as he realized the tearing noise had been his own leg muscle ripping apart.

With more strength than he knew he had, he raised his head, looked straight at his assailant and said, "Fuck you, asshole!"

With blood veins pulsing, the General screamed, "Kill!" and the two Rottweilers relaxed their grips, reared up on the hind legs and attacked again. This time one going for the soft tissues of the stomach and the other going for the throat. Neither dog would stop until they had ripped their target apart.

As the light faded from the FBI agents eyes, his last thoughts were of how they'd found out and who had betrayed him. As his view finally darkened, all he could see were the faces of his loved ones.

Chapter 2

Lieutenant John Deacon slowed from his morning's jog around the inside perimeter of the Naval Amphibious Base Coronado. Born in 1981 and raised in Norfolk, Virginia, his life had always centered around the Navy. His father had joined up aged twenty-three, directly from university, ending up commanding an attack submarine. His mother had been an accountant, but both were now retired. The middle of three children, his sisters were happily married with the elder having two young boys who adored their adventurous uncle. Tall and muscular he'd always been incredibly fit, playing American football at college and in the high school swimming team. Graduating Columbia University in Political Science and Mechanical Engineering, he'd also chosen the Navy specifically with the SEALs in mind. He'd finished high in each of the rankings, performing particularly well in swimming and unarmed combat. He had a wry sense of humor, was equally at ease talking with an Admiral or a dockworker, was always willing to push himself to extremes and was 100% dependable.

At a little over six foot tall and with short dark hair, he'd never considered himself particularly good looking, especially with the scar across his chin - the result of falling off a motorbike he'd been trying to repair when he was fifteen, but women didn't seem to agree. Slightly rugged and with dark brown eyes he always found it easy to have a lady on his arm when it suited. Still keen on fitness, every morning, where possible, he would rerun the initial SEAL endurance test; a five-hundred-yard swim, followed by forty-two push-ups, fifty-six press-ups, six dead-hang pull-ups, and finishing with a ten-mile run.

Hands on hips and breathing hard he stopped as he saw a Humvee approaching.

"Lieutenant. Base Commander wants to see you in fifteen. Jump in, I'll give you a lift to your quarters," the driver called.

Climbing in, the Humvee sped them away.

Ten minutes later, showered and changed into fresh BDU's, Deacon was walking across the parade ground to the offices of the Base Commander, wondering what was up. He'd been back from vacation over three weeks now. The vacation had been for the marriage of a former SEAL's widow, and Deacon had proudly walked her down the aisle and given her away. He'd then taken a ten-day break sailing from San Diego up to Los Angeles via Catalina Island, along with some friends and Rachel Sanchez - his long-time girlfriend who lived in San Francisco. Since returning, he'd been running training courses and exercise regimes for new recruits before waiting to be posted back overseas to re-join his team. He'd also fitted in a two-day trip to the Pentagon.

During his last mission, he'd been involved in the rescue of five young American female aid workers who had been kidnapped and held in Mosul, Iraq. During the rescue, he'd found one of the girls about to be raped by two of the kidnappers. He'd shot and killed both of the attackers, and they had eventually all made their escape. However, he believed the girl had been suffering from Stockholm Syndrome - a phenomenon first identified in 1973 in which hostages express empathy and sympathy and have positive feelings toward their captors, sometimes to the point of defending and identifying with the captors. After her rescue, she had accused Deacon of murdering her 'boyfriend' and had gained attention with the news media. Smelling blood, a gung-ho new-age anti-government news reporter, Lynda Anderson, had picked up on the story. Other news outlets and TV stations, eager for newsworthy stories, had followed suit and eventually public opinion had pushed for a hearing to determine whether Deacon had used unnecessary force and committed murder. The Navy had already decided there was no case to answer, but the hearing had gone ahead a few weeks previously, and Deacon was still waiting for it to be officially closed. Maybe it was something to do with that, or maybe Deacon was being sent overseas again, he mused.

Arriving at the Base Commanders office, he knocked and waited.

"Come."

"Sir, you wanted to see me."

"Yes, Lieutenant. Take a seat. The official word has now come back from your hearing. I think it's bullshit, son, but the Navy is taking it to a full court-martial."

"What the fuc–."

The door opened behind Deacon, and a figure entered. "Lieutenant," the Base Commander continued in a louder voice, "You are to be placed under arrest with immediate effect to await trial at a future date. I'm sorry, Lieutenant, I've done all I can. Attention!"

Standing to attention while trying to understand what was happening Deacon felt his hands being pulled behind his back and handcuffed together.

"Is that really necessary?" the Base Commander asked.

"Standard procedure, sir," the Chief Master-at-Arms holding Deacon's wrists said. "Lieutenant, let's do this quietly," then turning towards the Base Commander he said, "Thank you, sir," before leading Deacon outside and marching him, aided by two other Master-at-Arms, to the main cell block.

On arrival, the Chief Master-at-Arms removed the handcuffs and placed Deacon in a cell. Waiting to meet him was Captain Charles Santori. After introducing himself, Santori said, "Lieutenant, I am from the Judge Advocate General department. I will be representing you. You are being Court Martialed under the Uniform Code of Military Justice (UCMJ) charged with two counts of second-degree murder of Masoud Saadi and his accomplice, identity unknown."

"But this is bullshit, sir. The bastards were about to rape her."

"I've read the action reports from you and your men. I've also reviewed the hearing notes. Personally, I think the outcome of your hearing was decided prior to its end by social media and publicity. Lynda Anderson managed to rally enough support to accuse you of the wanton murder of Masoud Saadi and his colleague and this was supported by evidence from Laura Williams herself, although the other girls, including her sister Michelle

Williams, have confirmed her infatuation with Masoud. However, with two men dead and only your word against hers, JAG decided they need a full investigation. To make matters worse, we have a presidential election coming up, and both candidates are worried about being seen as soft on crime and punishment or even worse, covering things up. The press and news media are clamoring for a trial, and I believe that is what has swung it in favor of a court-martial."

"So what happens next?" Deacon said.

"We go to trial in ten days. I will be representing you. My colleague, Captain Wilma Gregson, will be prosecuting counsel. The Judge overseeing this will be Vice-Admiral James Bainbridge. He is the Judge Advocate General of the Navy. Because this involves the alleged murder of civilians by a serving officer, for a crime of this severity, there will be a jury panel of up to eleven officers. The trial will be held behind closed doors - there will be no public access.

"The important thing now is to tell me everything. Don't leave anything out. I need to get as much collaborative evidence as I can. So let's start at the beginning ..."

For the next two days Deacon went over and over every detail he could remember. Santori had access to Deacon's and his men's action reports, and they went over them with a fine toothcomb. Santori also had a detailed transcript of the recent hearing with witness reports from Laura herself, plus her sister Michelle, as well as from colleagues Cheryl Thompson, Emily Baker, and Debbie Morgan. This too was repeatedly examined for any possible flaw or error.

For the remainder of the time Deacon just sat there worried at the possible outcome.

Chapter 3

The morning of the trial started as most other Californian days start. The weather was warm and sunny with a gentle breeze blowing in off the sea.

The eleven jury officers had been flown in from various locations. Deacon didn't know any of them. He had been introduced to Vice-Admiral James Bainbridge and also to Captain Wilma Gregson, both based in Washington, who'd also flown in the night before.

The room being used was a smaller version of a traditional courtroom you'd see on TV, with the eleven jury officers being seated on the left. The judge sat facing the court on a raised platform with a long table in front of him. Tables and chairs were arranged for Deacon and his defense counsel to be seated to the left in front of the judge, and the prosecuting counsel to be seated to the right. There were two armed guards outside the door, and the Chief Master-at-Arms was stood just inside. In the corner sat the court stenographer, a lady in her mid-fifties. The room smelled of polish with just a faint background smell of tobacco smoke.

"Gentlemen," Vice-Admiral Bainbridge began, "This will be a closed hearing. We have a Press Office who will deal with the public. I suggest if any of you are approached directly, you merely refuse to comment and leave any interaction with them to us. Although we have two ladies present, I will be addressing the court collectively as Gentlemen."

He then explained the court would be relying on first-hand accounts, from written statements from men still overseas, from notes from the civilian hearing and finally, there would be a video link to receive live questioning directly to the same men serving overseas. The format would be for the prosecution to state their case this morning. After lunch, the defense would state theirs. He expected the case would be concluded by mid-afternoon. Finally, he banged his gavel on the desk once before calling the court to order.

"Lieutenant John Deacon. You are charged under the Uniform Code of Military Justice with two counts of second-degree murder of Masoud Saadi and his unknown accomplice in Mosul, Iraq, on the night of June 3rd of this year. How do you plead?"

"Not guilty, sir."

"Noted. Prosecution, your first witness."

Captain Wilma Gregson then took to the floor.

"Lieutenant, it is alleged that on the night in question you chose to murder two Iraqi nationals in cold blood on the pretext of rescuing Laura Williams from the hands of her kidnappers. It is further alleged that you made personal threats against Miss Williams at the time and in the hours following the rescue ..."

Over the next two hours, Gregson read aloud report after report from the previous hearing, stating Laura Williams had become Masoud Saadi's lover, with the plan for him to help them escape. Gregson claimed Laura Williams had become intimate with Masoud Saadi of her own volition and that Deacon had rushed in and shot and murdered both men in cold blood.

After lunch, the court reconvened, and Captain Charles Santori took the floor.

"Gentlemen, sirs. This complete case is built on fantasy imagined by an impressionable eighteen-year-old girl who fantasized about romantic rides over sand dunes with her handsome Arabic lover. A fantasy fairy tale romance completely at odds with reality. The reality was somewhat different. In fact, the defendant saved her from being raped at that time by at least one terrorist kidnapper, possibly two. We will show how only by his and his men's brave actions she is alive today and able to tell her tale. Lieutenant Deacon should receive a medal for what he and his men accomplished, not be on trial here today.

"Lieutenant, please take the stand and explain, in your own words, what happened that day. We've all read the mission notes so start from when you were dropped near Mosul."

Deacon saluted and walked to the stand. He took the oath then started his story.

"Sirs, as you know, the mission was to rescue the five female American hostages being held in central Iraq. We had information confirming where they were being held and we were using a local, Hakim Gerbali, who thought he was working for both the Jordanian Intelligence Service and the USA, in fact, he was working for Mossad and for us. Anyway, we parachuted in a few miles upriver and swam towards Mosul. Hakim met us on the riverbank and led us through the sleeping town to what

15

we hoped was the correct building. When we arrived, we disabled the gate guard, and Chief Martock and I made our way downstairs under the main building to where we thought the girls were being held. I left Hakim up near the gate and Petty Officer Hancock upstairs where we'd come in on guard as there were unfriendlies in the vicinity. We made our way downstairs to the basement where we found a locked door with an empty chair outside. We forced the door and found four of the five girls sleeping. Laura's sister, Michelle, confirmed Laura was missing. I sent the four girls upstairs with Martock while I checked the rest of the basement. Moving along the corridor, I heard murmuring and came to another closed door with light shining from underneath. As I pushed open the door, I could see who I assumed to be Laura laying on her back on a filthy mattress with her skirt pulled up to her waistline, and her blouse ripped open. There was one male kneeling by her head with one hand holding her wrists together above her head and his other hand rubbing her naked breasts. The other male in the room was kneeling between her thighs with his shorts down. He was massaging his erection, and it was obvious he was about to penetrate her. She was struggling, and the sound I'd heard was her crying and saying 'no' through a rag stuffed in her mouth. She certainly didn't look like she was enjoying it. I shot the one holding her hands in the head then kicked the other one off her before shooting him twice in the chest. I identified myself then helped pull her clothes together and picked her up to carry her upstairs. She began to panic and started saying he was her boyfriend and she loved him and that I was a murderer."

"What happened next, Lieutenant?"

"I tried to quieten her down. There were unfriendlies in the building upstairs and we were right in the center of town in the middle of the night, surrounded by ISIS. She started struggling and began to cry. Then I heard her inhale ready to scream. My only option was to put her in a sleep hold, which I did, and we made our exit. We all managed to get out of the building safely but unfortunately, within minutes ISIS had detected our escape and we had to fight our way out. However, we suffered no injuries to ourselves or to the rescued hostages."

"Did you threaten her or any of the girls again?"

"At one stage about thirty minutes later, we were waiting by the riverbank about to escape by boat when Laura started crying louder and louder. I grabbed her and threatened to leave her there or something if she didn't keep quiet I think."

"Any other time, Lieutenant?"

"Not that I can remember, sir."

"What about your men. Did any of them threaten any of the girls?"

"Yes, sir. We had made our first part of the escape and had commandeered a fast launch. Some of us were wearing Arabic clothing in disguise, and it was working well. As we were passing under one of the major road bridges under the eyes of ISIS looking down towards us, Laura suddenly leapt to her feet and started screaming. They immediately began to fire on us, and we had to take evasive action to avoid being hit. Chief Martock slapped her hard across the face and demanded she stay quiet. After that, she remained quiet for the remainder of the journey."

"So, Lieutenant, would you say she put you and your team along with her colleagues in danger?"

"Sir, she's a young girl having suffered a traumatic event of being kidnapped and almost raped. Her crying out didn't help the situation, but we were surrounded by the enemy, under intense pressure and fleeing for our lives. Therefore I don't believe her actions made the situation particularly worse."

At that stage, Captain Santori connected the video screen, and the image of CPO Martock came onto the screen. Under questioning, Martock confirmed much of what Deacon had said.

After completing the questioning, Captain Santori sat down.

Captain Gregson took to the floor and addressed the screen.

"Chief Martock. Just one question. You didn't actually see the two men Lieutenant Deacon killed holding down Laura Williams or about to allegedly rape her, so all you had to go on was the word of the Lieutenant. Is that correct?"

"Yes sir, but I had n–"

"Yes or no, Chief Martock."

"Well yes, bu–"

"No buts, Chief. Let the record show Chief Martock answered he only had the accused's words to go on."

"Thank you, Chief. No more questions of you," Captain Gregson said switching off the screen. "Gentlemen, Sirs. We only have the word of Lieutenant Deacon as to what happened down in the basement. You have all read Laura Williams signed statement that she and Masoud Saadi had become lovers and that he was helping them to plan an escape. In her statement, she clearly says Lieutenant Deacon shot and murdered both men in cold blood. She claims they both had their hands up surrendering but that Lieutenant Deacon took no notice and executed them anyway. She also states she was constantly threatened by Deacon during the remainder of the rescue and was so frightened she was unable to mention this to anyone until after she had been returned safely to America."

"Objection. You mean until she had met an ambulance chasing lawyer who thought she can get money for this fantasy story," Captain Santori said loudly.

"Gentlemen. GENTLEMEN. I will not allow shouting out in this hearing. The objection is overruled, and the jury will ignore it. We will break for fifteen minutes then I will hear closing arguments," Vice-Admiral Bainbridge said.

In the closing arguments, Captain Gregson highlighted the reckless manner of their escape from Mosul, how Admiral Carter had said their escape plan was 'crazy', that Lieutenant Deacon had become a 'loose cannon' who took matters into his own hands including choosing to murder two innocent Iraqi's doing their best to free the hostages and who had surrendered.

Captain Santori then stood and addressed the audience. He stated how Laura was distressed and shocked and her word cannot be relied upon. She was a young girl first time away from home and kidnapped and terrified at the possible outcome. She had become infatuated by her kidnapper, and it was only by the fearless actions and rescue by Lieutenant Deacon and his men that she is alive today and free to tell her story.

Thanking both counsels, Vice-Admiral Bainbridge took to the floor and said, "This case is quite simple. Did Lieutenant Deacon use excessive force and murder two innocent Iraqi's who were trying to help free the hostages and who had surrendered, as Laura Williams states, or were the men killed legitimately as part of normal enemy action? This is for you, the jury, to decide. This case has generated lots of publicity. It has been reported in the national newspapers above the fold for 1 day, below it for 1, before moving on to pages 5 and 6. It has also been discussed by all the major international news stations including CNN, Fox, the BBC, and Al Jazeera. Many eyes abroad have taken an interest in whether members of the United States Military are seen to be above the law. That is not for you to decide. Your decision must be based on the evidence presented here today whether Lieutenant John Deacon is guilty of murder or not."

Deacon was escorted out under guard to a waiting room while the Judge and jury deliberated. Sat there, Captain Santori put a hand on Deacon's shoulder and said, "They don't have a case. It's all supposition. Her word against yours. Don't worry, it'll be thrown out."

"What did the judge mean 'above the fold?'" Deacon asked.

"He was referring to important stories being printed on the top half of a broadsheet page so to be seen while folded. Less important stories on the front page are lower down or on inside pages. Just referring to the amount of Press interest, that's all."

Thirty minutes later they were called back in.

Captain Santori, Captain Gregson and Lieutenant Deacon stood rigidly to attention.

Vice-Admiral Bainbridge took to the floor again and said, "Members of the Jury. Have you come to a verdict on which you all agree?"

"Yes sir, we have," the jury foreman said.

"Please state your verdict."

"Guilty on both counts of second-degree murder!"

Chapter 4

Deacon just stood there unable to believe his ears. Guilty? Of second-degree murder? For just doing his goddam job? For killing two dirty little ISIS terrorists who'd kidnapped American girls, were holding them hostage and were about to rape one of them? No, this couldn't be happening.

Turning his head, he could see the shocked look on Captain Santori's face. Even Captain Gregson looked surprised at the verdict. He suddenly felt his arms being clasped and being moved away.

"What?"

"Lieutenant. You weren't listening. I called for a two-hour recess where I will take advisement on your sentence," Judge Bainbridge said, as Deacon was led away back to the cells.

Almost in a daze Deacon was led back outside and across the courtyard to the cell block. Once inside, his handcuffs were removed, and even the Master-at-Arms said he was surprised at the outcome.

Two hours later, he was re-cuffed and marched back to the courtroom.

Deacon stood to attention next to Captain Santori.

"Lieutenant John Deacon," Judge Bainbridge said, "you have been found guilty on both charges of second-degree murder of two innocent male Iraqi's. The usual sentence for this crime would be fifteen years confinement for each crime to run consecutively. However, due to your exemplary record while serving this country, I have taken advice, and the decision of this court is not to award a custodial sentence in this instance. You will, however, be immediately dishonorably discharged from the United States Naval Service with the immediate loss of all benefits. You will be escorted from here to your quarters where you will have fifteen minutes to gather your personal belongings. You will then be escorted to the Master-at-Arms office where you will sign the relevant paperwork and then, Mister Deacon, as a civilian you will be escorted off the base. You have brought dishonor to the fine tradition of the US Navy SEALs, to the US Navy as a whole and to the long and unblemished record of your father. You should hang your head in shame and be eternally thankful this court has chosen to be lenient with you. Now, as a civilian, this base is off-limits to you, so please leave. Dismissed."

Twenty-five minutes later, a shell-shocked Deacon drove his truck out through the main gates of the Naval Amphibious Base in Coronado, a medium-sized leather holdall in the rear. Most of his belongings were supplied by the Navy - even his watch. He had grabbed some loose shirts, jeans and chinos, some T-shirts, swim shorts and underwear and a leather jacket. He had a personal cell phone and some CDs, but everything else had been supplied as part of his position. Word had quickly spread, and most of his friends and colleagues had come and shaken his hand, wishing him well, not believing him guilty, but a small number of former colleagues had turned and walked away when seeing him, making it clear they thought he'd brought the service into disrepute. Outside the gatehouse, two television trucks were parked with crews and news reporters partly blocking the road. He slowed and suddenly found himself confronted by hand-held microphones and cameras thrust into his face through the open driver's window.

"How does it feel to be a murderer?"

"What do you think of the court sentence? Shouldn't you be in jail?"

"What are you going to do now?"

"Your father was a successful Naval Officer. How does it feel to have brought shame on his name?"

Shouting through the window for them to stand clear, he accelerated and headed south down Silver Strand Boulevard, his mind still in a daze. Three hours previously he'd been Lieutenant O-3 John Deacon of the US Navy SEALs Team 3 with a full career path laid out in front of him. Now he was a civilian again with no job and nowhere to live; just a truck, a few clothes and a little over 15,000 dollars in the bank.

He stopped at a gas station and filled the tank, grabbed a dried-out looking sandwich, a couple of energy bars and some water before climbing back into his truck, tuned the radio into a local rock station, and drove away.

Chapter 5

It was late October and winter had come in hard and fast. Snow flurries blew across the road, and the sky was grey. The forecast had said there'd be a heavy snowfall this evening which would actually warm the outside temperature slightly from today's 35F, but the wind would cause problems. The road was already icy, and a layer of snow on top would make it worse. But people living in this region of northwest America were used to harsh winters.

In the three months since he'd been discharged Deacon had tried to keep a low profile. The news people had lost interest a day or two after the court's announcement - news only sells when it's hot and current, and Deacon had dropped out of sight. The first night he'd driven north to Escondido and rented a cheap motel room before driving up to San Francisco to stay a few days with Rachel. Their time together had been tense, but their relationship had held. He still hadn't come to terms with what had happened, and the anger inside him grew. They'd gone out to a bar, and his picture had appeared on the TV on a 'News of the Week' review program. Some smart ass in a group had recognized him, and a scuffle had started. A table had been broken, and a couple of bottles smashed, but Deacon managed to get himself and Rachel away before the police had arrived. But he knew he needed to leave. The following morning they kissed warmly before he climbed back into his truck and drove away.

Since then, things had gone downhill.

Apart from when he was on missions and had needed to blend in with the locals with longer hair, he'd always kept it short and stayed cleanly shaven. Now he couldn't be bothered. It was down past his ears, greasy and lank. He also had three to four days of stubble, and his clothes hadn't been washed for almost a week. He'd traveled around and tried to get some bar work, but none of the jobs had held. He'd got into a couple of bar fights and had been arrested twice, luckily once in California and the second time in Nevada. Both times he'd spent the night in the cells but been let off the following morning with a warning, but twice in the same US State would have seen him charged.

Now he was heading north on Interstate 15, just south of Helena, Montana. It was late afternoon and what sun had been glimpsed was fast disappearing down over the hills. There were spent food wrappers covering the footwells of the truck and empty beer cans strewn around. He had an open Coors in the coffee holder and had just taken a mouthful when a strong side gust of wind made him cross the white lane divider momentarily.

Officers Larry Merit and Chuck Gibbons were having a quiet shift. There wasn't much traffic around today. Most daytime driving offences up in Montana were related to cars speeding or drivers not wearing seatbelts. Large trucks rarely broke the speed limit as truck fleet owners had found keeping their drivers to lower speeds significantly improved fuel efficiency and had fitted speed governors. But a lot of private car drivers still felt the seat belt law shouldn't apply to them. Larry Merit always said to those hc caught that if they'd ever seen the aftermath of a road crash of somebody not wearing a belt, they'd never argue about it again. He and his co-trooper had seen far too many young bodies broken and twisted beyond recognition from drinking, speeding and not wearing seatbelts to last a lifetime.

With the weather worsening, the duty sergeant had already radioed them and asked them for another six-hour shift overtime from 18:00 tonight as they knew this evening would be full of traffic sliding off the roads and vehicle strandings. With a reluctant sigh, but pleased for the extra money, the two Montana State Troopers readied themselves for a busy evening.

Heading south in their heavy and powerful Ford Interceptor cruiser, Chuck Gibbons had noticed the small truck approaching on the other side of the median. The outline shape of the driver could be seen, and he had his hand up to his mouth, and head tilted back. He was either eating or drinking while driving - both offences in Montana - and Gibbons was just about to say something to Larry when the wind blew stronger, and he noticed the truck swerve over the white line a little.

That gave them the excuse, not that they actually needed one, to pull the truck over and have a word with the driver.

Rapidly slowing down, they lit up their roof rack of flashing lights, pulled across the frost-hardened grass of the median and turned north in pursuit, quickly accelerating.

Deacon saw the red and blue flashing lights in his inside mirror and cursed. He took his foot off the accelerator and pulled gently to a stop, part way on the blacktop, partway on the grass verge. The police cruiser pulled in close behind.

Looking in the mirror, Deacon could see the passenger getting out and strolling towards him in the fading light, one hand unbuttoning his holster as standard procedure demanded with the other hand holding a Maglite torch. The driver had turned in his seat slightly and was apparently using the onboard computer to verify name and registration.

Officer Chuck Gibbons stood slightly to the rear of Deacon's door, leant forward and tapped on the glass with the base of his Maglite.

Winding the window down Deacon said, "What's the problem, officer?"

Gibbons could see the mess in the vehicle of the food wrappers and paper. He could also smell beer fumes drifting out through the open window. He loosened the restraining strap on his holster a little more and slipped his hand around the butt of his weapon. Gibbons loved the feel of his old Colt Python, a .357 Magnum revolver. He'd owned it for years, and it had never jammed, never failed. It was perfectly balanced in the hand and overall a beautiful piece of engineering. But two years back the department had changed en-masse to SIG Sauer P229 .357

semi-automatic pistols with a 12 round magazine. He'd never really liked it, and it never felt the same. He thought it was too plasticky, too gimmicky, so he'd kept his original weapon. The Python only held six rounds, but if you couldn't put your target down with that many, he thought, you don't deserve more.

"License and registration please," Gibbons said.

Deacon looked up slightly before replying, "Two and five?"

Gibbon looked him straight in the eyes and replied, "Two and five."

With his seat belt already undone, Deacon quickly thrust the driver's door open, catching Officer Gibbons on his right arm and shoulder. As Gibbons fell back slightly, Deacon was out and on him. Gibbons managed to get his hand to grip his gun butt and pulled it clear of its holster as Deacon's hands closed over his. Struggling, Gibbons dropped his Maglite and brought his spare hand also onto the gun butt. With a deafening bang, the gun went off, the round hitting the blacktop a few feet away sending chips of gravel and tarmac flying. Twisting the weapon until it broke free from the officer's hands, Deacon thrust his right shoulder forward directly into Gibbons' chest, sending him stumbling backwards.

Raising the officer's weapon, Deacon shot Officer Chuck Gibbons directly center-chest before turning it towards the Police cruiser.

Larry Merit failed to see the first interaction due to looking at the computer screen, but he'd seen the two of them struggling as the gun went off. Trying to grab his own weapon while at the same time twist and get out of the car cost him a second or two and he heard the second shot in time to see his colleague fall back onto the road. As he opened his door, he saw Deacon aim towards him, and he rapidly ducked down just as Deacon fired again and the windshield shattered. Jamming the gear stick into reverse, Merit jammed his foot hard on the accelerator, and the cruiser began to leap backwards, wheels spinning trying to gain traction as the driver's door mirror exploded.

Deacon cursed and shifted his aim slightly. The next round went through the stared windshield and hit Officer Larry Merit in the sternum, blood spraying everywhere.

As the officer slumped over to the left, his foot eased off the accelerator, and the cruiser slowly rolled back down into the ditch at the side of the highway.

Grabbing the prone body of Chuck Gibbons by the collar, Deacon dragged him quickly down out of sight and left him next to the almost completely hidden police cruiser. Satisfied that only the very top of the cruiser could be seen and most traffic would pass by not noticing, Deacon tossed the large-barreled weapon away, quickly jumped back into his own truck and floored the accelerator just as he could see other vehicles approaching in the distance.

Chapter 6

Deacon knew he had to get off the main roads and get as far away as possible. Those missing police officers would be found soon and the chase would be on.

His first instinct was to turn south, away from where he'd been heading and away from Helena, but once the two officers were found, the police would assume the perpetrator would be running and would set up roadblocks. In this sparsely populated land, it would be easy to capture him. He also had to get rid of his truck in case the driver had gotten a license check off in time, but a stranger to the area hitching at this time of year, or waiting for a bus or train would stand out like a sore thumb. No, sometimes it's best to do what the enemy doesn't expect. Helena was only another twelve or fifteen miles north and presented better options.

He pulled off the Interstate as soon as he could and kept to back roads but still headed north. Entering Helena from the south-west, he followed signs for St Peter's Hospital and parked it in the underground visitors parking. Grabbing his bag and slipping on a thick Parka coat, he began walking briskly towards the Ascot Airport Hotel. By now darkness had completely fallen. The heavy snow was still due, but only flurries had arrived so far. As he approached the hotel fifteen minutes later, he saw a sedan pulling in and parking. A young couple got out and took a suitcase into check-in. Assuming they would be there all night and not notice their car missing until the morning, he quickly forced the door lock with a large screwdriver he'd brought with him from his truck, before hotwiring the ignition and forcing the steering lock.

All my training has come in handy, he thought with a grin, as he pulled away, the heater on high. Turning on the car radio, he heard the news the officers had been found. After failing to answer repeated radio calls, an alert had gone out, and a passing 6-axle truck had radioed in about an apparently abandoned police cruiser parked in a ditch by the side of the highway. All the main routes were now being monitored with roadblocks.

Pulling to a stop in town Deacon rummaged through the glove box. He found the car's registration papers and also found what he was looking for. Unfolding the map, he traced a route he thought would keep him away from the busier roads. Ideally, he wanted to head south towards Idaho, but those roads would be monitored and likely blocked, so instead, he headed out onto the 270 through Silver City, hoping to get over the hills before the main snow dump arrived. If he didn't make it, he had no worry about spending a night or two living in the car - he'd done far worse during his SEAL training, but he was hopeful things would work out ok. As it was, the snow God was on his side, and although it did start falling, it was a light fall until he started coming back down off Mountain Highway, and he'd already found snow chains in the trunk and fitted them. Two hours later he arrived at the sleepy town of Westerton, population 124, in Powell County. The only lights showing were at a run-down diner, and a few hundred yards further on from a snow-covered sign outside a sleazy looking motel offering vacancies. Pulling in around the motel's rear, Deacon parked and walked through the fresh snow to reception. He could see an empty reception desk and the flickering light of a television reflecting on the office wall beyond. Banging his hand down hard twice on the desk he called out for service. Moments later a large, overweight, balding guy with greasy hair and smoking a cigarette lumbered out of the office.

"Yeah?"

"Wanna room. Just for one night. One at the rear."

"Seventy-five bucks."

"No way, pal. This time of night fifty, max."

"You passing through, mister?"

"Yeah, be gone tomorrow. But too much snow tonight. Fifty?"

"Yeah, OK fifty. Room 9. Ground floor." As he tossed a key to Deacon while folding the cash and putting it in his shirt pocket.

Deacon went back out and moved his car to directly outside room 9. The room was basic. A double bed with a flower-patterned cover. The pillows looked old, and overall the room wasn't particularly clean, but it was better than sleeping in the car. Sitting on the bed Deacon could feel the mattress springs were gone, but it was warm and dry, or at least would be warm when the small wall heater eventually came to life. He checked the shower in the tiny bathroom, inspected the closet and found some spare blankets.

Leaving his holdall on the bed, he walked back outside and locked the door. The snow was heavier now, and everything looked peaceful. Walking back past the reception he could see the flickering shadows of the TV again and hear its sound faintly, but as he walked on, he was surrounded by a blanket of silence with only the soft crunching of the snow underneath his boots disturbing the peace.

There was only one other customer in the diner - an old guy drinking a beer. Taking a seat with his back to the wall Deacon flicked through the well-thumbed menu.

"Hi, I'm Lily. What can I get you, hon?"

Looking up, he saw an early twenties plain-looking bottle-blond waitress facing him.

"Medium rare steak, baked potato and corn, please. And a beer."

She took his order and brought the beer a few minutes later. Three times she tried to engage him in conversation, but he really wasn't interested. Finally, when she brought him the food he asked for another beer, and she seemed to get the hint.

The TV above the counter was showing some typical game show when a 'Breaking News' alert came on. A blue-eyed, blonde-haired female announcer came on screen announcing two Montana State Troopers had been ruthlessly shot and murdered after a standard traffic stop today. The suspect's vehicle was a red and white Ford truck which the police were searching for. The person of interest was John Deacon, ex-US Navy SEAL, dishonorably discharged three months' ago for the murder of two innocent Iraqi's in Mosul, Iraq. The screen then showed an identical truck to Deacons before showing a picture of him clean-shaven and in military uniform. He was considered armed and extremely dangerous and shouldn't be approached.

Trying to keep his head down and eat and cursing quietly to himself, he noticed Lily looking at him a couple of times but then she went about her normal duties and seemed to forget him. Finishing as quickly as he could, he left enough money on the table to cover the food and drinks as well as a ten-dollar tip, before putting his coat on and heading out.

Arriving back at his motel room, he locked the door before stripping off for a hot shower. The wall heater had finally warmed the room enough, and after drying, he slipped his shorts back on and got into bed.

At 2:44 am his instinct roused him. Just as he was coming to and looking around, the room door was kicked open with an almighty crash, and five large men rushed in. He fought as hard as he could. One attacker suffered a broken nose and jaw, and another would have to use a stick to support his shattered knee, but even his training failed with five against one, and when a large baseball bat was swung hard against his thigh, his leg collapsed under him. He heard the whoosh of air but didn't see the final blow coming as it swept down viciously from above the attacker's head to crash heavily just below his ear into the side of his neck. Lying on the floor, barely conscious, he felt his hands being tied behind his back while a dark hood was pulled over his head. As he was dragged outside someone punched him with a hammer blow directly to the solar plexus, and the lights finally went out.

Chapter 7

The first thing he began to notice as he came round was the cold. He seemed to be tied to a chair but was still naked apart from his shorts, and it was cold. Extremely so. He could hear voices, but the hood over his head muffled their words.

An icy shock hit him and he couldn't help gasping as a bucket of water was tossed over him. His hood was yanked off, and he found himself squinting in the sudden light from naked bulbs. He could see the shapes of two men in front of him as his eyes began to adapt to the gloom and bright lights. One of them said, "You're awake" as he slammed a fist into Deacon's cheek.

Spitting a little blood out, Deacon said, "I am now pal, but I don't think much of your early morning wake-up call policy."

The one who'd punched him said, "Huh?"

The other shape said, "So we have a wise-ass here, do we?"

Deacon heard other voices behind him. He tried to turn his head to see, but they were still out of eyeshot. One voice was Lily's from the diner. She said, "He tried to look away when they showed his face on the TV, but it's him. See?"

A figure wearing Army-issue fatigues came into view. Quickly glancing at the chest and shoulder insignia

Deacon realized there were no official markings and these had likely been purchased from a services surplus store.

"So who are you?" Deacon asked.

Turning slightly, the new guy waved a hand, and the first two thugs moved back in and started punching Deacon again.

"I speak. You answer," the new guy said.

Leaving his thugs to have a few more punches each, the new guy moved around more in front of Deacon. Waving his hand for the beating to stop he looked down at Deacon.

"Who are you?"

Spitting a larger globule of blood out onto the dusty concrete floor, small speckles of blood splashed onto the new guy's polished shoes.

"I said, big guy, WHO ARE YOU?" as he kicked Deacon hard on the inside of his left knee.

"Nobody. Just a stranger passing through. Now, why don't we forget any of this has happened. Untie me, and I'll let you guys off," he hissed through gritted teeth at the pain.

"Funny man. I won't ask you again. Who are you?"

"I think you know who I am. Your goons took me from my room, and I expect they took my clothes and things too, so you have my wallet and driver's license. If you can't read it, General ButtFuck, go get one of your goons to translate."

"Do you know who I am?" he said, his low voice full of contempt.

"Ranger Smith with Yogi Bear and Huckleberry Hound here?" Deacon answered, nodding towards the thugs.

Bracing himself for the next round of beating, he waited until it was over and the lead guy moved back closer.

"I am General Boyd Lucas, and these are my men."

"You could be General Zod for all I care."

Taking an automatic pistol from his battle dress pocket, he slipped the safety off and pointed it directly at Deacon.

"Last chance. Who are you?"

"I'm John Deacon. Formally Lieutenant John Deacon of the US Navy. As you already fully know."

"What are you doing here?"

"Look, I was just passing through. Your goons broke into my hotel room and dragged me here. I was sleeping and would have been gone tomorrow."

"Why here? Why Westerton?"

"The snow was getting heavier. I needed food and didn't want to stay in my car all night. This town was the first place open I came to. I don't know who you are or what this place is and I don't care. You let me go, and I'll be on my way."

Lily moved into view again and said, "You're a cop killer. You're a wanted felon. I saw your face on TV."

Lucas put his arm around Lily and moved away with her while two thugs moved in again and started another round of punching Deacon. Head down and dazed, Deacon stared at the floor while he waited for his senses to clear. He realized now that he was in a large barn. The floor was concrete and covered in bits of straw and mud. He couldn't see or hear any animals, but they apparently used this place. Six naked light bulbs were hanging from the roof illuminating the barn, but someone had set two extra arc-lights about a dozen feet away pointing at him. That was why everyone was still mostly in the shadow.

His arms and shoulders were grabbed roughly, and he was untied from the chair. His hands were re-tied behind him, and he was half walked, half dragged out through the entrance into the cold night. The sky still looked to be full of snow, and it was falling heavily. He was dragged across a large flat area, the snow lying pristine and showing quite brightly even though there were no lights to be seen. His naked feet numb from the snow, he was pushed in through the doors of a cellar where his hands were released. One of the guards seemed to take extra pleasure in punching him a number of times in the kidneys. His Parka jacket along with his boots was already lying on a wooden bench, along with a dirty pillow and a thin, filthy mattress. With a resounding 'click' the door was locked behind him. A dim light offered just enough brightness for him to see as he staggered to the bench and quickly slipped his jacket on before thrusting his frozen feet into his boots. As the guards left, the light was switched off. Left in total darkness, he felt around, but there were no socks or other clothes, although he found two thin blankets folded under the pillow. He did some exercises to warm up and get the circulation flowing, before wrapping the blankets around himself and curling up into as tight a ball as possible on the bed. The only sounds were the far away howling of wolves, drifting gently on the breeze. Estimating the time at around 04:30 with daylight not breaking until around 07:30, he tried to get a few hours' sleep.

At 07:45 the outer door was opened, and three guards came in. One was carrying more of Deacon's clothes while the other two had M4 rifles. In the dim light Deacon could see the two guards stayed far enough out of reach while the clothes guy unlocked the internal cell door.

Tossing the clothes on the floor, he said, "Get dressed. The General wants to see you."

Slipping his coat off, Deacon quickly dressed before putting his thick coat back on, pleased to be a little warmer now.

Marched across the snowy compound, this time they went to a large hut. One guard, the same one as the previous evening, jabbed him repeatedly in the back with the barrel of his M4. Looking around, Deacon could see people emerging and beginning their daily chores. Some were armed with shoulder-slung rifles. All were wearing faded green battle dresses covered by large winter coats, also camouflaged. Some were younger, but most seemed around the early thirties range. There were also women and children wandering about.

On entering the large central hut, it was obvious to Deacon that this was Boyd Lucas's main offices. At the rear, leaning against the wall, were five burly men wearing camouflage and all carrying side arms. Sitting at the centrally located desk was the man Deacon had seen last night.

Showered, clean-shaven, and wearing a perfectly laundered BDU, he said, "Mister Deacon. As I said last night, I am General Boyd Lucas, and I am in charge of the people here."

"What is 'here' exactly?"

"This is a utopia for many. I lead the Brethren of White Christians . We are a peaceful movement and we own this land. In fact, we own everything on it. That means we now own you."

"Nobody owns me."

"While you are on this land, I do. Now shut up and listen. I know what you've done. There is a massive manhunt going on trying to find you. Both those cops you murdered had young families, and the County Sheriff wants revenge. If we throw you out of here, you won't last two hours. So you tell me why we shouldn't do the right thing and call the police to hand you over?"

"Well, I guess this isn't the sort of place you want to welcome the police to," Deacon said looking around.

"You'd be surprised," Lucas said. "We are a registered church and charity. This land, all of it, is church land. We pay our dues, and we're 98% self-sufficient. We school our own here and have sufficient healthcare. The local police have never had any problems with any of us or our followers. We are a major contributor to our local town and a financial contributor to the local police department. We even purchased a new police cruiser for Sergeant Dobbs last year. No sir, we have an excellent relationship with the local townsfolk and the police."

In other words, you've bought everyone local off, Deacon thought.

"Well then, perhaps you should do the righteous thing and hand me over to the authorities," Deacon said.

"I am still considering, Mister Deacon, I am still considering. You see, we are always on the lookout for fit young workers to help the cause. And your ... how shall I put it ... your 'skills' could come in mighty useful. Why don't you tell me a bit more about yourself and whether you think you could fit in here?"

Deacon sat down and started talking. He spoke about his upbringing and in joining the SEALs. He didn't discuss individual missions but ended by saying, "I'm pretty pissed off with the Government right now. I did my duty and went into harm's way more times than I can remember. Finished up rescuing some damn fool American hostages who'd wanted to go over to Iraq and 'save the world' but had ended up getting kidnapped themselves. We got them out, but one of the girls claimed I killed her Arabic lover. He was about to rape her, and I get blamed. Goddam Navy took her side, and I get dishonorably discharged. Me. After all the years I've put in. Dirty murdering little fuck deserved to die but this fucking politically correct government is so far up its own ass it's afraid to say boo to a goose, so I get hammered. This good old government is so politically correct over helping the bad guys they shaft their own. Well, fuck the lot of 'em. It's John Deacon first now and fuck 'em all."

Getting nods from the others listening, he went on, "Back after WWII America was the hero. We were the apple in everyone's eye. We became the world's police because no one else was powerful enough to do it. And everyone wanted us. We were liked the world over. We

43

were held in awe. Everyone wanted to come to America, and they were grateful for our views. We ran the oil production in the Middle East, and we headed up NATO. When we spoke countries listened, and when we shouted countries trembled. Now countries despise the US and want to destroy it. Half of the US is owned by foreigners, and this government is too frightened to do anything, even the Republicans. There's too much kowtowing to the Chinese and the Arabs. You can't even trust the police nowadays. They're so far in the pockets of politicians. We need a government and a leader that wants America strong again and fuck the consequences. But that ain't likely to happen, so why don'tcha call the local police and turn me in. I'm done. I've got nothing left to give this fucked-up country." His rant over, he sat there shoulders slumped in despair.

Boyd Lucas sat there contemplating for two long minutes. Then he slowly stood up, looked directly at Deacon and said, "No, I ain't ready to turn you in yet. You stay here today. We'll feed you and even send in some company so you don't get bored but you stay in your room, understand? There'll be a guard outside, and we'll talk again tomorrow morning."

Turning around he had some quiet words with a couple of the other men in the office before Deacon was taken back outside by two of them. This time he was directed to a different building, a long two-story wooden building. He hadn't been handcuffed, but the guard from earlier still seemed to take delight in prodding him with the barrel of his rifle. Deacon just sucked at his gums a little and chose not to react. The other guard introduced himself as Noah Turner and gave him directions.

After being herded towards the correct room, Deacon went inside. It was a downstairs room with an outside view through a small window. There was a steel-framed bed and small cabinet next to it. The mattress looked reasonably clean, the pillow also. When the guards left and locked the door behind them, he heard the scrape of a chair being placed in the corridor just outside. Checking the windows, he found heavy steel bars protecting them. Realizing he hadn't many options he banged on the door and shouted, "Hey, I want to use the bathroom and have a shower. Then I want some food." The chair scraped back, and he heard footsteps moving away. A few minutes later the footsteps came back, and a voice called through, "Yeah, in ten." Then he heard the creaking sound of someone sitting on the chair again.

Almost thirty minutes later the chair creaked again, and he heard voices. The click of the key was followed by the door swinging open. Two guards, including the one that didn't seem to like him, had their weapons trained on him.

"Shower block's next door. Come on," said Noah.

"What about my other clothes? They were in my motel."

"All here now, asshole, along with your wheels. No one there knows you even existed," the other guard said.

Entering the open shower block Deacon began to strip.

"Soap?" he said, "And a towel."

Following the pointed finger, Deacon grabbed a half bar of soap as the water began to run warm. Standing underneath the hot shower his thoughts turned to how the day was forming. After five long minutes of enjoying steaming hot water, Deacon switched the taps off and said, "I need a towel."

Handed one the size of a handkerchief, Deacon spent a few minutes drying himself before donning his clothes again.

"What about food?" he asked.

"Back in your room," came the reply, and he was escorted back to his temporary accommodation.

He saw his holdall lying on his bed waiting for him. Looking briefly inside he could see all his clothes and his few possessions from the motel room.

"Food'll be here soon," Noah said while Deacon got changed.

A few minutes later a young very pretty girl of about eighteen arrived with a tray of food and a large mug of coffee.

"Hi. I'm Terri-Anne. I'm yours for the day," she said, smiling.

Taking the tray and placing it on the bed, Deacon thanked her, softly gripped her shoulders and turned her around before gently pushing her back out through the door, saying, "I'll be fine here all alone today, thanks, Terri-Anne." He then told Noah to close the door before he went back to the bed and ate a breakfast of lukewarm coffee, bread and cold pancakes.

Chapter 8

By seven o'clock the next morning Deacon was dressed and waiting on the edge of his bed. He'd been left alone all the previous day until early evening when Terri-Anne had brought his evening meal of meat stew and dumplings, with a side of mashed potato and bread, and had taken away the breakfast tray. She had again asked if he wanted her to stay, and again he'd said 'Thanks, but no thanks', amused at her soft pout at rejection. He'd used the bathroom once more in the day and again after the evening meal. For bathroom use overnight he'd been given a metal bucket and the thought of someone cleaning up after him as he'd pissed into it made him smile.

Terri-Anne arrived at 07:45 again with his breakfast tray, this time the plate had hot scrambled eggs and bacon on it, along with his coffee that he wolfed down. The old SEALs adage had been to eat whenever you can - you don't always know when your next meal will be.

Another guard had been on duty overnight, but Noah had relieved him at 07:30 and soon after 08:00, Deacon heard the lock click open, and Noah called him to come.

Waiting outside was the other guard who immediately prodded Deacon and shoved him forward.

"Hey pal, take it easy. I'm not causing trouble. What's your problem?" Deacon said.

"Not so tough now are you, cop killer?"

Ignoring him, Deacon glanced around. It had snowed lightly for most of the previous day and night, but now the sky was clear and blue, and the sun was dazzling. The hills in the distance were brilliant white with the dark green and black of trees showing clearly. The firs and similar were laying heavy with snow bending their boughs down almost to the ground while the deciduous varieties had become black skeletons against the white brightness. Most of the snow within the compound was undisturbed and it was easy for Deacon to quickly see the main routes of interest from where the footprints led.

Heading back over to the meeting building of the day before, Deacon could see men and women beginning their daily chores. Overall, they seemed happy enough, but that wasn't for Deacon to decide.

As he entered the office, he saw Boyd Lucas sitting at his desk with the same five people around him. Lucas pointed at the chair and instructed Deacon to sit. Before he could begin to move, he was prodded forcibly in the kidneys with the rifle barrel.

Turning, Deacon looked the guard straight in the eyes and said, "Do that again and I'll hurt you."

"Huh, you think you're tough enough? You might be tough shooting cops but I co-- " the guard said while constantly prodding Deacon in the chest with the barrel.

With a blur of motion Deacon swept the muzzle aside and grabbed the barrel with his left hand, pushing it back towards the guard, making it awkward, if not impossible for the guard to pull the trigger. At the same time Deacon's right hand slammed upwards, the heel of his hand striking an enormous blow just above the guard's top lip shattering the guard's nose.

With a look of amazement on his face the guard just stood there, already unconscious. As gravity took effect and the body began to fall, Deacon wrenched the rifle from his hands and turned back towards Boyd Lucas.

Lucas had hardly moved and two of the other five men had just begun to slide their hands towards their pistols when Deacon slammed the rifle down so hard on Lucas's desk it seemed to shake the entire building. Sitting down as the guard's body was still settling, Deacon kept his hands in full view in his lap and waited.

With four handguns now pointing at his head he just sat still and said, "Well, I did warn him."

"Holy shit!" Lucas gasped and then just sat there for a few seconds. "Boys, put your weapons away. I think Mister Deacon has made his point. And get rid of him," he said, pointing at the body on the floor.

One of the five went outside and returned almost immediately with two others who removed the body of the unconscious guard.

"So, ex-Lieutenant John Deacon, what are we going to do with you?" Lucas said.

"A man like you with skills you just demonstrated... a man like that could be useful at times ... Would seem to be a damn shame for a man with your kind of skills to spend the rest of his life in prison just waiting for the needle, only to die tied down like some wild animal like a hog or a steer, just waiting for that amber fluid to be pushed into his veins ..."

"I'll take my chances," Deacon said.

"Son, you think they were tough on you for killing them Arabs? You gone and killed two State Troopers, boy. Shot them down where they stood. People around here don't like that sorta thing. Not honest, hardworking God-fearing folk. You're getting the needle that's for sure. Unless they shoot you for trying to escape first and save the legal people all that trouble."

"How the fuck did you get my service record? That's classified," Deacon said, looking down at the desk. He was amazed to see a manila folder with the emblem of the US Navy on it and his name in the top corner amongst the paperwork on Lucas's desk.

"Just 'cus we're up here in the middle of nowhere don't mean we don't have resources. You came here telling a fancy story. Well, I wasn't still sucking on my Momma's tit yesterday. I've had you checked out, and your story seems to hold. So, ex-Lieutenant cop-killer John Deacon, as I see it you have two choices. We take you into town to the Sheriff's office saying we found you wandering about. We get his thanks for apprehending a dangerous murdering criminal, and you're fucked. Or ..."

"Or?"

"Or you join our merry group."

"Ok, tell me more," Deacon said after almost twenty seconds of thought.

Offering a cigar to Deacon, who declined, and before lighting one himself, Boyd Lucas said, "Let me introduce you to some of my fellow worshippers. You've met Brother Noah Turner. He's my go-to man. Anything you need here within the compound he'll sort for you."

Turning and pointing to the other five men who were standing behind him, Lucas said, "Wade Horton, Travis McCabe, Dwight Emery, Travis Polanski, and my second-in-command Brother Fuller Simpson," as he pointed left to right at the men. "Fuller is an ex-Army, so you two have a lot in common. And it was through his connections that I got your file."

Glancing at Fuller's eyes, Deacon could see the hatred and jealousy behind them. Fuller Simpson had obviously been top dog in this community with his military background. Although he'd been one of the men whose hands had reached their holsters, it was obvious to all concerned that Deacon was the faster and better of the two men. But Deacon knew he'd have to keep a close eye on him and that he was trouble.

Chapter 9

Lucas continued, "Like I told you before we are a two-hundred-plus strong peaceful religious group. We believe God knows best and man has corrupted God's teachings. We are striving for a simpler life where hard work and daily chores equal a healthy, satisfied life. The people here love me, and for them, this is utopia. I formed this group almost seven years ago. We are fully registered, we own this land, and we pay our way. The local townsfolk also love us, and we don't ever cause trouble."

"So why call yourself General, not Preacher or Reverend?" Deacon asked looking around, "And why the weapons if you are a peaceful religious group?"

While Boyd Lucas was answering Deacon slowly looked around the hut. All the buildings seemed to be of similar construction. A concrete base with walls and roofs of wood. The internal wood in this hut was smooth but not polished or varnished. Lucas's desk was old and heavily marked, and there was a three-drawer metal filing cabinet stood in the corner. The only item out of place was a polished leather briefcase made of either crocodile or alligator skin leaning against the filing cabinet.

"Every community needs structure," he heard Lucas explain to him, "even the simplest of family groups need structure. From the father down through the mother to the children. There needs to be law and order. The father sets the law, and the wife and children obey. If they break that law, then they suffer the consequences and maybe get extra duties to perform or may even suffer a beating. Well, we have a structure here. I make the law and my 'children' follow it. If any break my law, they are punished. It is simple military structure. Through history, the most efficient groups and leaders have observed the same military command modelling. Attila the Hun, Genghis Khan, Adolf Hitler, Saddam Hussein, even Osama bin Laden have all followed the same model."

"But these were evil men, and many went to war. Are you planning on going to war?"

"They were, but they were great leaders as well. They inspired loyalty, and they achieved great things. Things that many said couldn't be done. No, I don't want to go to war, but I do want to achieve greatness."

"You need guns to impose your law?"

"No, the weapons are not used against my children," Lucas said, "The problem in many families around this once-fine country of ours, is they live in fear of 'outsiders'. We live a peaceful life here in the wilderness but sometimes strangers come-a-knocking, and we need to be ready to defend our home. We have money here, and some outsiders would want to steal it. Many would be jealous to see what a fine life we have here and would want to ruin and take. The Lord says a man has the right to defend his home against beggars and thieves and that's what we will do."

Stopping to draw deeply on his cigar, Lucas swept his arm around as if pointing towards the encampment.

"We desire a simple life where God gives, and God takes away. The problem now is man is too greedy. Everything is wanted now. Young people don't want to wait and work for things, they want it all now. And who leads this idea? Who pushes for 'now'? Banks and bankers, that's who. The good Lord said 'The love of money is the root of all evil'. That is as true today as when it was stated two dozen centuries ago. The government is corrupt, and politicians are corrupt. We want to go back to the time soon after the depression - when everyone thanked God and life was simpler. People now are too focused on possessions. They want, want, want. Women go out to work. That ain't right. They should be at home bringing up them babies. A women's place is beside her husband doing what he tells her. Gambling is evil. Homosexuality and prostitution are evil. Faggots should be killed - it ain't right what they do. It ain't natural. But God will exact revenge this year. They're sinners. It's against God's teachings. All are the work of the devil and against God's work. The new city of Sodom and Gomorrah will perish in fire and brimstone just like its ancient cousin. Women nowadays are sinful. They flaunt their bodies in their short skirts and open tops. Men are weak. They're attracted to these wanton women. Man must stop wanting, and those that don't will perish. Banks and money lenders are still the root of all evil. Jesus despised them. They fuel the people's lust for want," Lucas said, eyes wide and with spittle forming at the corners of his mouth, his voice having raised in volume and pitch throughout his speech.

Realizing he was losing it a little, Deacon tried to calm him down.

"I agree. I agree. But surely living your lives as you do is away from all of that?" Deacon said.

Having regained his breath and calmed himself from his ranting, Lucas said, "The community here is self-serving. There are almost 230 people here; men, women and children. We have a fully-trained medical nurse, running fresh water and power. We have mechanics, carpenters, farmers and a teacher. We have vehicles. We are self-sufficient, and we grow a lot of our own food and buy in what else is needed. We don't want interference from outside. The local police know of us but leave us alone."

"And the cell where I was kept the first day? And the beating I received?" he asked.

Noticeably calmer now, Lucas inhaled on his cigar before continuing.

"Even good people have bad days. We praise and we punish. Like a father may choose to take his belt to an unruly child, I will administer whatever punishment I believe is appropriate. As for your beating, you were an unknown source. You are a murderer, a fighter, as you've again shown this morning. We needed to be sure you were secure or we'd hand you over to the police. But let us put that behind us now. You are welcome to join the Brethren of White Christians. You'll receive no money, but you'll be fed and housed. You'll work six days a week as instructed, with the Sabbath your day of rest. You will be known here as Brother John Deacon. You will not have any communication with the outside world, and for the next month at least you will not be able to leave until the police search for you is reduced. Or Noah here will drop you in town, and you can take your chances. Your choice."

After silently counting to ten Deacon said, "Well it looks like your flock has just grown by one, General."

Rising from behind his desk, Lucas extended a hand of greeting before leading Deacon over to the other five men who each, in turn, shook Deacon's hand and offered a welcoming smile or greeting. Apart from Fuller Simpson.

Expecting trouble, Deacon made sure his hand firmly clamped into Simpson's. The simplest handshake trick was to close your fingers quickly before your opponent's hand was completely within yours, thumb to thumb. Then when you grip you squeeze excessive pressure across their knuckles sometimes breaking or at least dislocating one or two. But Deacon knew of that trick and hundreds of others. Staring straight into Simpson's eyes and with their hands firmly locked, Deacon felt Simpson start to squeeze. Hard. And he squeezed back. Harder.

"Brother Simpson," Deacon said.

"Brother Deacon," came the reply, tension noticeable between them. With each squeezing harder and harder their handshake had already taken almost ten seconds. Eventually, Lucas slapped them both on the shoulders, saying, "Boys. Boys. Enough of the horseplay. BOYS!"

As they separated, Deacon could feel the hatred flowing between them.

Chapter 10

The next days and weeks seemed to roll into one. Six o'clock was when everyone started their day, with group prayers at 06:30 followed by breakfast at 07:00. There were always ample amounts of food, with bread, porridge and coffee on the menu but Deacon quickly bored of it. On Sundays, the cooks included cold meats with fried and scrambled eggs. Lunch was served at midday and consisted of hot soup and meat sandwiches and a hot evening meal was served at 19:00. Both meals had group prayers immediately prior. Lights out was at 21:00.

For the first week, Deacon was kept under close scrutiny. Travis McCabe became his shadow, instructing him what and when, and Deacon's chores ranged from gardening to rubbish collection to vehicle maintenance. McCabe didn't seem to do much himself, being one of Lucas's inner circle. Under advice from Lucas, Deacon let his beard grow longer to blend in closer with the other members of the group, but most of the group seemed to ignore him. Whether they'd been warned about him or were just unsociable Deacon never knew, but the only person who regularly spoke with him was McCabe when issuing orders, or Terri-Anne.

On the fourth day, Lucas walked over to see him, with Terri-Anne in tow.

"Brother Deacon, you're doing well and settling in. As a reward, you have been assigned Terri-Anne for the next week," at which point Lucas gave her a brief pat on her shoulder and passed her over.

"Huh? What do you mean, General?"

"She's yours. Your wife. A gift. She'll explain. Now get back to work."

While Deacon carried on the rest of his daily chores, Terri-Anne moved Deacon's small amount of belongings from the single bed and cupboard he'd been using in the main living quarters to a larger private cabin with a small lounge, bathroom and bedroom fitted with a double bed. Lucas also mentioned that the man-hunt for Deacon had begun to slow down with the police reporting they assumed he'd left the state.

Later that evening, while they were eating their evening meal in the dining area, she explained. Most of the men at the compound were single. Those that were married shared their wives with the single men. This was to stop jealousy and fighting. Lucas would choose which women went with which men and for how long. He had the pick of them all. Terri-Anne wasn't married to anyone yet, but being one of the youngest and prettiest, she was regularly sought after. Lucas and Simpson had already used her regularly for their pleasure, sometimes both together, and had grown bored with her, preferring two up-and-coming younger girls of fourteen and fifteen who had become their personal playthings. Terri-Anne, however, was still for the personal pleasure of the others in the inner circle and Travis McCabe lusted after her the most and wanted her all to himself, but Lucas demanded everyone shared. As for Terri-Anne, she thought Deacon looked fit and muscular, and being new blood she was looking forward to their time together.

During dinner, she kept putting her hand on his forearm, squeezing it. Deacon glanced up and could see Travis McCabe watching them - the jealousy and hatred in his eyes clearly evident. That's the second one I need to look out for, he thought.

Back in their room later that evening, he made it clear that they were not going to be intimate.

"But don't you want me?" she said.

"Very much. You're an extremely attractive woman, but I don't think I will be here all that long, and I'm not willing to play Lucas's game and become a gigolo. You shouldn't be being forced to have sex with men of all ages here. Lucas is making you an unpaid prostitute. You should be with someone nearer your own age."

"But I will be beaten if I don't satisfy you," she added. "Anytime a man complains the woman is beaten until she satisfies him. McCabe has complained about me twice, and both times I got into trouble."

"Why did McCabe complain?"

"He's horrible. He's got bad body odor and bad breath. He's rough as well. Not just with me, with all the women. We all complain, but Lucas always takes the man's side unless we're seriously injured. Then the man gets beaten as well. One of the men got into trouble last year. He smacked Jess around and broke her nose. She even had to have stitches. Lucas and some of the other guys took him out of the camp and up into the forest and beat him up. I guess he left 'cus I haven't seen him since," she said, hands moving over his chest to undo his shirt.

"No, just lay here with me," Deacon said, gently moving her hands off his buttons. "Why did he complain about you?"

"He'd been drinking heavily and was breathing right into my face. It made me feel ill and I guess I just laid there. He didn't like that and slapped me and then I started crying. He bruised my face and then was too drunk to finish. He complained about me the next morning, and I got punished."

"What happened?"

"I had to satisfy him another way, but I don't want to talk about it," she said cuddling into Deacon.

"Ok, sorry to have brought this up. Why don't you just tell me a little more about this place?"

Over the next hour, Terry-Anne explained to Deacon where Lucas originally got his money from. His grandfather, Jeremiah Lucas, became wealthy during WWII. He already owned a fledgling engineering company and received multiple orders from the US Military for specialist weapons. The company expanded quickly, and after the war, Jeremiah realized homecoming servicemen would want vehicles and houses. They'd want to get married, and their spouses would want energy-saving white goods. He cleverly diversified, started making fittings for cars, pre-fabricated housing, cookers, and washing machines. He was a very talented and astute businessman, and as his company grew, he made millions. His son and Boyd's father, Gideon Lucas, took over in the early sixties and the growth continued. All along the plan was for Boyd to take over, but Boyd had other plans. Not wanting the conventional business life, Boyd had attended UCLA in the late '90s but dropped out. The Lucas family had always been strictly religious, and Boyd found himself becoming more and more devoted to religion or at least his variant of it. Gideon Lucas died almost ten years ago from a sudden heart attack, and his shares passed to Boyd. Seeing his opportunity, Boyd sold up and overnight became worth tens of millions of dollars and as many people who suddenly become rich, went on a drugs, drink and gambling spree. After having lost almost half his fortune, having gained multiple STD's and substantial damage to his kidneys, he sobered up two years later and started the Brethren of White Christians to save mankind from evil.

"How sure are you about all this?" he asked.

"Very. My Mom and Pop were two of the original attendees here, and Boyd used to tell everyone about where he'd come from and why he opened this sanctuary. I was only ten then, but I remember it started really well. Others joined, and it grew in size, and we even started our own school here, so my friends and I didn't need to go to school in town every day. But then it began to change. We had one couple who came here but started stealing, so they were thrown out. After that he began to impose rules, stupid ones. Everyone had to learn to shoot, and all the barbed wire went up. He started to get really religious at times - often quoting from the Bible. Sometimes it's like he's off in another world, quoting this scripture and that. It's almost like he believes he's there. You know ... Like he's there in front of God. It's really weird. Anyway, then his inner circle team joined, and it got stricter again. Some people tried to leave, but he didn't like that. He made it more like a military camp."

"Where are your parents? Are they still here?"

"No, they finally left about two years ago. They live in southern California now, but I rarely hear from them. Maybe just one letter a year."

"They left you here? All alone?"

"They had to. Boyd had already taken me as his lover and wasn't willing to give me up. Fuller Simpson had joined by then, and he and Lucas shared everything. Including me. Simpson was rough. Knew what he wanted and was rough about it. Unlike Lucas. He was just vicious. I think he's a sadist. If he didn't hurt me and make me cry he wasn't having fun. He would bite me and bend my arms around my back until I screamed. He hadn't started like that, but he got worse and worse. My parents had asked to leave and take me with them. I was just sixteen then. And then they suddenly went. Here one day, gone the next. Boyd said they'd had to move quickly and gave me a letter from them although I didn't even recognize my Mom's handwriting. She told me she loved me but I should move on with my life here, and they would get in contact again sometime. I've only received one more letter from them since, and they didn't even give me their address."

"How do you know they live in southern Cali?"

"Boyd told me when he gave me their letter last year," she said.

"So what happened around the time your parents left? When things really changed?"

"That's when he began to call himself General, and the beatings started. Until then we'd been able to go to town once a week. Suddenly that stopped, and all outside contact with anyone was ceased. Guards patrolled and a curfew was imposed. Anyone caught outside within the compound after lights out now receives a beating. There are more men here than women and Boyd declared that all women are possessions to be shared by everyone. Even the married ones. Anyone can take any woman for a night or two. All they do is go ask Boyd, he decrees it, and the woman has to oblige. Any woman. In fact, any girl over 14. Then if she doesn't satisfy the man, she gets a beating and is still forced to please him. Luckily for me, by now Lucas was getting fed up with me and wanted someone younger. I was then made available to everyone. Because of the beatings and hurt I'd got from the two of them at least I knew how to keep a man happy. Then a new girl arrived. More a women really. She was a few years older than me and the two of them made a beeline for her. She wasn't here long, though. Suddenly left one night. She might have got lost in the forest 'cos some of the men went out looking for her, but she wasn't ever found. I was told the wolves might have got her. Same thing happened to a guy that came here. Nice man. He just turned up one day saying he was fed up with life and all that. He was here about three weeks. I liked him. Friendly, like. Then he disappeared too. Told he went for an evening walk up in the forest to get some wood. He must have got lost too 'cos same group went out to look for him. Never found anything. Not even his bones. Most likely wolves got him too I was told."

"What about the residents of Westerton? What do they think of this little community here?"

"We're not allowed to talk to them much but most seem to like us. Lucas buys supplies from in town and he bought the police some equipment. We don't get bothered by them none," she said.

"And what about the girl, Lily, from the diner? She's the one who told Lucas who I was."

"Yeah, since he got all religious and the wire went up he pays some people in the town as lookouts. They report back any strangers asking questions about the community. I overheard him talking to Brother Simpson soon after you arrived. He told him to give her a bonus for flagging you, whatever that meant."

Lying next to each other on the bed, the heat from their bodies made her drowsy and gradually Terri-Anne's voice dropped away as sleep took over. Deacon, however, was fully awake, his mind racing. It was some hours before sleep finally came to him.

The following morning, after prayers and breakfast, McCabe approached Deacon and ordered him to work in the vehicle shed again. This was one of the buildings furthest away and gave him ample time to casually look around as he walked there.

From what he could see, much of Lucas's land was in a large tree-filled gently sloping valley. This was an ancient forest, wild and randomly spaced - not a managed, maintained forest where trees are planted in rows to facilitate easy felling. Looking as he walked, Deacon could see patches where the trees were so dense it would be almost impossible to squeeze past. What few tracks meandered up through the trees were random and narrow, often looking overgrown with gorse and fallen vegetation. It was also very dark near ground level, the tree canopies having grown and intermingled together until it looked almost solid and was an easy barrier to the weak November sunlight trying to penetrate.

The sun had just risen but was still at a low angle casting long shadows over the raw sleeping land.

With snow flurries swirling around his feet, Deacon walked slowly up the gentle slope. The main building he'd just left was 'U' shaped, with barns converted into sleeping quarters for single men. Both arms of the 'U' were for sleeping, and that was where Deacon had initially slept. It was a conventional open plan barracks-style, with each bed having a small metal 3-drawer storage unit and a metal wardrobe next to it. The bottom of the 'U', or the central part of it, was large and was the main dining and meeting room. The building itself was of wooden plank construction set on a concrete and wooden floor. It was fairly basic, and evidently money hadn't been wasted on finishing touches. There were various outbuildings including some small dwellings that were the married and family quarters. There were also some spare double sleeping quarters where the single men would sleep with the married women. Further away across what could be considered a parade ground was a long building with adjoining huts. This was Lucas Boyd's place plus that of his trusted 'inner circle' colleagues. There were various toilet and shower blocks further down the slope, segregated into male and female. Along the side of one arm of the 'U' was the kitchen and next to that was a large underground storage area with enough tinned and frozen food for 12-18 months, with various deep freezers running packed full.

Far to the right of the compound was a fast-flowing stream. The water-wheel generator in the adjacent building powered the entire site, but there was also a diesel generator backup with an underground storage tank containing enough diesel fuel to run for over two years. Further to the right facing east was the church. The entire compound was about 1,000ft by 1,000ft and all surrounded by a fifteen-foot fence topped with razor wire, with secondary wire fencing twenty foot further away, also topped with razor wire. Two Rottweilers, Satan and Lucifer, were patrolling in the gap between. At each interchange were well-defended gun pits. Further away was the armory and further away again was the chemical storage building.

Over to the left of the compound, outside the fenced area, were six ploughed fields and a large garden area. This time of the year the fields were virtually barren, but Terri-Anne had said wheat, barley, potatoes, sugar beet, and various greens were their main cash crops with any surplus beyond what they needed being sold for profit. Deacon could see that the compound itself seemed self-sufficient with its own freshwater stream providing drinking water. The buildings were in the middle of a dense forest area on private land of almost 60 square miles. The next nearest buildings were approximately 11 miles away as the crow flies with only one track off-site. Within the forest areas would be plenty of wild animals including both black and grizzly bears, coyotes, lynx, and wolves. The entire compound was pretty secure. The single track was partially-blocked with angle-iron tank traps efficiently stopping any rapid vehicle approach. Solar powered Wi-Fi cameras and sensors along the track with a large padlocked gate at the site entrance would give ample notice of anyone approaching. There was no cell phone coverage, and any landlines were in a secure main control room behind Boyd's private quarters. There was only one door and a single window in the control room, but it was always guarded. Although isolated, Boyd had all the power he needed and the satellite antenna on the roof would provide him with full internet and TV coverage.

The remaining buildings were the stable block where Deacon was initially held and beaten and the nearby lockable cell. The furthest building in this direction was the one Deacon was walking to - the garage, and it housed various vehicles including vans, Jeeps, pickups, tractors, a backhoe digger, a minibus, some SUVs and a BMW sedan.

With all contact with the outside world banned and stuck in the middle of nowhere, Deacon realized he was trapped.

In the last few weeks, he'd twice seen a Montana State Police cruiser come down the quiet track. The first time Boyd Lucas had gone out through the gate and shaken hands with the driver, Sergeant Dobbs. Deacon had stood well back out of sight but heard Boyd ask Dobbs how the cruiser was going and how his family was. Both questions received positive answers, and he heard Boyd confirm that no strangers had been around and of course the

Sergeant would be the first person he'd call if anyone turned up, especially if it was that cop-murdering bastard from the news. The second time the cruiser had arrived Deacon was in the field ploughing. He couldn't hear what was being said, but Sergeant Dobbs left with a smile and a friendly wave.

Boyd Lucas walked up to him afterwards and said, "That was the local police again. Dobbs confirmed the search has moved towards Washington State where they think they've had a couple of sightings in and around Seattle. It's unlikely he'll be back. Tomorrow I want you involved in something else."

"What?"

"See me after breakfast. Now get back to work."

The following morning Deacon arrived at Lucas's office at 07:15.

"Today, Brother Deacon, I want you to show some of these guards how to defend and shoot accurately. We have a target range up in the forest. After the firing, I'd like you involved in hand-to-hand combat. How to disarm etc. OK?"

"Sure! You're the boss!" and Deacon spent the remaining days of that week and the following two showing how to strip down, clean and reassemble weapons until the guards were doing it in their sleep. He also explained to them how to breathe slower when shooting and to reduce any slight movement by exhaling just before pulling the trigger. All pretty basic stuff they could have gleaned from the internet, but useful to have someone showing you.

In the main meeting hall they laid spare mattresses down and used the area for hand-to-hand combat training. Deacon taught them basic skills of how to disarm someone carrying a knife, a gun, or a baton. Some of his students were quite agile and learned quickly while others were slower on the uptake, but over the duration of a few days, everyone learned some new techniques.

Twice Lucas asked him about explosives and how to blow up a structure, but Deacon merely said there were many ways to do that. He said he'd need to know the type of building in question, whether it was brick with hollow walls, reinforced concrete, how thick the walls were to offer the right advice, but each time Lucas declined to provide extra information. However, it was clear that over those couple of weeks Deacon became a more trusted individual and more people started to acknowledge him.

Terri-Anne stayed with him throughout this time and Deacon took great pleasure in kissing her and putting his arms around her when Travis McCabe was looking. However, each night they just lay together with Deacon refusing to become more intimate.

Chapter 11

The young couple had flown into Vegas from San Francisco for a four-day vacation over the forthcoming Thanksgiving holiday weekend. Their romance was still in its early stages, and he was still trying to impress his lady. He bought her flowers and treated her well, and she had already begun to fall for him especially after the previous dreary boyfriend she'd been with. He took her out at least four times a week, and they enjoyed meals together and just socializing. They'd already met each other's friends and seemed to hit it off well.

This trip was completely unexpected, and he had surprised her at work where she was an office manager. A large bouquet of flowers had arrived with attached card and envelope. In front of all of her co-workers, she'd had to open the envelope, and she'd gasped in surprise. Two return tickets, a Limo pick up from the airport to the hotel, and four nights in the newly opened Beldorf Palace - the newest and most luxurious hotel-casino on the famous Las Vegas Strip. Buzzing with excitement, she wondered whether she would see anyone famous.

Although they'd already been intimate, she brought some of her favorite sexy underwear to please him. On their way in a taxi on route 101 waiting to get to the airport, she cuddled her salesman boyfriend tighter, confident she was going to have the best weekend ever.

On Interstate 15, a father was getting tired of driving but looking forward to arriving shortly. They'd set out almost seven hours ago from Anaheim, but a number of accidents had slowed traffic and the journey time had nearly doubled. To make matters worse, the wife had refused to take a turn driving due to the heavy traffic and the kids had begun to get bored. They'd stopped twice for food and drinks, once in the small town of Barstow where they'd had burgers and fries and stretched their legs, and the second time just for drinks at some crazy Greek-style cafe out here in the middle of goddamn nowhere. But they were almost there now and the next few days off work beckoned. The biggest problem had been the boredom while on the road. The kids had started complaining but eventually dozed or played on their various electronic gadgets, and his wife had been mainly silent. Mile after mile of two-lane driving on roads straighter than a billiard cue, under a crystal blue sunny sky. He yawned, rubbed his face, stretched his neck, but could still feel himself near sleep. But it was only another sixty or so miles, and the new fancy hotel would be worth it ...

<><><>

The Chinese tour group were in town just for the Wednesday and Thursday. Then they were off to the Grand Canyon before heading on towards Monument

Valley. There was twenty-seven in the group in total, most of them strangers to each other, but six of them had become friendly on the flight over. Chinese people love to gamble and these two days at gambling heaven in the new hotel was going to be the highlight of the four-week trip. They'd be able to talk about it for years to come.

The old lady was nearing sixty-five but still insisted she was in her late forties. She looked good for her age, but only her eyes would pass her for late forties. Her husband of thirty-five years had died almost two years ago leaving his chain of golf shops to her. She, ever pragmatic and not a bit interested in golf, had immediately sold them to his biggest competitor and had moved to Vegas, living permanently in one of the quieter hotel-casinos. Free to indulge her hobby daily, she was well known around all the casinos, sometimes losing, sometimes winning, but usually ending each week about equal. The opportunity to play in the newest glamourous casino put a spring in her step she hadn't had for years.

The athletic looking salesman was in his mid-forties, quite good looking, and he knew it. He sold marketing ideas and was the top salesman in his company. The others shared secretaries, but he had his own personal assistant. He also had a healthy travel budget for her to travel with him at times. His wife, a mousy haired petite woman, was happiest at home looking after their two boys and was jealous of the attention he gave his PA. He still loved his wife of sixteen years but had the hots for his female assistant - a twenty-three-year-old blonde beauty. She was tall, pretty, kept herself in shape and, as far as he knew, every man in the company wanted her. She had traveled with him and seemed to like him, but he hadn't managed to bed her. Yet. He'd cancelled their return flights without her knowing, saying the airlines were overbooked and forcing them to stay over the Thanksgiving holiday. He'd apologized profusely and said he'd managed to get them rooms at the newly opened Beldorf Palace. He planned to wine and dine her over the next couple of nights, and put on all the charm, but if that failed, he had a backup plan. A little something to drop in her drink to make her slightly more receptive.

The British man and his wife had wanted to visit Vegas for years. It was on both their bucket lists. They were nearing retirement age, and their kids had already flown the nest, so they were trying to catch up on lost time and view the places they wanted to visit the most. It was their thirty-year wedding anniversary this weekend so they'd come to the States on a four-week vacation and had already done most of the 'tourist' things on their list. Young at heart and still pretty fit, they'd visited Los Angeles and been to Disneyland and to Knott's Berry Farm. They'd also completed studio tours at Universal and Warner Bros. They'd taken their time and been awed by the Hoover Dam and stunned by the Grand Canyon. The lights and activity of the Vegas Strip made them giggle almost like children, and they loved the buzz and excitement. They now had a few days in Vegas before flying to San Francisco to visit Alcatraz, drive down Lombard Street - the most crooked street in the world, and see the Sea Lions on Pier 39.

The croupier was single, gay, and enjoying life. Work was hard, but his friendly manner and happy smile to his customers seemed to work well. He'd worked in five casinos before and had applied to this one as soon as he knew they were hiring. After getting onto the shortlist he'd passed the trial period with flying colors. Punters staying at the more popular and expensive hotels always seemed to spend more, and his smile and attitude meant he received more tips than most of his fellow colleagues and his table was always busy. His rent took almost half his salary, but the good supply of tips meant he was well on the way to getting his new motorbike, a fancy gold and red Yamaha.

Chapter 12

Fuller Simpson had been busy. For the past two weeks, he'd been working in a large tent erected over two hundred feet away from the chemical shed. It was also where they kept the explosives. He and two colleagues had been working there almost twenty-four hours a day under daylight and battery light. Nothing that could possibly cause a spark was allowed anywhere near them. Even the tools they were currently using were wooden. They had started with sixteen empty plastic barrels. Fourteen of them were now full and were stored another three hundred feet away under a tarpaulin. The latest mix would fill the last two barrels, and at last, he and his colleagues could breathe fresh air.

Mixing the ammonium nitrate fertilizer with the correct amount of diesel was an imperfect science. It needed to be thoroughly mixed, so it was moist throughout, but not too wet to be running with diesel. Fuller told the other two that the simplest way to check was to grab a handful of mixture and gently squeeze it. Small dribbles of diesel should escape through your fingers. The main problem was the chemical reaction between the ammonium nitrate and diesel. It caused large amounts of heat to be generated. This made it too hot to hold and squeeze. It also made it extremely volatile with the slightest spark likely to trigger it. They kept a large amount of sand outside which could be quickly added to the mix to neutralize it, if need be.

The second problem was the fumes. These would produce the strongest type of headache imaginable. Even ex-Army breathing masks couldn't filter all the ammonia out, and all three of them were suffering the kinds of headaches normally only found with severe hangovers. However, when the last two containers were finally filled, the lids placed lightly on top, they were also moved to the other outside stack and covered. Over the following twelve hours, the heat would gently dissipate, and the containers would be less volatile. At that stage, the lids could be placed firmly closing them, and they would be as safe as possible for travel.

Dwight Emery drove the stolen white GMC Savannah panel van out from the garage. It had been taken over a year ago from Kansas City. Since then, the van had been fully serviced and all recognizable features removed or resprayed, including the fitting of fake license plates that were copies of another white Savannah van in Utah.

Gingerly they placed all sixteen containers into the rear of the van and strapped them in. The tops had already been fully sealed after passing a close inspection by Simpson.

Two of the containers also had a stick of conventional dynamite attached to a blasting cap, and then both were wired back to a cheap electronic timer, currently with the batteries removed. Inside the truck were large sticky pads containing old nails, screws, nuts and bolts, and ball bearings, all stuck to the inside walls of the van. On detonation, this shrapnel would hurl outwards at hundreds of miles an hour causing additional damage to structure and flesh.

With back slaps all around, fist pumps and shouts of 'Wah hoooo', Dwight gently drove the laden van out through the gates and onto the track facing north. Just before he began to carefully accelerate, Fuller Simpson swung in on the passenger side. They had almost 860 miles to cover, and it would take them over fourteen hours. Heading south on the I-90, they joined the I-15, and that would take them directly to downtown Las Vegas.

Taking turns driving every few hours, they drove south within the speed limits, mile after mile, determined not to draw attention to themselves. However, in the event of trouble, both were carrying handguns and two replacement magazines each. Arriving in Salt Lake City that evening, they chose a quiet out-of-town, less glitzy than some, motel and checked in. Next door was an equally run-down diner, but the food was wholesome and ample in its quantity. They parked their van as far away from their room as possible, just in case anything happened, but the night passed without incident.

Following a cooked breakfast in the same diner the next morning, they were on the road again before eight o'clock.

The ride was boring and long, but between them, they talked and listened to the radio. Again, careful not to speed or do anything else that would draw outside interest to them, they relaxed and just drove and drove. The weather stayed calm, and the countryside slowly changed from the frozen lush green of the north to the straw brown of the desert.

Chapter 13

With some supplies running low, Lucas called Travis McCabe and Deacon into his office.

"I need you to go into town today and pick up some essentials. Brother Deacon, keep a low profile, but with your beard and the old photo the police were using, I don't think you have anything to worry about. Go straight there then come straight back. Understood?" he said, passing a list of requirements to Travis.

Climbing into the passenger side of the Ute, Deacon decided to needle Travis.

"Sure am going to miss little miss sugar lips while we're gone," he said. "She kisses real sweet and she's got the hottest bod around, don't ya think?"

"Shut the fuck up."

"I'm just saying. She's been with me every night for the last three weeks and boy, have I enjoyed her. Smooth, soft skin, pert litt–"

"I SAID SHUT THE FUCK UP," Travis shouted, weaving all over the track and almost crashing the pickup.

"Not jealous, are you Travis? Not jealous of me slipping into that hot, tight body every night while you just play with your limp dick, are you? She said you only had a little dick," Deacon teased, waving his little finger in the air.

With that, Travis jammed the brakes on and turned in his seat, trying to aim a punch at Deacon's head. With practiced ease Deacon grabbed the bunched fist in his own right hand and twisted clockwise as he leant over with his left and grabbed McCabe's left shoulder across his throat and then leaned his elbow in.

With his left hand being twisted almost to breaking point and with Deacon's elbow firmly in his throat crushing off his air supply Travis could only gurgle and gasp as Deacon increased the pressure. As the world began to spin and the edges of his vision darkened he could feel himself slipping towards unconsciousness when Deacon suddenly released the pressure.

"C'mon asshole. Drive. We've gotta job to do. You think you're tough? Well, I'm tougher. Next time you're with Terri-Anne overnight and you ain't happy with her, you keep your fuckin' mouth shut. Or you'll answer to me. Understood?"

"I said understood?" Deacon said again and louder a few seconds later after getting no response.

"Y .. yeah, understood," Travis muttered.

"Good. So drive on, asshole. I fancy a beer."

"But we've gotta go straight back. Orders!"

"Well, why don't I twist your wrist again 'til it snaps. Then you can shove it up your ass along with your orders?"

With the conversation ended, Deacon sat back and enjoyed the remainder of the 30 plus mile drive into the small town of Westerton.

The track to the compound gradually improved until it was a wider dirt road before becoming loose stones and gravel. Eventually, it led onto a poorly maintained pot-holed tarmac road before again improving and finally joining a narrow two-lane standard road which led into Westerton. The outside temperature was just a little above freezing and snow flurries scurried across the road in front of their wheels. As they bounced and drove over puddles Deacon could clearly hear the thin layers of ice cracking and creaking.

Arriving from the west, Deacon recognized the motel he'd stopped in over three weeks ago and the diner he'd ate at. Glancing through the window as they drove by he thought he could make out the shapely outline of Lily, the waitress, and wondered how many others she'd ratted out for her pieces of silver.

As they approached the General Store Travis reversed into a parking slot at the rear. Within twenty minutes or so, they had loaded the required provisions, including twenty large sacks of flour, ten sides of beef, ten of lamb and fifteen of pork, and a mass of other things. Pulling the covers over the rear of the Ute before climbing back in the cab, McCabe started the engine and Deacon growled at him, "The bar!"

Reluctantly, McCabe drove them to the other end of Main Street and parked to the side of 'Jeb's Bar'.

Walking in, Deacon ordered two beers and took a seat at the bar. Travis came and sat next to him and together they downed the first glasses within seconds.

"Same again," Deacon said to the server and pointed at the empty glasses. He quickly topped them up before moving off to the other end of the polished wooden bar.

On the third glass, McCabe began to loosen up and started talking.

"You wanna be careful. The General don't like his orders not being carried out."

"You let me worry about that. When I want a beer, I want a beer. How's a self-appointed, dressed-up tin-can General gonna stop me?"

"He'll set Brother Simpson on you."

"What? That pussy? Oh, I'm sure worried now! Actually, where was he going? Him and Brother Emery?"

"You'll hear tomorrow. A great day for the General. He's been planning it for years. We're gonna be letting that Democratic waste of space in the White House know where we stand."

"But we have a new Republican President being sworn in in what, 8 or 9 weeks?" Deacon said.

"Not a moment too soon, Brother. Not a moment too soon. The General will make the announcement tomorrow."

Finishing his third beer Deacon said he needed the bathroom before heading back to camp. Leaving McCabe sitting at the bar, Deacon slipped past the toilet entrance and to the far side of the bar where a pay phone was hanging on the wall out of sight.

Lifting the receiver and slipping some quarters into the slot, Deacon heard a dial tone and quickly dialed a number from memory.

On the third ring, the pay phone clicked, and the money was deposited directly.

"Hello?" Deacon heard just as he looked up and saw McCabe moving from the bar and looking around to find him.

Putting the phone down quickly while trying to keep the noise to a minimum, Deacon side-tracked and appeared to exit the Gents bathroom.

"You ready? Let's go." McCabe said, looking a little suspiciously at Deacon and then at the phone, the handset cable still gently swinging.

Chapter 14

After a long day of driving and having stopped a few times to stretch and get food, Simpson and Emery arrived on the outskirts of Las Vegas on the evening of 23rd November. The loom of the city lights reflected off the partial clouds and had been visible for the past hour. Simpson was always surprised at how much the sky was obliterated by man-made light pollution, especially when compared to the vast skies of darkened Montana.

Coming in from the north-east, they kept slightly north of the city before heading into one of the more downtrodden areas before turning onto the quiet back streets. Shortly after, they turned into an ally before turning again sharply into a back street body shop. After waiting for the doors to close, Simpson finally turned off the engine, climbed out and stretched his aching back. The body shop owner, Carl Hobbs extended a hand in greeting.

"Fuller. Good to see you, man. Any trouble?"

"Nah, piece of cake. All good here? Everything arrived?"

"Yeah, ready when you are," Hobbs said.

That evening Simpson and Emery ate pizza and drank beer after Carl Hobbs went home. They stayed out of sight and slept on sofas at the body shop. Hobbs had left them a DVD player and some porn discs, so they sat and watched TV until falling asleep.

The following morning, November 24th, Carl Hobbs turned up at 07:30 am, along with his chief mechanic, Dwayne Scott. Between the four of them, they washed the truck from top to bottom. They even raised it on jacks and power washed the underside to remove any evidence of road grit or mud. Dwayne then climbed back into the cab and wiped every surface with a cloth soaked in bleach - the idea being to remove every fingerprint or particle of DNA. Finally, wearing latex gloves, Dwayne ran a simple toggle switch cable from the control column out under the dash to the ignition wires running to the engine. Placing the switch in the 'on' position allowed the truck to start as normal. Flicking it to 'off' killed the ignition, and although the engine turned over on the key, it refused to start.

After the van exterior had dried off, the four of them, wearing latex gloves, carefully positioned the large vinyl stickers before peeling off the backing paper and firmly pressing them into place along the sides, rear and front of the van. Within the hour, the simple white van that arrived the evening before was adorned with the logos and colors of one of Vegas's most popular hotel food and beverage delivery companies.

Finally, after placing the switch back to 'on' and fitting local Nevada plates, all that remained was the connecting of the electronic timer's batteries.

Leaving an armed Dwight guarding the van with Dwayne and Carl keeping him company, Simpson borrowed a car and headed towards the Strip.

Even in the daytime, the sidewalks were busy with tourists and locals enjoying Thanksgiving Day. Vegas never shuts, and the casinos were already busy and expecting the evening to be busier.

The Beldorf Palace Casino Hotel was the newest and plushest of them all. Opened just six months before, it was where everyone wanted to be. They'd had the biggest opening event in Vegas history, had the most stars at the opening ceremony and the complex had cost almost a billion dollars.

In a city where everything is brash and bold, where glitz and glamour outdoes itself, and where money seems to be no object, the Beldorf Palace Casino Hotel now outshone them all. Even the luxurious Bellagio and the Luxor were being seen as down-market compared to the Beldorf.

But in a city where everything is focused on the chance of making money, where there are even slot machines to play in the restrooms, mistakes can easily be made.

Security is good, but there is always room for improvement. Guests on vacation don't want the hassle of being screened and metal detector wanded every time they walk in or out of a place. The casinos rely on foot traffic and on gamblers trying their luck wherever they are. With large amounts of food and alcohol being consumed daily, commercial delivery vehicles need quick delivery and turn-around times. It's in these instances that security measures may be breached. Fuller Simpson had already spent a number of days in Vegas the previous month looking at possible access routes while planning the attack.

Usually, driving up and down the same street a number of times might be viewed as suspicious and possibly raise the attention of the police. But in Vegas it's different.

The Las Vegas Strip, or just Strip as it's known locally, is actually a 4.2-mile section of the South Las Vegas Boulevard. The Strip isn't officially in Las Vegas, this section is just outside the official city limit, but it has retained its name and is world famous. Many of the largest and most famous hotels, casinos and resort properties in the world are located along this short piece of blacktop. With millions of light bulbs and over 15,000 miles of lighted neon tubing crammed into that 4.2-mile section, the Strip has truly earned its place in history and is a favorite tourist viewing spot each evening.

All eight lanes of this section of road are often full of slowly crawling traffic, and many people repeatedly drive along its length to enjoy its scenes from as many angles as possible.

A simple dark grey sedan traveling its length three times in one hour stood out as much as a single grain of sand in the desert, and it allowed Fuller Simpson to check and recheck his timing and the plan.

Chapter 15

By 8:48 pm on Thanksgiving Day, every casino was buzzing. The Strip was crowded with both traffic and walkers enjoying the scenes. Every fifteen minutes the music would play, the fountains would turn on, and one of the best free music and water shows would perform outside the Bellagio to the waiting enthralled crowds.

Tonight Vegas was full. Virtually all hotel rooms were booked, most shows had sold out, and the streets were heaving.

The young couple had enjoyed the day and were amazed at the size and opulence of Vegas. Although they'd seen it on TV, it wasn't the same as actually being there. They had gambled a little last night, and he was almost two-hundred dollars up. Their room at the Beldorf was the largest she'd ever seen, and the double-King-sized bed was both enormous and felt as soft as silk. She was wearing some of her sheerest lacy underwear, and he was already aroused at the thought of undressing her later that night and at what fun beckoned.

The father had quickly recovered from the long drive earlier and was really enjoying himself. Not needing to worry about driving, he could drink beer when he wanted. He and his wife had spent the day with their kids but the nights belonged to them. They'd had an early evening meal as a family and then put the kids to bed - the hotel operated a child-minding service - allowing the parents to spend as much time elsewhere in the hotel as they wished. They even supplied the parents with a beeper that the kids could contact them on if they became too lonely. The only stipulation was the parents had to remain within the walls of the Beldorf.

The six Chinese friends had been gambling almost non-stop since they'd arrived. Many Chinese like gambling, but this group were hooked and serious. Hardly stopping for food or drink, they'd been at the tables non-stop since eight o'clock that morning. Each was down over $500, but they were determined to win it back. The bright lights of the Strip or the dancing showgirls were not for them.

The old lady was currently up over $1,000. She'd won, lost, lost a little more, then won and won again. She was looking pleased with herself. She planned to play until 9:00 pm then leave, no-matter-what, planning to be back tomorrow. For her, the days merged into one. Having retired, every day was a possible gambling day and Thanksgiving Day was no different.

<><><>

The salesman hadn't managed to clinch the deal yet. Try as he might, his sexy-looking secretary had resisted his charms. He had given her $200 to play with today, and she was currently up $90, so quite happy to stay around him. She'd spent some time in the gym and the beauty bar earlier, before swimming in the indoor heated pool. Watching her from behind a pillar as she climbed out of the pool, water cascading down over her shapely breasts and backside he'd felt himself become aroused. Just looking at her now, siting at the bar with her long sexy legs on show, he became aroused again. She was drinking quite cheerfully and was just a little tipsy. He was still trying, but he was only going to leave it until about ten o'clock then slip that little pill into her next drink. When she woke the following morning in his bed, it would be too late.

The man and wife celebrating their anniversary had started the day with a champagne breakfast. The day had been great, just an easy going day with some shopping and sightseeing. A light lunch and an hour or so on the slots. A little time on the tables now before a romantic meal overlooking the fountain would be the perfect end to a lovely day. Tomorrow they'd visit some of the other casinos but today had been all about relaxing and enjoyment. And the Beldorf was the perfect place to relax and enjoy.

<><><>

The croupier was in a great mood. His shift today had started at three in the afternoon and finished at midnight. Tomorrow was a day off, and he planned to spend it relaxing with his new friend. He glanced at his watch. It was 20:48.

<><><>

At 20:49 time stood still and then all hell broke loose.

Chapter 16

Fuller Simpson returned to the body shop late afternoon. He'd checked his route twice and was satisfied nothing had changed since his previous inspections weeks before. With the outlet contacts disconnected, he plugged a new battery into the electronic timer, set the alarm function to five minutes and pressed the switch. After exactly five minutes had passed, the timer alarm went off, and Simpson smiled. Confident everything was ready, at 20:00 he reset the timer to five minutes and reconnected the outlet contacts of the timer to the blasting caps.

At 20:30 Simpson drove the van out of the body shop and headed downtown on one of the busiest days of the year. At 20:38 he drove south along South Las Vegas Boulevard where he passed the Stratosphere Casino and the various small wedding chapels offering instant marriage and lasting happiness. He drove a little further south onto the main 'Strip' before turning right onto Spring Mountain Road and then left onto Frank Sinatra Drive. This was the primary delivery access road to all the casino hotels on the west side of the strip and it provided him with the easy access he'd been looking for. As the clock hands showed 20.42, he turned off this road and through the delivery area, taking a sharp left turn in part-way under the hotel building canopy, before clicking the new switch 'off'. As the engine died, he coasted to a stop close to the wall before trying to start it again. With the switch still 'open', the engine turned over but wouldn't start.

Sergeant Hank Zuniga had always taken his job seriously. Ever since high school, he wanted to join the Army but failed the initial physical because of being asthmatic. The police was another option for him, but they also required the same level of fitness, so he'd taken the safer route of private security. He'd started as store security at WalMart and gradually been promoted over the years until he was in charge of the complete security team at the Miracle Miles shopping mall. Married and with two teenage daughters he was settled and comfortable.

When he received the call out of the blue and was asked to attend an interview he was surprised. When it turned out he'd been headhunted to fill the new vacancy at Vegas's latest and greatest hotel/casino, the Beldorf Palace, he knew all his dreams had come true. The hours were long but the money was good, and the promotion possibilities seemed endless.

He'd seen the food delivery truck turn in off the ramp and head towards the delivery dock. It had slowed before finally stopping close to a sidewall and under part of the main building. He could hear the driver trying to start the engine again as he sprinted over to the broken down van.

Raising his voice and shouted, "Hey, you can't stop there. Get it moving."

The driver, a tallish white guy with a ginger beard and dark sunburned skin, wearing a pale blue thin jacket leaned over and lowered the passenger side window, looked at him and explained he couldn't get it started.

"Well, we will have to get it towed. You can't park it there," Hank said.

"See if you can start it?" the driver said, so Hank Zuniga quickly climbed into the driver's seat and turned the key. After ten seconds of turning over but not catching, Hank released the key, turned towards the passenger side wall and found himself looking straight down the suppressed barrel of a Colt handgun. Beckoned to move closer, he slid across the plastic bench seats and Simpson fired two quick shots straight into his chest. With a final sigh, he collapsed and slipped down off the bench seat into the footwells, completely hidden from view. Simpson flicked a switch to start the five-minute counter, walked across the roadway shouting towards the van that he was going to call for a tow truck, and disappeared from view. As he sprinted up two flights of stairs to an access door, Simpson stripped off his outer jacket before turning it inside out and then refitting it, now looking a pale yellow sun color. He also pulled a baseball cap from his pocket and placed it on his head after tugging his ginger beard off and putting it, along with the sunglasses, into an inside pocket. A final sweep of his fingers through his darkened hair, along with the fitting of tinted reading glasses completed his new look and moments later he was walking through the main part of the hotel and out towards the front doors of the lobby.

It was 20:45.

Chapter 17

Inside the GMC Savanna panel van parked under the edge of the Beldorf Palace, the cheap battery-operated timer, part of a travel alarm clock, finished its countdown to zero at 20:49 exactly. The alarm was triggered, and the 9-volt battery sent a trigger pulse to the buzzer to wake up. However, instead of being connected to the usual buzzer, the wires disappeared into two small metal blasting cap detonators, each containing over twenty grams of black powder and each inserted into one stick of dynamite. The detonators immediately exploded causing the dynamite to undergo an instant transformation from a relatively safe stick of compressed chemicals to a small raging fireball of superheated gas. The pressure wave and heat produced by the two sticks of dynamite triggered the 16 barrels of ammonium nitrate and diesel oil to explode outwards with tremendous force and heat. The panel van actually swelled in size momentarily before its seams split, releasing the fireball and shockwave, turning the air around it red hot due to friction and its speed. The blast extended outwards traveling at just over 3,000 meters per second. One-millionth of a second later, the roof under which the vehicle was parked took the full upward pressure wave of the explosion, along with the wall next to the parked van. The pre-stressed concrete was not designed to withstand such a force and shattered and almost dissolved, projecting upwards and away from the

94

origin of the blast. The ball-bearings, nails, nuts and bolts attached to the inside of the van peppered the concrete, shattering some of the flying remnants into deadlier smaller pieces. Other vehicles nearby were completely ripped apart by the pressure wave followed by the nuts and bolts, with two cars immediately exploding into fireballs further adding to the flames and fury. Two-millionths of a second later, the shattered roof and walls blew up straight into the casino.

Chapter 18

The croupier who stood on the carpeted floor was the first to feel a slight movement. Before his brain could register what was happening, he was lifted bodily off the floor, his limbs were torn from their sockets and what remained of his torso was thrown towards the ceiling, his head hitting first and turning into a pulped mess. The shock wave, cement particles, shrapnel and superheated air next hit the six Chinese friends sitting around his table. The force of the energy exploded their bodies outwards. The heavier boned areas of chest, pelvis, thigh bones and skulls separated into flying missiles while the softer tissues just dissolved.

The hand and arm of one player decapitated a person over twenty feet away, while bones and solid body parts ripped through others. The remains of their torsos and their table hurtled outwards. The roulette chips lying on the table, being of a harder substance, became missiles, flying hundreds of feet and killing with the power of machine gun rounds. The old lady at the next table was next to be hit. As the shock wave lifted her backwards, three roulette chips hit her in the head, one taking her jawbone with it, while another entered her left eye socket and exited at the rear of her head along with most of her skull and brain matter.

As the shock wave caused her to fly backwards into other bodies, her right leg and foot were forced from her torso and smashed into another man who stood behind her. The jagged point of her knee traversed straight through his stomach, cleaving the man's spine in two and ended up sticking hideously out of the man's back. The man and wife celebrating their anniversary had just raised a glass to each other and started to say the word 'Cheers'. Before the word could be correctly formed, a dozen or so roulette chips hit his wife in the face and chest, turning her body to puree before the heavy metal of the roulette wheel itself sliced her torso in half. The shock wave expanded rapidly, and the pulped and dismembered body of her husband was thrust across the wife in an ordinarily intimate but now obscene manner.

The mother and father had been walking towards the center of the room when it happened. Shards of metal and pieces of concrete some as large as footballs headed towards them slicing them into pieces. Parts of their arms and legs were broken off in various directions. One particular fragment the size of a tennis ball hit what remained of the wife in the neck annihilating her head before continuing on into people standing behind.

The salesman's luck had finally turned. His determination had won out, and his personal assistant was feeling grateful for the weekend away and was feeling aroused. The alcohol had helped, and she was slowly coming to terms with sleeping with him that night. As she looked him in the face, the last thing she registered was his eyes exploding forward into hers as his head exploded as a stranger's foot hit his skull. They were both then slammed towards the next roulette table as more fragments tore into his back turning his internal organs to mush before they traveled on through her body doing the same. As their mutilated bodies bent and twisted under the pressure wave, they slammed into the far wall with the remains of the salesman's head finally coming to rest ironically on his PA's chest.

The young couple were in the early stages of a kiss when the blast hit. As he leaned forward towards her mouth, lips already parted, the explosion ripped across them sideways removing their clothes and the flesh around their faces. A forearm slammed into her side carving her chest in two as a shard of metal passed through the bones and soft tissue of his head. As their bodies cartwheeled away, parts of their torsos struck others.

The shockwaves kept spreading, funneled towards the outer walls. With few windows available for the blast to escape through, it continued upwards and outwards. Many more people were injured as the glass on the slot machines prevalent throughout the floor had exploded under the pressure wave. The ceilings and light fittings began to collapse, and then the fire wave hit.

An explosion of this sort has three main elements of damage. First, the immense pressure wave flattening everything in its path. This is followed rapidly by shrapnel and flying debris adding to the carnage. Third is the fire. The pressure wave had already superheated the air as it compressed it. By now everything was extremely hot and spontaneous combustion occurred destroying most remaining items. It also combusted what oxygen remained in the rooms thereby suffocating any remaining casualties.

The shockwave had to disperse somewhere and it continued out into the larger casino area, flattening and destroying everything as it went. The large front plate windows blew out, hurling giant shards of glass into passers-by out on the busy Strip. With a low rumble, part of the floor immediately above the explosion collapsed down into the turmoil. Less than three seconds had passed since the bomb had been triggered. The blast noise echoed up and down Las Vegas Blvd bouncing off buildings and structures.

Then the screaming started.

Chapter 19

Fuller Simpson was already almost 500 yards away from the casino when the explosion happened. He, along with everyone else, felt the shock wave before hearing the blast. Cars and taxis immediately outside the side of the Beldorf were hurled sideways and a couple were overturned. People walking towards or away from the hotel were blown over like tenpins, many suffering severe injuries. Buildings along the strip to the left side of the Beldorf Palace received the full blast of the shock wave funneled by the concrete structures and tunnels that are used for delivery access. Multiple windows blew out, falling on people walking below, and two giant illuminated billboards buckled under the pressure wave and collapsed, further adding to the carnage.

Simpson turned to look, along with thousands of other spectators. Even he was surprised at the effects of the blast. The human brain cannot register the sudden change from enjoyment to terror instantly, and it took a couple of seconds for people to comprehend something terrible had happened.

Then panic took over.

Some would stay there, wandering around dazed, unable to understand what had happened and would need to be helped and guided to safety. Others would immediately try to offer help, but for the majority, survival instinct would kick in, and they would panic and want to escape.

Within seconds the crowds turned desperately wild to get away after the first shout went up that it was terrorists attacking and more bombs were due to go off. Traffic was already stopped or moving very slowly on the Strip before the blast, as it was a busy evening. Now, as people rushed away and started crossing the roads, some drivers panicked and tried to accelerate away hitting and trapping some people between vehicles and crushing others under their wheels. Fights broke out as some considered others were not moving fast enough and they punched and fought the slower movers out of the way.

Las Vegas Metropolitan Police Department patrol cops Todd Wood and Harry Che were part way through their night shift. No major trouble had been expected today, but it was Thanksgiving and one of the busiest days of the year, there would always be some. Usually, it would be from some of the many pickpockets that casually walked the Strip, waiting for easy pickings in the crowds. Sometimes, later on in the evening, it would be from some of the hundreds of hookers that frequented the area looking for a winning 'john' or even a losing one wanting to drown his sorrows, as long as he could still pay. Occasionally it would be drunks - some were winners who had partied too hard, others were just too drunk to remember which hotel they were staying at. They'd seen most things in their years in the department, and they were pretty sure they could handle most situations.

But not this.

They had been driving slowly up and down the Strip looking for any trouble. Both in their mid-twenties, Harry was engaged to a dancer from one of the clubs, but Todd was still single and enjoying the life on offer for a single guy living in one of the most exciting cities in the world. They were heading north and were just passing the Excalibur while discussing where they were going to go for a drink on the weekend, when the clock display flicked to 20:49. Although a quarter of a mile away from the blast and too far to be directly affected, it took them a few seconds to realize what had happened.

"Holy fuck," was all Harry could say, watching the fireball churn and twist up into the night sky.

Quickly realizing the traffic was blocking them from the scene, Todd climbed out of the car telling to Harry to follow him.

Thumbing his transmit button Todd half shouted into his radio mic, "Ten Mary Four to Control, we have a major explosion in the vicinity of the Beldorf Palace. Multiple injuries, I say again, multiple injuries requesting immediate backup," as they both ran towards the horrific scene.

Fuller Simpson had stayed amongst the crowds. As they had panicked and tried to move away, he'd gone with them. He knew from past experience when the police later investigated the attack and checked people's camera footage and street camera recordings that they would be looking for anything out of the ordinary. Anyone seen rushing away from the Beldorf immediately before the explosion would raise interest. That was why Simpson had casually strolled out of the front doors, along with many others. As he walked down the drive, he'd deliberately not looked at his watch or walked too fast, even though he was counting down the seconds in his head. He'd kept close to a group of visiting Asians and kept pace at their slow walking speed.

Now after the event he moved with the masses. Any photos or video of him would show a face partially covered by tinted glasses and a baseball cap. He also kept his face mostly tilted down - all tried and trusted methods of obscuring the clear image that any facial recognition software would require.

It was less than five minutes since the explosion, and already the mass wail of fire engines, ambulances and police car sirens could be heard approaching. Some people, thinking they were far enough away from the source of the explosion had now stopped to look. Cameras were everywhere with virtually everyone trying to film and record what was happening on their phones rather than actually help those in dire need.

The Chief of Police, Maxwell Navarro, just arriving and always aware of doing the right thing as he was planning on running for office later this year, tried not to panic. It was too soon to understand if this was an accident or a terrorist attack and if it was an attack whether it was a one-off or part of a wider attack plan. To play safe, he chose the worst case scenario of an ongoing attack and immediately raised the emergency status to 'Supreme Red', meaning a total lockdown and emptying of all public areas of hotels and casinos. As fire and emergency alarms were activated in each casino to ensure rapid evacuation, it actually made matters worse as thousands more people rushed out onto the already overcrowded Strip.

In the total mayhem and confusion that followed it was child's-play for Simpson to stay hidden amongst the crowds, as the second wave of police vehicles drew up, and the sound of multiple fire engines and ambulances approached. To ensure he wasn't caught on camera he ducked behind one of the many advertising billboards along the Strip and removed his jacket, turned it back the original way and refitted it. Removing his baseball cap and glasses, he slipped them into his pocket and pulled out a woolen hat. Stepping back into the throng of people he was quickly lost amongst the panicking crowds. He'd now changed his appearance twice and would be lost forever in the crowd.

Carl Hobbs was waiting for him, parked near the junction of Swenson and East Flamingo. Sliding into the passenger seat, Carl drove them back to his body shop, keeping clear of downtown Vegas. When they arrived, Carl shook hands with Simpson and drove home after instructing Simpson and Dwight to stay in the building overnight and for them to leave early the next morning.

Eating yet more pizza, Dwight handed Simpson the first of over a dozen beers he would drink that night. After congratulating him on a job well done, he picked up a large slice of meat feast pizza, folded it in two and turned to Simpson.

"So didn't you sees enough killing when you was in the Marines?" he said as he started eating.

Simpson looked up, leant over and smacked Dwight across the face, "Marines? I weren't no fucking Jarhead. I was Army. Was a grunt and proud of it."

Over the next two hours, Simpson gradually relaxed after the tension and excitement of his mission. He became drunk and talked too much.

"Ain't tired of killing people yet," he said. "Done two tours in Afghanistan and two in Iraq. Killed loads of them A-rabs. They deserved it. Them thinking they better than us. One of them - I clean blew his fucking head off with a grenade."

"What?" Emery said, his mouth full of beer and pizza.

"Yeah, mouthy fucker. Him and his family. Spoke English and wouldn't show me his papers. Claimed we were invaders. So we tied his hands behind him and arrested him. Was gonna take him back to base for interrogation, but little fucker kept shouting at me. His wife started crying and all, then started her goddam wailing so I slapped her, real hard, like across her face. Little fucker then starts shouting at me saying how's I'm abusing his wife, and shouting about Allah, and then spitting at me. So's I thought 'fuck this' and pulled a grenade from my belt, popped the pin and jammed it in his mouth. Should've seen the terror in his eyes! Kicked the little fucker over and ran into the other room just as the grenade exploded. Blew his fucking head clean off. Brains everywhere. All over his screaming wife and kids. She came screaming at me, fists raised, so I shot her in the face. Had to do the kids as well 'cus they'd seen me."

"Cool!"

"Yeah, but some of the others heard the grenade and came rushing in. Saw what I'd done and some fucker reported it. I got charged by ACIC (Army Criminal Investigation Command) and spent 3 years in Leavenworth before being dishonorably discharged."

"So what happened next?"

"I was just drifting around. Met Boyd in a bar. He asked me to join him. We think alike. We think everyone should be free to do what they want, and we don't want or need the government ruling our lives. The USA was founded by Christian white folk and that's who it should be for. Too many goddam blacks and spics. Shoot the fucking lot of them, I say, unbelievers, the lot of 'em."

"Yeah, but won't that all change with the new president? He's on our side - a Republican, ain't he?"

"Yeah, but he's a businessman first. Better than that good-for-nothing Muslim fucker and them Clinton traitors before, but he'll need all the help he can get. Only way to save the great US of A is to go back to being Christians again."

"So why'd we blow up Vegas then?" Dwight asked through a drunken beer haze.

"Cus anyone who'd gamble on Thanksgiving Day, the day we thank the Lord for saving our asses and providing food on the table for us, anyone who'd gamble on that day don't deserve living none," Simpson replied, equally drunk, before eventually slipping off to sleep.

Chapter 20

The first hurdle to overcome was in trying to get to the scene of the explosion against the tide of panicking civilians who were trying to get away from it. Officers Todd Wood and Harry Che were the first responders, and as they raced towards the source of rising smoke, they began to realize what they were running into. As they got closer, they could see some of the less-injured victims. These were the ones hurt by flying glass or rubble. They were cut and bruised, and some had broken limbs. One or two might succumb to their injuries, but they had a good fighting chance, and some members of the public were already trying to help them.

Then they got to the hotel entrance, and the scene changed. There were bodies everywhere. Most were covered in blood having been cut by flying glass, and many were unmoving. Some had been trampled underfoot. Realizing there was nothing either of them could do to assist, they ploughed on further into the once magnificent foyer of the latest Vegas creation. The power had gone off so they used their torches to light the way and moved inside.

Grabbing his radio mic, Todd thumbed it and half-shouted, "Ten Mary Four to Control. Onsite at the Beldorf Palace. Major explosion with multiple injuries and fatalities. What is the status of support? Over."

The reply came back moments later that all available police, ambulance and fire services were en route but all roads close to the Beldorf were crowded with pedestrians trying to leave.

Moving further into the wrecked foyer, worried at the possibility of further building collapse, Officer Che suddenly stopped, turned, bent double and was violently sick. Todd turned towards him, saying, "Hey man, what's wron–," when he saw what Che had seen - a part of a foot sticking out of what remained of a woman's back.

Trying to stop himself from gagging, Officer Wood moved on towards the main scene of destruction. He'd only gone twenty feet when the sights and smells of dismembered bodies and burning body parts caused him to also violently lose his lunch.

Ashen-faced, they both staggered back out towards the entrance as the red and blue flashing lights of the emergency responders began to light up the carnage.

Over the next hour, the first responders managed to save as many lives as they could, patching injuries and shipping survivors off to the hospitals able to offer trauma support. The entire area was cordoned off by the police who had already identified a van parked in one of the delivery bays earlier as the source of the explosion, but the primary concern was whether further vehicles were set to explode elsewhere in the city. The sky above the Strip was buzzing with police helicopters monitoring the area, along with at least six news helicopters offering live coverage to viewers across the U.S. and the world.

Ninety minutes after the explosion, the Chief of Police, Maxwell Navarro, made the first of many official statements:

"A major explosion occurred here at ten to nine this evening. Initial reports indicate a van making a delivery at the rear and parked partly under the hotel exploded. The ensuing explosion was directed into part of the casino causing multiple injuries and fatalities. Part of the floor above also collapsed down onto what remained of the gaming tables. Police and law enforcement are treating this as a deliberate act of terrorism against the law-abiding citizens of Las Vegas and the United States. The Department of Homeland Security and the FBI have been called in, and this will be a joint operation to find those responsible and bring them to justice. There is a risk more explosive devices could be active, and I would advise everyone to stay at home or in their hotel rooms until further notice. Under the emergency powers act related to a potential terrorist attack, I have ordered all casinos to be closed immediately until we can guarantee the safety of our citizens and visitors."

That night for the first time in the living memory of many residents of Las Vegas, the advertising lights of the Strip were turned off, and the streets were mainly empty apart from emergency services vehicles.

With all casinos closed most of the public retired to their hotel rooms or homes, leaving the police and emergency services free to investigate. During the night with no further explosions occurring, Police Chief Maxwell Navarro took the unusual decision and confirmed the attack as terrorist-driven. He'd also called in Hal Caperton - the District Director of Homeland Security of Las Vegas, and Bill McLain - the Las Vegas FBI Divisional Director.

Together, they held a press conference at midnight stating the 3-party working relationship, with the FBI taking the role of lead investigator. Under the 2015 Interstate Emergencies Act, the Nevada State Governor had agreed to keep all casinos closed for a further 24 hours to allow time for the investigation to proceed.

As this additional closure period meant all casinos were closed until at least Saturday lunchtime, many visitors decided to leave.

The following morning the exodus began.

From just after daybreak, the roads became crowded as Thanksgiving Day tourists decided to call it quits and head for home. At McCarran International Airport, every seat of every flight was snapped up, some people paying three or four times the face value price to guarantee themselves a way out of town.

At 09:15 Fuller Simpson took to the driver's seat of a five-year-old Pontiac. Sitting next to him was Dwight Emery. In the rear of the car was Angelique Hobbs, the wife of Carl Hobbs; and also Krystal McKens, the latest girlfriend of Dwayne Scott. They headed out of Vegas on the now busy I-15 north and kept well within the speed limit. Ten miles outside the city limits the police were stopping and checking all vehicles but didn't know who or what they were searching for. With the limited information that it had been a terrorist attack, any vehicles containing just one or two men inside were stopped. Those with men that could loosely be called of 'middle eastern' appearance were stopped and searched vigorously.

Vehicles containing a mixture of men and women or those which included children were just waived through the road blocks with barely a question. Simpson's vehicle was stopped, but Simpson and Emery merely said they were in Las Vegas for the weekend with their wives, who smiled sweetly and waved at the traffic cop. The cop barely looked at them before waving them on.

"Brother, it was a good idea to include the girls," Dwight said as Fuller accelerated away.

"The General thinks of everything. He knew the police would be too busy to hold and check everyone so knew they would rely on profiling. Two couples sharing a car for a Thanksgiving gambling weekend down from Salt Lake City just wouldn't raise any flags," Simpson replied.

Every hour they listened to the news channels. They heard Police Chief Navarro stating one-hundred-eighty-four were confirmed dead so far, with a further two-hundred-and-seventy-two suffering injuries ranging from mild to severe or life-threatening. All the major hospitals in Las Vegas were operating on an emergency basis with all non-essential surgeries cancelled or postponed. Fifteen of the most severely injured had been airlifted to Mercy Hospital in Los Angeles.

The FBI Divisional Director, Bill McLain, took to the microphone at the eleven o'clock briefing, "We believe this was a one-off attack. The attacker appears to have driven a white van loaded with explosives under the rear wing of the Beldorf Palace Casino Hotel. The van was loaded with a mixture of ammonium nitrate and diesel oil and exploded a few minutes later. This is a similar type of explosive as used in April '95 by Timothy McVeigh in the Oklahoma City bombing of the Alfred Murrah Federal Building. We have CCTV footage of the driver arriving in the van. We believe he may have overpowered the building guard, Sergeant Hank Zuniga, a twenty-year security veteran. The CCTV footage shows Sergeant Zuniga approaching the van and talking with the driver, before climbing into the driver's seat. The footage then shows the original driver running towards the stairs leading into the casino hotel. No more movement is seen from the van until it exploded almost five minutes later. At this stage, we don't believe Sergeant Zuniga was involved. We also don't know if the driver escaped or is one of the injured. All we can confirm so far is the driver appears to be a well-built, five-foot-eleven or so male. We would ask the public for access to their cameras and cell phones for any footage immediately before and after this heinous attack. If you have any footage or even still photos, I would ask you to make contact with your local FBI office and arrange to pass these images over to us. The phone number showing on the bottom of the screen is the local Las Vegas FBI office. If any of you are traveling home, please get in contact with your local offices. In the meantime, I advise everyone to be alert and report anything suspicious. We'll update you more as further information comes available. Thank you."

With no other updates, the news services kept repeating the same announcements throughout the day. The only thing different was the number of dead and injured that continued to rise. Over the coming weeks,

Officer's Todd Wood and Harry Che would become celebrities, being regularly interviewed and questioned on TV for being the first responders on scene. One reporter also confirmed the Beldorf Palace would need major repairs and would be closed for at least six months.

The four of them followed the road north stopping for a quick lunch in Cedar City before continuing and dropping the two women off at Salt Lake City airport at 16:30. Angelique purchased two one-way tickets from Salt Lake to Las Vegas on her credit card after flirting with the ticket salesman telling him that they'd been up north attending a bridal shower. Fuller knew both Angelique and Krystal would be sworn to secrecy by Carl Hobbs and Dwayne Scott. Both men were ex-cons and still involved in criminal activity. Both were experienced in persuading their women to keep silent.

Seven hours later, just before midnight, their headlights bounced off the dirt and gravel road and reflected off the wood and metal gates topped with barbed wire. Hitting the horn caused the darkened compound to partially come to life, and two guards carrying rifles hurried to open the gates.

The happy smiling face of Boyd Lucas came into view out of the darkness in the loom of the car's headlights.

Chapter 21

Dwight and Fuller were pulled from their vehicle amidst back-slapping and cheering. Bottles of beer were thrust at them, and they were half-carried, half-dragged into the main meeting hall.

"Brothers and sisters. Today, Brothers Simpson and Emery have made us proud," Boyd Lucas shouted above the cheering, "Tonight we celebrate. They have struck the first blow in our quest. Sinners and gamblers shall be punished. They have lost the pathway to God, and they will burn in eternal damnation in Hell. This is a mighty day for us. The next blows will be against those that are ungodly, those that crave riches and against those that suck at our very blood. They're the evil ones. They'll suffer and perish," Boyd continued, spittle flecks flying from his mouth and with a crazed look in his eyes.

The cheering and back-slapping continued, and the atmosphere turned into a party mood.

Deacon casually sought out Boyd who was still celebrating with Fuller and Dwight. Deacon clasped both their hands and shook them warmly, congratulating them on a job well done.

Laughing and smiling, he turned to Boyd and said, "So why Vegas and what's next?"

"Them gamblers and fornicators got what they deserved yesterday. Thanksgiving is all about praising the good Lord and thanking him for protecting us. Not gambling and stealing money from righteous folk. That city is like Sodom and Gomorrah. Full of gamblers and hookers. Men full of greed and women with no morals. They got what they deserved. Even might get blamed on them Muslims. That'll be real good," Boyd replied, "News report said there were some anti-Muslim protests starting."

"Is the Brethren going to admit responsibility?"

"No, Brother Deacon, not yet. Our jobs not done yet. We have three more tasks given to us by the Lord to complete before that day dawns. You'll be helping in those."

"But we have a new President-Elect to be sworn in on Inauguration Day, Jan 20th. He's a Republican and already in favor of tightening border controls and removing unregistered Mexicans. Won't that change matters and these problems go away?" Deacon said.

"No Brother," Boyd said, the beer beginning to take effect and make him slur his words, "He's a Republican, but he's a rich money maker. All he's interested in is making more money. He's better than that current Democrat traitor who's a Muslim to boot, but we need a genuine President who can make us strong again and bring back our old family values. We're just gonna help the new President to see our way of thinking and help set the scene for him," Boyd slurred before wandering off to drink some more.

The following morning started late for most of them. The celebrations had continued until after three, and few were awake and working at the regular work hour of 08:00.

Sitting in the main mess area eating breakfast, Deacon was joined by a red-eyed Fuller Simpson.

"You and me. Today. We gotta show a couple of ways of blowing up a tree. We grunts do it one way. You SEAL pussies do it another. The General wants to see both."

"What do we have available?"

"We got loads of ANFO and standard dynamite. That's all."

"What are you going to use?"

"Dynamite," Fuller said.

Later that afternoon, Deacon, Fuller Simpson and the other 'inner circle' walked up into the forest. Boyd Lucas picked out two similarly sized trees and gave Fuller and Deacon one each to demolish.

Simpson went first. He placed two sticks of dynamite on either side of the trunk. He then ran a cable from a safe distance to a blasting cap he'd pushed firmly into one stick.

Moving back, he connected the wires to an old plunger-style dynamo, shouted, "Fire in the hole" and pushed hard on the plunger.

With an enormous explosion and a sound that echoed throughout the forest and the valley the trunk by the explosives shattered into fragments. The tree crashed down, and Boyd slapped Fuller on the back.

Turning, they smiled at Deacon and Simpson mouthed 'Your go!'

Deacon had spent an hour in the chemical shed and had brought a rucksack with him. He went to his tree and extracted a standard auger with a half-inch cutting blade. Placing it against the trunk, he drilled two three-inch-deep holes either side of the trunk. He then took a plastic food container from the rucksack and gently prized the contents into two sausage shapes before pushing them gently deep into the drill holes. Instead of a blasting cap, he merely cut back the end wires until about a half-inch of copper wire was showing before pushing the two wires into one of the sausage mixes.

Retreating to the others, he primed the plunger dynamo before whispering 'Fire in the hole' as he pushed the plunger down hard.

The muffled bang would not be heard from over two hundred yards away. Instead of blasting the trunk to smithereens, the explosion just caused the wood to splinter. The tree toppled and crashed to the ground, making more noise landing than the blast had done.

"How the hell did you do that?" Boyd asked

"What I did was make two small shaped charges with a modified ANFO mix. I added aluminum powder to the mixture. The downside is it makes the mix much more unstable. The upside is it more than quadruples its effective explosive power and makes it far easier to detonate just using a battery. The smaller amount means less noise, but the amount of damage is the same. Both methods are good and both are effective, but I wanted to show you there are options depending on the situation,"

Deacon said, feeling the envious look from Simpson boring into him.

"Many times we want the end result but maybe with less indication of what happened. The advantage of using something like this is ANFO is available worldwide so identifying and tracing who caused an explosion becomes harder. Also means we can do more with less explosives," Deacon continued.

Walking back down through the forest, Boyd Lucas seemed deep in thought. He could already see the advantage of having Deacon assist with the next missions. Arriving back at the compound he detailed two of his men to carefully set about making a new ANFO mixture until they had enough to fill approximately twenty barrels.

Chapter 22

Five days later the police and FBI had gotten nowhere. Las Vegas itself was slowly getting back to normal, but visitor numbers were down by over sixty percent. The television crews had been running twenty-four-hour coverage and lead anchor men and women from the major networks worldwide had been in attendance, but the information coming out was becoming old news. The outgoing President had visited and done a number of photo calls speaking with the injured, and the President-elect was due in a few days - also keen to get his face on as many cameras as possible. Tributes and condolences had been flooding in from leaders and organizations worldwide. It was the second worst terrorist attack on US soil, 9/11 being the worst.

Even Bill McClain from the FBI was having trouble coming up with anything new. He'd admitted, off camera, that you need three things to solve an incident like this. You need a motive and so far, that was unclear. He and his team couldn't understand who benefitted from these deaths and injuries. You also needed method and opportunity. The method was clear, and opportunity had been the lack of security and ease in which the van had gained access to the rear and underside of the Beldorf. But the motive was what stymied him. Could it have been a competing casino worried about the business the Beldorf was taking? Highly unlikely as all the casinos were suffering from reduced numbers now and anyway although officially legitimate businesses, most of the larger hotels and casinos still had strong ties to the underground crime cartels and they'd be damaging their own money sources.

Camera images and CCTV footage had been replayed and reviewed, and there was evidence to suggest the bomber had changed jackets and walked out the front of the Beldorf Palace along with other leaving gamblers or guests. However, the footage didn't give a clear image, and he disappeared in the throng of people. The last views of him were amongst the crowds who were beginning to panic, on the Strip, and he was lost completely soon after. The police and FBI issued the video picture and detailed it as a 'person of interest', but the quality was so poor, even after the FBI labs had enhanced it as much as they could.

Casualties had increased to two-hundred and seventy confirmed dead with four-hundred-and-forty-nine injured. Some of the injured had escaped death but suffered terrible life-changing injuries including missing limbs and major body trauma. Over the coming weeks, eighteen more of the seriously wounded would succumb to their injuries.

No one credible had claimed responsibility, and there had been no warning. ISIS had claimed responsibility, as they often do after an attack or accident, that the attack was by one of their disciples, but there was no evidence to support that theory, and the police and FBI were not taking the claim seriously.

Experts would spend the following weeks carefully examining every single particle to try to determine the source of the bomb and the identity of the attacker or attackers, but would eventually come to a dead end. Remaining parts of the truck were examined, and the Vehicle Identification Number (VIN) was found. It was discovered the truck had been reported stolen almost two years previously from a car park in Denver but hadn't been seen since. The ammonium nitrate fertilizer was available from many sources, as was diesel fuel. A forensic examination determined the dynamite as likely to have come from a batch stolen from a quarry in Nevada over a year previously, but even that assumption was open to some doubt. The heat from the fireball that followed the initial explosion removed what little evidence had survived the blast.

As often happens when evidence is scarce, the conspiracy theories started. Websites sprang up accusing the government of setting off the explosion to kill some unidentified terrorist or warlord; others claimed it was the Russians who had also been involved in the presidential election. Some claimed it was competing underworld gangs and that the Albanians or the Russians were trying to take over the Mob, and the most extreme was that it was aliens. A few sites ironically were closest to the truth. They claimed it was God's work against the evils of gambling and that everyone must repent.

Boyd Lucas's planning of the operation had left little to chance. He'd tried to guess all potential outcomes and allow for the unexpected.

<>< ><>

The following morning he called Deacon to his office.

"The next mission is in North Dakota. You will work with Brothers Todd Polanski and Travis McCabe. Brother Simpson will take the lead. The mission is to destroy part of the existing Keystone pipeline."

"Why should I help you?" Deacon said.

"You said you wanted to make a difference. You said you wanted a better America where people respect each other and value people over things. People are too self-centered nowadays. Too quick to travel and move around. I believe we were better off when we lived in smaller towns where everyone knew each other. Then people respected each other. The Keystone pipeline brings in almost fifteen percent of our daily oil requirements from Canada. Half of all Canadian oil comes through that pipe. Close that down and fuel costs escalate, and people stay at home more. I've had a vision from our Lord. He's instructed me to close down the oil, and the country will begin to heal itself," Boyd said.

"But that's only one pipeline. Only fifteen percent. What about the rest?"

"Brother John, we are just starting. Vegas was the first. Our mission is to do as the Lord demands. First, the gambling. Reports show Vegas hotels were only half occupied this last week since the explosion. When the time is right, and the Lord instructs, we'll send more teams to finish that den of evil for good. In the meantime, the Lord instructs me to close this pipeline. We will attack refineries another time as other followers join our cause and when the Lord commands. Are you with us, Brother Deacon?"

Taking a moment to reflect, Deacon stood, clasped Lucas's hands in his own and said, "Yeah, General, I'm with you. What the hell, I've got nothing to lose."

Later that evening the five of them met to begin going over a plan. Lucas had printed out a general overview of the pipeline. He also brought detailed satellite images and printed Google Earth pictures. Looking through the paperwork and maps, Deacon said to Lucas, "Where did you get such detailed information from? Isn't a lot of this classified?"

"I told you before, just because we're up here in the boonies don't mean we don't have connections."

Lucas then continued, "The Keystone pipeline runs 2,151-miles from Alberta, Canada, to Oklahoma. It has a thirty-inch pipe mostly buried underground as it crosses North and South Dakota and has 37 above-ground pumping stations here in the US. It pumps 590,000 barrels of light crude oil from the Canadian tar sand fields each day, where it is then processed. Due to the marshy terrain, in Canada most of the pipeline is above ground, but in the US only twelve percent of it is, mainly in North Dakota, again due to the marshy ground. The rest is buried almost twenty feet deep and well protected."

"God's plan is for us to destroy a long section of above ground piping within North Dakota, ideally close to the many ravines and streams in that area. Doing so at this time of year in early winter will make it almost impossible for repair until the land thaws out and the rivers and streams begin to dry up," he continued. "I also want two adjoining pumping stations destroyed and some of the piping in between. This should ensure the pipeline is out of action for a minimum of six months, possibly longer."

"When does this attack need to take place?" Deacon asked.

"It's just over three weeks until Christmas. I want it done in two weeks' time on a Saturday. I want it done on Saturday, December 17th."

"Why that exact date? What's special about that day?"

"That is what the Lord has instructed me to do. It must be on December 17th," Lucas said, offering no further discussion.

Looking at pictures of the pipe structure Deacon could see it was mounted on large concrete blocks spaced anywhere from 60 to 120 feet apart, set into the marshy ground.

"What explosives do you have? Just ANFO and dynamite?" Deacon asked, receiving a nod in reply.

"We could use dynamite but it's not the best solution."

"Why not?"

"The area is marshy, and we will likely have to walk across country to get to the actual pipeline. Correct?" he said.

Getting nods, he continued, "We need to be as far away from any service roads as possible to make any repair difficult. We would need reasonably large amounts of dynamite to blow even one reinforced block to guarantee total destruction. It depends on how reinforced the concrete is, but too little dynamite and it will just crack it and leave it serviceable. Ideally, we need to blow two or three blocks simultaneously. That way the pipe will sag and drop to the ground. We can then blow sections of the pipe which will cause the oil to spill and ignite."

Looking at the maps and satellite photos Deacon and Fuller both agreed the best place would seem to be southwest of the small town of Langdon, North Dakota. The entire surrounding area for many miles around looked to be extremely marshy with hundreds of lakes and streams. The pipes here were supported every 60 feet, mounted on reinforced concrete pillars. The land was also very uneven meaning standard vehicles would have trouble gaining access, even in the spring when the weather warmed. Any destruction would pollute the area but would also make repairs very awkward especially during the cold winter as everything would be covered in ice. No complete repair work would be possible until late in the spring thaw.

Deacon said, "All of the US located pumping stations seem to be above ground while the remainder of the piping to Oklahoma looks to be buried. The pump stations are automatic and only manned some of the time, maybe just for routine maintenance."

"Yeah? How do you know that, college boy?" Simpson sneered.

"Look at these satellite photos," Deacon said, passing various images around. "You can even see it in these Google images."

"What? What can you see, asshole?"

Ignoring Simpson's tone, Deacon pointed at the images. "Look closely. There are only three pumping stations in this entire region, and none of them is close to towns. But look, no vehicles are showing in the photos. So how do people get there and back without trucks? There're parking slots - you can see them here, but no cars or trucks, yet these two stations are something like thirty miles away from the nearest town."

"Good point," Boyd said, "Go on."

"Being unmanned, it will be easy to blow the stations. But those stations will also have access to the pipes for launching or recovering PIGs - Pipeline Inspection Gadgets. Place explosives and a timer onto a PIG and launch it down the pipe. The PIG will flow along with the oil at 6-7mph. Estimate where you want it to detonate, set the timer and boom! The explosion will destroy the pipeline underground and pollute the area," Deacon said.

Boyd Lucas smiled as he thought through the after effects. He said, "With the pipeline broken and at least two pumping stations destroyed, the USA will lose over half of Canada's daily export. Canada supplies almost 1/10th of USA oil. This won't cripple the US, but the shortage will drive the price of oil up, and many Americans might stop driving and go back to simpler ways."

"But won't it just cost people more? Why will they stop using cars?" Deacon asked. "In the past people have just absorbed oil price rises. Maybe some have stopped driving, but only a small number."

"You're wrong, Brother Deacon," Boyd said, "With the messages we will be giving out people will see the light. They will go back to simpler days and buy less."

Not convinced, Deacon just smiled slightly and nodded his head in basic agreement.

Boyd studied the maps and photos before eventually saying, "I need the four of you to go and reconnoiter the area and plan the exact site. Go the day after tomorrow and come back to me with a detailed plan."

"So is that it?" Deacon said.

"What do you mean, 'Is that it'?" Boyd said.

"Shutting off a bit of oil is hardly going to bring the country to its knees, is it? Twenty cents on a gallon isn't suddenly going to turn us all into the Waltons. It isn't gonna be 'G'night John Boy', is it?"

"It's a start. The good Lord has instructed me, and I have instructed you. The Lord has other plans, but I am not at liberty to disclose them to you yet. Once this mission has succeeded, then you will be informed of the others. Okay?"

Realizing that was as best an answer as he was likely to get at this time, Deacon wisely decided to back down and live to fight another day.

After the team split up, Boyd called Fuller over and said quietly, "Brother Deacon seems too good to be true. I know you were a grunt but his training as a SEAL means he's carried out lots of demolition. His knowledge and experience could be crucial to the success of this mission. But keep an eye on him. He now knows one of our plans. If he steps out of line, kill him."

Chapter 23

The following morning Travis McCabe and Wade Horton headed into Westerton to fill up with supplies. Deacon decided he wanted a beer, so he went along for the ride. They had a full truckload on order to pick up from the General Store. Arriving close to lunchtime, Deacon stood there for a couple of minutes watching then turned and said, "Boys, you fill the truck. I'm going for a beer. Pick me up when you're done," before walking back down the High Street.

Stood at the bar in 'Jeb's' he ordered a beer then headed to the restroom. Slipping three quarters into the payphone coin slot, he dialed a number from memory. After a brief fifteen second call he saw the truck pull up outside, so he hung up and nipped into the Gents bathroom. Staying there for almost three minutes, he washed his hands and walked out, straight into McCabe.

"Where were you?" McCabe asked.

"Taking a shit. Do you wanna see it, pal?"

"We should go," McCabe said, turning towards the door.

"I'm drinking my beer first."

"Well, I'm leaving."

"You leave now, pal, and you'd better keep on driving. I'm gonna stand here and drink my beer, and unless you want me to break your fucking legs you'll be outside waiting 'til I'm ready, capisce?"

The journey back to the compound was in silence. On arrival, McCabe reversed the truck to the kitchen stores area and opened the back, just as Deacon got down and began to walk off.

"Aren't you gonna help us unload?" he shouted.

"Nope, that's your job. Me? I'm off to take another shit," Deacon said, smiling as he walked away.

What Deacon failed to see was Fuller Simpson looking at him before he walked up to Travis McCabe to have a word.

<><><>

The following morning, early before sunrise, the four of them met in the mess hall for an early breakfast. They'd take turns driving but it was a long way, and the weather didn't look good. The temperature was hovering around twenty-five Fahrenheit and snow flurries were blowing across the yard, with heavier snowfalls to come. This morning's breakfast was ham, eggs, toast and coffee. The cook had also packed sandwiches and filled three coffee flasks for them.

Climbing into the Jeep, Deacon offered to take the first spell driving. Boyd Lucas had a quiet word with Fuller before they set off and then Deacon navigated the snow-covered track along to the one-lane road before it turned into the standard blacktop. Passing through Westerton, they headed across country to the I-90 before heading east and joining the I-94. With almost nine-hundred miles to go and the weather staying clear, keeping to a safe speed of around fifty it would still be a long day. The plan was to get to Minot and stop overnight, spend the following day in and around Langdon, Devil's Lake and St John, before heading back.

The drive there was entirely uneventful. The heater in the Jeep didn't work, and the average inside temperature hovered around freezing all day. Those not driving mostly just dozed. They swapped driving roles every ninety minutes or so and stopped for lunch near a small town called Glendive. During the entire day they only passed a few cars and traffic heading towards them was negligible. Heading north on route 83 they were the only vehicle in sight. As late afternoon turned to evening and the sun set, thicker dark clouds began to move in from the west. Arriving at a cheap rundown motel with a bar next door on the outskirts of Minot, Simpson went in and booked two twin rooms. Deacon and Todd Polanski shared one room while Simpson and McCabe took the other.

Sat in the bar that evening they were careful not to be overheard. The bar was very basic. The long counter was badly scratched and faded but an attempt to polish some life into it gave it a reasonable shine. There were basic wooden chairs and tables set around the room and multiple animal heads adorned the walls.

The barman and owner, an older, overweight man with thinning hair, served them beers before trying to start up a conversation.

"So we don't see many travelers this time of year. What are you boys up here for?"

"We're contractors working at the Airforce base up the road."

"Doing what this time of year?" the barman persisted.

"Can't rightly say. You know, classified and all that. Nothing real secret like, but not allowed to discuss it, if you don't mind, bud," Simpson said, touching the side of his nose.

"Hey, no problem boys. We're all on the same side. Let me buy you all a beer," which not only finished the conversation but allowed the four of them to speak quietly without raising suspicion.

The following morning, after leaving the motel and stopping at a truck stop cafe for breakfast, they headed out towards Devil's Lake. It had looked perfect from the satellite photos but now the entire area was covered in ice and snow. Although this would inhibit any heavy repair vehicles gaining access, it would also limit their ability to get close to the pipeline in their Jeep. The dark grey shape of the Keystone pipeline was clearly visible a mile or so away across the terrain, however the land was so flat anyone would see them moving towards it from miles away. There was also no place to leave and conceal the Jeep. They drove around the area for almost an hour, careful not to be seen or to draw attention to themselves before deciding they needed a better location.

Looking at the satellite images, both Deacon and Simpson agreed further north nearer the Canadian border might offer more hope.

Heading north, they arrived at the Turtle Mountain Reservation, close to the border. Here, the countryside was more crowded, with trees, small hills and multiple places they could hide. Passing over a small bridge, the road turned sharply back on itself and they managed to park behind a large group of trees and be entirely hidden from view from the quiet road. The four of them grabbed their backpacks and set out in the general direction of where they expected the pipeline to be.

The first few hundred yards was easy, but as they ventured further, the terrain worsened. The surface plant growth hid a watery sub-level eighteen or so inches deep. The thin ice layer creaked and groaned under their weight, and twice Polanski and Simpson slipped through. Under the water layer was another six or more inches of decaying plant life encompassed in a thick black muddy goo. With icy water up to their knees and the black goo holding them firmly, it took two others each time to pull the trapped one free. It took them almost two hours to travel the mile and a half to the edge of the pipeline with Polanski and Simpson suffering the beginnings of frostbite in their feet and legs.

Approaching the first concrete support, it was clear to see how strongly built it was. It's foundation disappeared at least six feet underground, and a large metal frame was bolted to its top. Two angular metal brackets were bolted to the frame and the flange of the pipeline was bolted to them. The pipe itself was held approximately twelve feet above the frozen soil and the heat from the oil within the pipeline could be clearly felt and was keeping the immediate area free from ice.

"Why's it hot?" McCabe asked.

"Warm or hot oil flows easier than cold. Coming out the ground it's hot, and the pumping stations are also heating stations, warming the thick oil. If it cools too much, it will solidify and block the pipe. Once cooled and blocked, the pipe will never open again," Deacon said.

"If we destroy the concrete supports, the pipe will sag to the ground and begin to cool. We can then blow the pipe, and the hot oil will initially spread out and warm the ground. It'll mix with the water around here and make it virtually impossible to repair," Deacon continued. "Although the water and ice will disappear in the summer, the oil will stay a soggy mess and make it impossible for heavy equipment to get close. When they stop the pumps from working the rest of the oil will cool and solidify. The entire 2,000 mile pipeline will become a giant lump of solidified oil. It'll never flow again."

For the next thirty minutes, Deacon made some quick measurements and drawings of the structures, deciding where to place the explosives.

On this ground which was particularly marshy, the concrete foundations were placed around one hundred feet apart. Deacon and Simpson agreed that if they could collapse three or four of them before blowing the actual pipeline up, the resulting oil spill and damage would make it extremely hard if not impossible to repair. Certainly, for almost a year any attempt at repair would be unfeasible as the ground would have to dry out in the spring and summer, before any mopping up and collection of the spilled oil could commence.

"The main problem I can see," Deacon said to Simpson, "is dynamite isn't the right explosive for this. We'd need to drill holes in the concrete to place the sticks in. Otherwise most of the blast will expand outwards."

"So what? Too important to drill some fucking holes?"

"No, but do you want to be the asshole carrying a big fucking drill and a power pack all the way from the road?"

After looking around some more and taking some photos, they headed back to their Jeep.

Chapter 24

It took them another three hours to drive to the nearest pumping station close to Burtsville. As expected, the site was unmanned. There was a camera focused on the padlocked gate and two more cameras located on poles aimed at the pump site buildings. The cables from the cameras ran towards a small outbuilding with an antenna located on top. Next to it was another small building with an electrical sign on the door.

"That's a wireless link for the cameras and next door is the back-up generator. The main building will be connected by cable or the internet for control and alarms, but the cameras are feeding live images somewhere. We disable that wireless link and blow the back-up genny and we can wander around without the alarm being raised until we actually gain access to the building. It won't be a problem," Deacon said.

"But won't guards be sent if the cameras fail?" Todd Polanski asked.

"Yeah eventually, but first they'll suspect it's just some technical fault. As long as the main building stays online and they can control everything as usual, they'll most likely just consider it a snafu and send a technician out to fix the cameras. That could take hours. As soon as we blast into the pump room the alert will go up, but we can set up the PIG and explosives before we do that. It'll take them time to get here and we'll be long gone by then. Also, when the control fails after the cameras have, they'll assume it's either a power outage or a bigger technical fault. They won't have seen us here," Deacon said.

From the maps and satellite images they'd brought with them and looking at the site through binoculars, it was easy to identify how the site operated. The cooling oil came in from the underground pipe and came up to a wellhead. There, the main pipe split into four, each smaller pipe going through a combined pump and heating system. Having raised the temperature of the oil by roughly fifteen degrees Fahrenheit and increased its pressure, the four outlets were combined again into one and the output pipe then proceeded underground. There were also two 'T' sections where a PIG could be introduced or removed from the system. The PIGs could only travel the distance between pumping stations, but they could all see how easy it would be to load the PIG with explosives, prime it ready and have it ready to be introduced to the downstream section as soon as they broke into the control room. From there it could be controlled and, once entered, would move at the same speed as the oil flow.

Deacon and Simpson looked at the map for the location of the next downstream pumping station and estimated it was almost sixty miles away.

Deacon said, "It'll take the PIG between nine and ten hours to get to the next station, so all we need to do is set the timer for some time in between. We can work out its progress on the map and choose a time when the PIG will be in the worst possible place to access it."

Looking confused Polanski said, "But will it destroy the pipe itself?"

"It will devastate it," Deacon said. "The blast will explode outwards and break the pipe. But because it is buried some of the power of the blast will be trapped. The pressure wave has to expand somewhere so it will follow the path of least resistance and actually travel up and down the pipe further compressing the oil. That will burst out at any seams it can, meaning more repairs, and it will also damage the next pumping station downstream."

It was now late afternoon and already getting dark. They climbed back into the Jeep and began the long drive home.

By seven-thirty the weather had worsened, and the snow was falling steadily. Approaching the small one-horse town of Glenfield, Simpson made the decision to stop for the night. The town had one small motel, a bar, and a diner that was already closed as they noticed passing it on the way in.

After checking in, again two to a room, they headed out to the bar for drinks and food. After ordering, Deacon went up to pay and spoke briefly with the female server. He slipped her two twenties as a tip wrapped around a note. She moved away down the bar, read the note, smiled and gave a faint nod to Deacon before she headed off to serve others.

An hour or so later they all headed back to the motel.

Deacon opened his eyes at exactly 05:45. He'd set his internal alarm clock the night before, and it never let him down. His breath showed in the cool moonlight as he slipped out of bed, quickly dressing. This time he'd shared with McCabe, who he could hear snoring gently. Picking up his boots he quietly let himself out of the room, where he finished dressing, put on his boots and his thick Parka before heading out into the snow.

The clouds had gone, but the temperature had plummeted. It was at least five below freezing, maybe lower. The snow reflected brightly in the clear moonlight, and he made good time walking towards the eastern end of the town. His footsteps left clear impressions in the new, crisp snow and each step crunched as the frosty snow covering collapsed under his weight. He could see for almost half a mile and the lights of the Blue Skies Diner were showing clearly. One of the first customers to arrive, he slipped into a booth one away from the corner but sat facing the entrance. As he sat down he could just make out the shape of someone sitting behind him and he saw the outline of a dark Buick in the carpark, snow and slush built up around the wheels and windshield.

"Hey, early bird. What can I get you, hon?" the waitress asked as she walked over carrying a steaming jug of coffee.

"I'll have the works. Bacon, sausage, eggs over easy, hash browns, wholegrain toast and keep that coffee coming please, Megan," he said, after a glance at her nametag.

"You got it, cowboy," she said topping up his mug before she walked away.

Over the next few minutes before his breakfast arrived, Deacon sat staring sideways out the window at the snow-covered road. Only one pair of vehicle tracks to the diner showed.

Twenty minutes later, just as Deacon was swirling the last piece of toast through the remaining yolk on the plate, the door crashed open, and the angry faces of McCabe and Simpson appeared, Polanski following in their footsteps.

"Where the fuck have you been?" Simpson snarled.

"Even a dumb grunt like you should've been able to follow my footsteps. As for him," he said, indicating towards McCabe, "he's so dumb if I gave him a mirror on a stick, he still couldn't find his own asshole."

"Whatcha doing here?" McCabe said while the waitress looked on, a smile on her face and trying not to laugh.

"Having breakfast. What does it look like, dumb-ass?"

"C'mon, we're leaving."

"Not until I finish my coffee. Now be polite to the lady, smile and sit down."

Not wanting to make a bigger scene than he'd done already, they sat at one of the empty tables and just glared at Deacon.

Taking twice as long as he needed, he drunk his coffee slowly before walking over to the counter, handing over a twenty and saying thanks to Megan.

"Sure, cowboy. You have a nice day 'n all. See you around," she said, smiling.

Chapter 25

Walking back to the motel, Deacon deliberately walked slower than usual then insisted on time in his room to brush his teeth. Eventually piling into the Jeep, Simpson instructed Deacon to begin the driving.

"Sure, no problem, pal. I've had a good meal, I'm riding in a fine and dandy limousine, and I'm surrounded by friends. What more could I want?" Deacon said, his sarcasm being lost on his fellow travelers.

The first part of the journey was boring. Flat, uninterrupted landscape covered in snow. Very little man-made life was to be seen, and the brightness of the sun reflecting off the snow made Deacon squint. It wasn't until they were a long way back inside Montana that the area showed a little diversity. They arrived back at the compound after dark and had to wait until the gates were opened before they could drive in and park. The cook had kept food warm for them so they all trooped off to the mess hall and ate. When they'd finished, McCabe and Simpson went and talked with Boyd Lucas. Deacon arrived a little later.

"Brother Deacon. I hear you went off this morning. That was wrong. You should have stayed as a group, as instructed," Lucas said.

"Quite simple, General. We'd had a few beers the night before, and I woke up hungry. The shithole of a motel only served bagels, and I wanted something hot. Didn't want to wake McCabe so went for breakfast. My tracks were pretty obvious. Anyway, more importantly, I have the details we needed to blow the pipeline. We need to change the plan a little, or we need a lot more dynamite and a large power drill with power pack."

"Will ANFO do?"

"Definitely not. It's got less explosive power than dynamite. That's why you needed so much in Vegas. With the dynamite you have here we would only be able to blow one concrete tower, and even that will be problematic."

"So what do you propose?"

"Instead of destroying three or four support towers, we destroy the metal mounts at the top of them supporting the pipe itself. The pipe will still fall off, and we can destroy it as before on the ground."

"What's the drawback to that and what's your reasoning behind it?" Lucas said.

"You don't have enough dynamite. The concrete supports are tougher than I first thought and you need more dynamite to destroy them fully. This way, you can still destroy the pipeline but it would leave the concrete supports easier to repair. They would still need heavy lifting equipment to bring in replacement sections of pipe but the repair will be easier."

"So if you were still in the SEALs how would you do it?"

"I'd blow it apart using det cord and C4. You'd only need smaller amounts of C4 at each support block to completely destroy them, and two hundred feet of det cord would wipe out that much pipeline."

"Det cord?"

"Yeah, detonation cord. It burns at over 6,000 meters a second. So fast it's the same as an explosive. Get a long length of that and lie it along the pipe and the whole thing goes up."

Boyd Lucas sat there gently rubbing his chin, deep in thought for almost five minutes. In the ensuing silence Deacon looked slowly around wondering if Lucas had fallen into a trance or even asleep when Lucas suddenly said, "Don't have no det cord, but would ten pounds or so of C4 change your mind?"

"You've got C4? Damn right it'll do. Where the hell did you get that from?" Deacon said.

"We've got some Claymore mines located at key points in the forest here. If I arrange to get them back here, you'd just need to remove the C4 from them. Can you do that?"

"With my eyes shut, General, with my eyes shut. Even Simpson could do that."

After being dismissed and instructed to begin reclaiming the C4 the following day, Deacon headed outside where he bumped into Travis McCabe.

"So you felt the need to go crawling to Lucas to tell him about my breakfast, eh? you squirming little fuck."

"So what if I did?" McCabe said.

Punching him once hard in the stomach, Deacon smiled as McCabe collapsed onto the snow. Leaning down close to him and lifting him partly off the ground, Deacon said, "Now I'm going to go to my nice warm room, have a nice warm shower and then fuck young Terri-Anne until she can't stand up, so why don't you tell Lucas that as well," he said as he dropped McCabe back down, the look of jealousy already burning in McCabe's eyes.

Knowing the thought of him with Terri-Anne would eat McCabe up inside for the rest of the evening, Deacon smiled as he walked away.

Back in Lucas's office, Simpson and Lucas were still discussing Deacon.

"I can't put my finger on it, but I still don't trust him, General."

"Keep a close eye on him. We'll use him for now, and he'll be the perfect patsy for the 17th."

Terri-Anne had been waiting for him the night before. As he'd told McCabe, he'd had a hot shower and then gone to bed with her. But then it had differed. As before, they lay together with her in his arms, and they'd talked a while. Eventually, both had drifted off to sleep. Rising a little late, they'd both gone and eaten breakfast before Deacon wandered over to the chemical shed and Terri-Anne went off to do her duties. Twice Deacon almost bumped into Travis McCabe, the black look of hatred showing clearly in McCabe's eyes.

Four of the other Brothers had been ordered to retrieve the Claymores, so Deacon sat around relaxing until they returned. Then he and Simpson started removing the composite C4 explosives from the ten Claymore mines.

C4 is often portrayed in the films as having an almond smell, but this is just Hollywood. In fact, C4 smells of engine oil. It's soft and pliable with a texture much like putty. It can be pulled apart and squashed together and even set alight quite safely. If lit, it burns with a bluish yellow flame but gives off noxious gasses. It feels a little oily and leaves a greasy trace on the hands. It is one of the safest explosives around until it is connected to a suitable detonator. Then it is deadly.

Compared to standard dynamite, C4 is approximately 1.6 times more powerful. Its blast is also faster and spreads farther. It can be molded to fit and is easy to mold into a shaped charge which can be used to direct its force more accurately.

Each Claymore mine weighed approximately 3.5 lbs. made up of 1-1.4 lbs. of C4, up to 700 steel balls, and the metal casing. Deacon and Simpson unscrewed the casing, removed the No. 2 type electric detonators and gently removed the steel balls. The composite C4 was cold and hard to remove so they placed the entire mine in hot water. Once warmed and pliable, they scooped the C4 out using a wooden spoon and gently squeezed and weighed it roughly into 1.5 lb. shapes. Simpson kept one Claymore separate, saying Lucas might need it at a later time.

That evening Boyd Lucas called Simpson into his office.

"What have you got?" he said.

"Over 12 lbs. of C4, split down into 8 charges. It's perfect. Deacon reckons he could blow three structures and we use the dynamite to blast the pipe off the mounts and also explode the pipe itself. The rest we use at the pumping station, dynamite at the station itself and C4 in the PIG. That'll give us the biggest blast underground."

"I've just seen the long-range weather forecast. There's a storm coming in late next week. It'll make a problem for us. You've done well. Let's talk again in the morning," Lucas said.

Chapter 26

Having breakfast with Terri-Anne, Deacon tucked into porridge, toast and coffee when Lucas and Simpson came and sat down, one either side of him.

"Brother Deacon, the plans have changed. There's a heavy snow storm coming in from the West next week, so I am bringing everything forward. The four of you will head back out tomorrow and plant all the explosives on the pipeline, but the detonations must still be set for 12:00 noon on Saturday 17th."

"But that's pretty early. What if it's found?"

"Brother Simpson thinks like I do. It's unlikely anyone will be out in a blizzard. It's far enough away from the road no one will see unless they go looking for it deliberately."

"What about the pump station? When do we attack that?"

"We'll still do that on the 17th. The roads will likely be cleared enough, but we're gonna get an almost five-foot dumping next week, and Simpson said getting across the ground to the pipe was already tough. With an extra five-foot or so of snow, it'll be impossible. So I need you to work together today to get everything ready," Lucas said, leaving little room for discussion.

Heading back over to the chemical shed, Deacon told Simpson to get the team together while he started checking the inventory.

The C4 was still there along with ten barrels of ANFO instead of the expected twenty.

When the group were assembled Deacon gave an overview of what he and Simpson had decided.

"Brothers. Brother Simpson and I have come up with a plan. The General has discovered the weather is worsening next week, so we will go back tomorrow and plant the explosives on the pipeline. We believe the chances of it being discovered before the planned detonation date of Saturday to be highly unlikely, but if the expected snow arrives access next week will be virtually impossible. Brother McCabe, I want you to get the timers together. We'll need three but bring four. Make sure all four timers work and that all the alarms are set and activated. We also need wire, rope and duct tape. Put new batteries in all of the timers. Brother Polanski, I need you to gather a dozen or so grey blankets and twelve pairs of heavy woolen socks, preferably grey or dark colors."

"What the fuck do you need blankets, socks and rope for?" Simpson asked.

"You'll see. Polanski, just do it. Back together in one hour then I'll show you how to use C4."

Ninety minutes later, Deacon pulled a bit of C4 no larger than a piece of chewing gum off the larger amount and began rubbing and rolling it between his fingers.

"This is totally safe like this. Look, I can even set fire to it," he said, lighting it with a match. As it burnt slowly,

McCabe and Polanski winced. "Get it warm, and it's easier to mold. It also sticks better," he said, blowing out the flame. He then led the team outside and over to a sapling where he brushed the snow off part of its trunk. Pressing the warm C4 into a short sausage shape and pressing it hard against the trunk, it caught on the rough textured bark. Deacon then placed a blasting cap detonator in the C4 before attaching the twin copper ends of a long piece of cable to the pair of wires sticking out of the blasting cap.

Unravelling the cable, Deacon walked backwards to the group twenty feet away.

"We'll use electric timers, but this is just to show you," he said, baring the cable ends.

He then counted down from three and stroked the bare wires across a simple 9-volt radio battery.

The sharp crack echoed around them, and the central two inches of the sapling trunk disappeared.

"To do the same with dynamite, I'd have to have tied the dynamite to the trunk, and it would have needed almost three times as much. Almost 80 percent of the blast would have been outward and therefore wasted. What we had with the C4 was a shaped charge and almost all of the energy was directed into the trunk, just where I wanted it to go."

"OK, so what about the pipeline?" Polanski said.

"We'll use six of the C4 bundles. We'll split each one in half, making twelve equal amounts - four for each of the three structures. We'll place all four amounts around one base equal distances apart and wire a blasting cap detonator into each. Then all four blasting caps are wired back to a single timer. This means all four will detonate at exactly the same time and although some of the charge will blow outwards, most will go into the structure. There's no way it will survive that. At the same time, we'll place more C4 on the connecting beams above that are supporting the pipe. Finally, we'll duct tape two or three sticks directly to the pipe. These'll trigger automatically when the C4 goes up. Finally, we'll hang the grey blankets over the charges, tied with rope. The blankets will blend in with the grey of the pipe but the snow will cover it anyway and it'll be invisible from more than a few feet away."

"And the socks? Is that 'cus you have cold feet?" Simpson sneered, smiling at his own joke.

"No, that's to keep the batteries warm for the four or five days, so they don't lose charge. Each timer goes inside four pairs. The wool keeps the batteries warm and working. Cold kills batteries as I am sure you know - this way they will work for weeks," Deacon said.

"And the rope?" Simpson inquired, less aggressively.

"How else do we get up the fifteen feet to the pipe itself? We can't take ladders. Just throw the rope over the pipe and climb up."

The rest of the afternoon was spent letting them play with the C4 and practicing wiring the detonators together.

Noticing a small piece of stiff wire lying on the ground, Deacon picked it up and dropped it in his pocket.

Finally, with the evening drawing near, Deacon arranged for them to lay everything out to ensure nothing was overlooked or forgotten. He then checked off explosives, timers, blasting cap detonators, connectors, duct tape, rope, electric cable, blankets, and socks. They also placed four rucksacks ready on the table.

Lucas joined them for their evening meal and got them to run through the plan again to make sure each knew what they were doing.

"General, when checking today I saw the C4 and the dynamite and ten barrels of ANFO. Where's the other ten gone?" Deacon asked.

Glancing at Simpson, Lucas answered, "Have no fear, brother. We have moved the other ten away to a safe place. As you yourself said, you don't need it for this mission. You'll be told more when you need to know," which effectively ended the conversation.

The snow was gently falling again as he and Terri-Anne headed back to their cabin. Later, lying in bed with her asleep against him, Deacon ran through the plans again and again, trying to find any mistakes or areas of doubt. Satisfied every base was covered, he got up and dressed quickly in the dark so he would not wake Terri-Anne. Too wide-awake to sleep, he quietly closed the door behind him and went for a quiet walk around the pitch-black compound after checking the contents of his pocket.

Chapter 27

Another early start. The high-level cloud had already arrived overnight, with the promise of heavier snow to come. It was at least twelve hours away, currently over the north Pacific, but the weather channel showed it lasting two or three days before high pressure would eventually push it further east and was warning of heavy snowfalls to come.

With the Jeep loaded, Deacon climbed in the back, having said someone else could start the driving. At least the heater worked now, one of the mechanically minded brothers had fixed it after being shouted at by Simpson, so the journey was more comfortable. The traffic was a bit heavier with everyone trying to get things done before the worst of the weather set in.

Arriving at the same motel on the outskirts of Minot, the owner greeted them as if they were old friends. In the adjoining bar later that evening, the bar owner tapped the side of his nose in understanding before buying them all a beer.

Offering a salute for the beer, Simpson thanked him and briefly explained this would be their last job before Christmas.

Apart from two locals, they were the only customers in the bar and were left alone.

The following morning they headed out just as the sky was beginning to lighten. Clearing almost a foot of snow off the windshield, they climbed in and started the Jeep, the engine sluggish in the cold. It had been gently snowing for almost forty-eight hours and the heavy low-slung clouds totally obscuring the sun looked dark and ominous. The winds had increased, and the temperature had plunged to 16°F.

Losing their way a couple of times and twice accidentally driving off the road due to snowdrifts, they eventually arrived back at Turtle Mountain Reservation. Even with snow chains fitted, it took multiple attempts to drive through the thickening snow close to the road, but they eventually found the same small bridge and parked behind the same clump of trees two hundred yards off the road where they'd stopped on their previous visit. The thicker snow made it more awkward to get there and twice the three of them had to push the Jeep to stop it getting stuck, but they were soon entirely hidden.

Deacon looked around then said, "Brother, take some branches off that bush and go brush over our tire tracks to hide them," to Polanski.

Grabbing their heavy rucksacks, they headed further into the trees towards the pipeline. The going was much tougher than previously. The snow was deeper and totally obscured the areas of water and ice. During the mile and a half journey, they all slipped and fell into the water and black muddy goo at least once before they managed to get to the pipeline itself. After checking they weren't being observed, Deacon pulled out the rope and after three failed attempts in the strengthening wind, managed to get the rope over the pipe. Getting McCabe and Polanski to hold the other end, he quickly scaled up the ten feet to the metal pipe support brackets. Sitting tucked in with one leg around the bracket, he pulled one of the smaller amounts of C4 out and began to massage and squeeze it until it was warmed and fully pliable. He pushed it into shape around the bracket and then pushed a blasting cap detonator into the mix. He rubbed his arm along the sides of the pipe six or so inches up from the bottom. The warmth of the oil had warmed the pipe and the sleeve of his jacket cleaned off any traces of oil. Using a long strip of duct tape, he stuck four sticks of dynamite around the bottom of the pipe with a blasting cap sticking out of one of them. He deliberately took his time with it being quite warm close to the pipe, while his colleagues shivered in the icy wind below. Eventually, sliding back down the rope, he and the others wiped the surface as clean and dry as possible with their jacket sleeves, before pressing four equal amounts of warmed C4 equally spaced around the base of the structure, with a blasting cap in each.

Deacon then grouped all the wires together before stripping the plastic from the ends of the wires and screwing them down into the multi-way connector. He had to take his gloves off for this and within minutes he was losing the feeling in his fingers in the biting wind. He then uncoiled a section of fresh cable, stripped the ends and connected it between the 'one' contact of the connector and through to the electronic timer. Getting the others to gather around, he showed them what he'd done.

"See, the timer feeds the multi-connector. That then goes to each of the blasting caps. So when the timer goes off, all the caps receive the charge at the same time. Everything explodes together. I even put one in the dynamite guaranteeing simultaneous detonation. The other sticks will trigger from it. All we need to do now is cover the area with the blanket, put the batteries in the timer and set it. Then 'boom', when the time comes. Now let's set the blanket, and then you go and do the other two."

Climbing back up the rope with a blanket, Deacon eased out from under cover of the pipe and stood as tall as possible on the windward side. Stretching up, it took him five attempts, but finally, he managed to get the blanket laid over the pipe and secured it with extra pieces of rope. Sliding back down, he pulled batteries from his pocket, blew on his hands and fingers to warm them and fitted the batteries in the timer.

"Twelve noon on the 17th. Correct? And the current time is 10:43 on the 11th. Check?" as the timer display sprung to life and he set the current time and the alarm time.

Receiving nods of agreement from the others, he slid the timer into multiple layers of socks before sticking them to the concrete with duct tape and tying the blanket over it.

"Done. Now you guys," he said, jamming his frozen hands deep within his pockets.

Moving over to the next structure it was Simpson's turn. The wind had strengthened further and it took a number of attempts to get the rope over the pipeline, finally succumbing to having a rucksack tied to it to act as a throwing weight. Simpson started to climb, but the cold had affected his hands, and twice he slid or fell back down. With Deacon and Polanski leaning against the structure, Simpson finally managed to get to the top and to the metal brackets. Sitting there, he waited almost fifteen minutes with his hands pressed against the warm pipe to bleed some life back into them. Using the same trick with the rucksack as a throwing weight he managed to get the blanket over on the third attempt after sticking the dynamite to the pipe. Sliding back down, together the four of them fixed the C4 around the structure and fitted the timer and the connectors. Again, they checked the detonation time and the current time before sliding the timer deep into the socks.

The third structure was the hardest yet. The ground around the concrete was gently sloping, and the warmth from the pipeline had melted the initial snow. However, the icy wind had frozen the wet grass, and it had become a small mound covered in ice. Even trying to stand upright was problematic. Where the other two structures had taken between twenty and thirty minutes each to wire up, this one took almost two hours. McCabe was chosen to scale the concrete and the others had to lift him as high as possible. Once the rope was over the pipeline it became a little easier, but by now the cold was eating into each of them and their movements and actions were becoming slower and slower as the early stages of hypothermia and frostbite began to set in. With fingers turning blue from the cold, McCabe twice dropped the timer and batteries. Finally, Polanski managed to wire everything up and Simpson set the timer.

It took them almost three hours to set the explosives and complete everything. It was extremely unlikely any inspection would take place between now and the 17th, but they took no chances. The blanket Deacon had put over the first position was already covered in snow and blending in perfectly. Even the warmth of the oil within the pipe didn't stop the snow from pitching on the top of it, and the grey of the blanket blended in well with the color of the pipeline itself.

Finally, with the last blanket tied down, they began to head back towards the Jeep. Simpson turned and rushed back to the first timer, the only one he hadn't set himself. Pulling it out of its protective socks he checked the current and alarm times before smiling and pushing it back home.

"Don't trust me, huh?" Deacon shouted over the noise of the wind.

"Just checking," he shouted back.

By now the snow was heavier. The flakes were larger and the wind had picked up even more. Visibility had dropped to less than fifty yards, and the fresh snow had already completely covered their earlier tracks. It was only by using a compass that they could be sure they were heading in the right direction.

Slipping and sliding and twice breaking through ice into the freezing cold water below, Deacon led the way towards the Jeep. Feet frozen from the earlier soakings, they stumbled towards the hidden vehicle like old men.

With a cry, Polanski suddenly fell through the ice into a deeper pond. One second he was there, the next he was gone. McCabe turned as Polanski disappeared from sight and shouted a warning. Within moments they were back to the ice hole, but Polanski was nowhere to be seen. The water under the ice in most places was static, but here it was slowly flowing, and Polanski had likely been moved downstream. With the ice covered by snow and no idea of how far he'd drifted, it would be impossible to find him without the tools or shovels to break through the ice.

Wet completely through and shivering in the cold, the three of them stumbled back to the snow covered Jeep. Brushing as much light snow off as possible, Deacon grabbed the door handle and pulled. Even the locks had frozen. It took almost ten minutes of breathing on the lock to unfreeze it when finally it succumbed to the heat of two of them pissing on it. Finally crawling into the driving seat, Deacon started the sluggish engine and put the heater and blower on full. Sitting there shivering, it took them almost a half hour to thaw out. Deacon then put the Jeep into drive and tried to move off. However the wheels wouldn't grip enough to push away the snow drifted up against them. It took them another twenty minutes of pushing the Jeep and revving the engine before the tires finally touched the blacktop, now completely hidden under two foot or more of white powder.

Driving carefully but as quickly as was safe, they headed back through Minot and down towards the highway, knowing the Interstate would be kept as clear as possible. Apart from seeing three other vehicles slowly driving in Minot itself, theirs was the only one on the road until they hit the I-94. Turning west, they managed to increase speed and made reasonable time close in behind a snow plough. They followed it for almost fifty miles towards the state line. Not wanting to stop except for fuel, they purchased sandwiches at a gas station and continued back to Westerton.

Although the snow was heavy, the main interstate had been kept reasonably clear, and they were keeping up an average speed of almost forty miles an hour. They arrived at the compound just before four in the morning.

Exhausted, they climbed from the cramped Jeep and fell into their beds.

Chapter 28

The weather during the rest of Monday was the same. Everyone stayed in the main buildings to keep warm. Simpson met with Lucas at 08:00 to give an update. Bleary-eyed he told Lucas of the problems they'd had and of Polanski's demise.

"Did Deacon have anything to do with Polanski's death?"

"No boss, he was leading us back towards the Jeep, then it was me, McCabe and Polanski at the rear. We'd all stepped over the same area and must have weakened it. He just fell through and went. It was only moments before we got back to him, but he was gone. There was nothing we could do."

"Was everything set OK?"

"I checked it myself, boss. 'Specially the bit Deacon did but it was all good, 'though I still don't trust him."

"Why?"

"Dunno, but we don't know anything about him really, do we? Just that he got kicked outta the SEALs."

Lucas sat there in thought for a few minutes before saying, "You make a good point. We should check out more about him. Get onto your guy. I want everything on ex-Lieutenant John Deacon. Everything. I want to know what he's had for breakfast every day for the past five years. I want to know where he's been and what he's done. If he's had a shit, I want to know when and where. Understood? Tell him he has twelve hours."

The remainder of the Monday passed quietly. The snow was heavy and the north-westerly wind kept blowing it into deep snowdrifts. All of the men were directed to keep the main paths clear while the women were instructed to help in the kitchen and keep the fires stoked.

The biting wind gradually took its toll as the men found that only an hour of shoveling was enough before numbness in hands and feet set in. They would then come back into the warmth for food or drink and to warm up before heading back out into the blizzard conditions.

As in most countries that are used to severe weather, the local townships and residents had effective action plans in place to cope. Most farmers during the winter would fit snow ploughs to the front of their pickups and keep the side roads from their property to the larger roads clear. They would also clear the major roads as much as possible. The state would have teams of snow ploughs out, and all major routes would continuously be ploughed and kept passable in all but the worst conditions. This meant by early Monday evening, as the worst of the snowstorm moved further east, eighty percent of the State of Montana's roads were already passable with care, with all major routes fully open.

At a little before nine pm, Lucas received a detailed email. Simpson's source had come through again. Calling Simpson to his office, he told him to sit down and listen.

Boyd Lucas read aloud, "*General, using facial recognition software against Facebook, I found a match on a cancelled*

Facebook account. Ex-Lieutenant John Deacon's face is in an image along with that of a woman, and the posting refers to a wedding back in July in San Diego. When I found this, I looked into it further and found Deacon and this woman, a Rachel Sanchez from San Francisco, had attended the wedding as guests. The account of this Rachel Sanchez was closed and locked a couple of months ago and all links deleted, which is suspicious by itself as most people don't cancel Facebook, and even if they do, it just makes their account non-active. This looks more like someone trying to hide something, so I investigated further. I found this Sanchez woman works as a geologist for the US Geological Survey Institute, in Menlo Park, SF. Through various means, I've found her home address, her phone number, driving license and IRS details. This Facebook account was closed and deleted on August 19th and this woman is not on any other social media sites ..."

Lucas stopped mid-sentence, put down the printed email and then said to Simpson, "Deacon told us both he was single and not in any sort of relationship. They look pretty close in this photo."

"July was just before his court-martial," Simpson said, "Perhaps that caused them to split up? Might explain her cancelling her account if she was embarrassed."

"Hmmm, it might. Although, as he says in the email deleting an account is unusual. Almost like trying to hide something. With next week coming up I think we need to have a quiet word with Miss Rachel Sanchez, Brother Simpson. What'cha think?"

Getting an affirmative nod with a leering smile, Lucas folded the paper and put it in his coat before they both headed over to Deacon's cabin and banged on the door.

<>\<>\<>

Deacon and Terri-Anne had retired back to their cabin an hour previously. The main compound building held a collection of books and novels and Deacon had grabbed a couple to browse. Terri-Anne was showering and getting ready for bed when Deacon heard the loud banging on the door. Quickly saying to Terri-Anne to stay quiet, he slid the latch up and swung the door open.

Lucas and Simpson were stood there covered in snow, with flurries blowing around them in the icy wind.

"Can we come in?" Lucas asked

"Sure," Deacon said, stepping back and opening the door wider.

Slipping off their snow-covered coats, they moved towards the large fire Terri-Anne had set. Deacon walked towards them, stood there in the glow of the flames.

"What can I do for you gents this time of evening?" he said.

"Brother Deacon, Brother Simpson and I have to head off early tomorrow morning. We will be away two or three days. I need you to work with Brother's Horton and McCabe and finish the other ten barrels of ANFO. Put them in a truck and wire it back to a fifteen-minute timer in the cab. OK? We'll need them for the weekend. Work with the others and do what Brother McCabe says, OK?"

"No problem. So what are we hitting next weekend and where are you off to?"

Not receiving satisfactory answers to either question, Deacon was left standing there while Lucas eyed the bathrobe covered body of Terri-Anne who'd just come out of the bathroom.

"We'll .., ah, we'll discuss that when we get back," Lucas said, moving towards the door again.

Closing and locking the door behind them, Deacon sat back down and continued reading, but his mind was elsewhere.

Chapter 29

It was just over 1,000-mile journey from Westerton to San Francisco, and Lucas knew it would take them almost 16 hours straight driving. With the snow he counted on an extra 3 or 4. They took two vehicles, a panel-van loaded with ten barrels of ANFO and wired with two sticks of dynamite and the same Jeep Deacon and his team had used. The Jeep had 4-wheel drive if needed and had good tires. The van was heavier and had bigger tires so was unlikely to get bogged down in any snow. Also, the weather in the direction they were heading would get warmer quite quickly. They headed south on I-15 through Idaho and into Utah to Salt Lake City then west through Nevada on the I-80 to the small town of Winnermucca where they stopped overnight. The snow as far as Idaho Falls had been heavy, but then it had cleared and the greens and browns of the landscape showed through. The interstate had been cleared of snow, as expected, and they'd made good progress.

Stopping at a cheap motel and eating in a local bar had been easy, with both places used to strangers passing through and the people used to not asking too many questions.

The following morning they left early, wanting to get to their destination by lunchtime. They followed the interstate through Sacramento and Oakland before heading across the Oakland Bay Bridge into the city.

As often in San Francisco, it was overcast and raining. As a stranger in any city, it's easy to get lost; in the rain more so. Coming off the Interstate in South Market they quickly realized they were in the wrong area. However, by keeping the business district to their right and looking to see where the hills were located, they managed to find the approximate location quite quickly. Once in the area, it was just a case of Simpson in the van pulling over into a side road and waiting while Lucas in the Jeep drove up and down the desired street until he'd found the exact spot.

Calling Simpson on his cell phone Lucas explained the exact location to park and where he would pick him up afterwards. To avoid being seen, Lucas then drove another few streets away and parked.

Simpson, in the meantime, traveled slowly along the street. Stopping twice at lights, he could feel the sweat forming on his brow. With enough explosives laced with bolts and ball-bearings to flatten an area of almost 1,000 square yards, he just wanted to park the van and get away. Finally, he approached the place Lucas wanted him to park. The space was quite tight and he had to reverse twice to get in close to the kerb, but he managed it. He was within twelve feet of the entrance door of the target building. Scattering some papers on the passenger seat and leaving part of a newspaper on the dash, he slid into the rear of the van and lifted the blanket covering the ANFO. Within seconds he'd plugged in fresh batteries, set the timer to the required time and day and watched the countdown begin. Pulling the blanket back over to cover everything, he slipped out of the driver's door before casually locking it and walking away. In the teeming rain, no one paid him any attention. He slipped off his latex gloves and put them in his pocket and was quickly lost to sight around a corner. He walked two more blocks before turning left and found Boyd Lucas waiting for him, parked halfway along on the left. Rolling the gloves into a ball, he stooped once and dropped them and the van keys down a road drain before sliding into the passenger seat, just as Lucas gently pulled away.

With a big grin on his face, Lucas turned briefly to Simpson and said, "Well done, brother. Two phases done, two to go. Now let's go and have some fun," as they headed south out of town and followed the signs towards the airport.

Rachel Sanchez was 28 and of Spanish-American descendant from Phoenix, Arizona. She lived in San Francisco after studying and graduating with double Masters' Degrees in Geology and Volcanology from the Carlos III University of Madrid. Working at the US Geological Survey Department in Menlo Park, her area of expertise was in co-managing the National Earthquake Hazards Reduction Program. She'd met John Deacon in 2012 when her knowledge of volcanoes and earthquakes had been used to help defeat an Al-Qaeda plot to destroy the eastern seaboard of the US. She'd stayed friends with Deacon ever since and they enjoyed an on-off relationship when he hadn't been assigned overseas. In July after the wedding of the widow of one of Deacon's friends, she, Deacon and two other friends had spent ten days sailing between San Diego and Los Angeles.

Now, after a hectic day of meetings and report writing about the latest landslip threat, she was heading home to enjoy a long hot bath followed by one or two glasses of Napa Valley's finest Merlot.

She lived in a renovated two-story two-bedroom townhouse in the residential suburb of Sunnyvale, on a quiet leafy street close to a small play park. Over the years she had decorated the house in a New England style with grey/blues and yellow. It wasn't particularly large but it was hers, and she was comfortable there.

It wasn't late but it was already dark when she arrived home and parked her car on the drive. Like any other day, she walked in, shut the front door, dropped her keys back in her purse and turned to switch off the alarm.

That was when she realized it wasn't bleeping its normal tone. In fact, it wasn't bleeping at all. It took a second or two for her to react and as she turned to run back outdoors, hands frantically scrabbling to get to her keys and her attack button on her key ring, she felt a hand snake around her head from behind and across her mouth to muffle her cries. Something wet and sweet-smelling was in the hand covering her nose and mouth, and as she breathed she could feel the sweetness draw down into her lungs. She tried to struggle but the assailant's other arm held hers in close. Remembering what Deacon had taught her in the event of an attack, she stamped her foot backward scraping the heel of her shoe down her assailant's shin while at the same time thrusting her head back to try to hit the person behind. With a heavy curse, she felt the hands holding her loosen slightly as her head bounced off the side of his face. As she struggled to get free or at least to free her mouth so she could scream, the fumes from the cloth over her face began to take effect, and she felt her knees begin to weaken as everything grew darker.

Back in the compound Deacon was just finishing cleaning up the chemicals. All ten barrels of ANFO had cooled and were stable enough to be transported. They were currently under a tent exposed to the cold which had helped bring their temperature down. Tomorrow he would help load and secure them in the one remaining truck and connect the dynamite and detonator together.

Still dizzy and feeling sick, Rachel slowly came round. Her arms and legs felt leaden, but as she tried to move, she realized she was tied down. She was blindfolded, had a gag across her mouth and she could sense she was tied at the wrists and ankles and lying spread-eagled on her bed. She was also cold and realized she'd been stripped to her underwear.

She began to shake with fear when she heard a voice she didn't recognize say, "We're not gonna hurt you. I'll remove the gag, but if you try to scream or shout you'll be punished. It will be very painful and the gag will be replaced. We are gentlemen and just want some answers. Do you understand?"

Beginning to cry, she nodded. She felt someone move on the bed and then the gag was loosened and pulled down as far as her chin.

"You are Rachel Sanchez, correct? If you answer all our questions, we will not harm you and leave peacefully. If not, Mr. Deacon will never see you alive again. Do you understand?"

"What do you want?" she asked, her voice trembling.

"Just for you to answer some questions. Now, what is your relationship with John Deacon?"

"He's a friend and he'll fucking kill you."

"Well, that's as maybe but he's not here and we are. Let me ask you again. What's your relationship with John Deacon?"

"Go fuck yourself!"

"Now that's not very polite language from a pretty young lady like yourself," he said, as he cupped a hand and gently slapped her across the face.

Over the next hour they asked her multiple questions concerning Deacon and his court case. During that time they never actually harmed her beyond a slap or a hard pinch, but she could feel the blade of a long knife lying on her stomach. Gradually his voice lost what little charm it had to begin with and grew harsher.

"What is Deacon doing now?"

"No idea and go to hell."

With that, his patience was getting short. He picked the knife up from her stomach, and she felt the tip touch her forearm. As she felt the stinging prick of the blade, she also felt her warm blood start running down her arm.

He asked her the same question again. This time she bit her lip and didn't answer. He tried once more and again she refused to answer. Without warning, a rag cloth was violently pushed over her mouth as the small toe on her left foot was suddenly crushed with pliers.

With the sudden intense pain, she gave a muffled scream and passed out. She awoke a few minutes later, tears streaming down her face and trying hard to fight back the rising nausea and bile in her throat.

"Just a simple question, Miss Sanchez. I'll ask it again. What is your John Deacon doing now?"

"Fuck you," she cried while gritting her teeth before she screamed again as her crushed toe was violently bent back. The blindfold made matters worse as she couldn't see where the two men were moving. Each time she screamed, her mouth was covered with a rag.

The pain and questioning continued for another two hours until she was totally spent. With four toes broken and crushed with pliers, three fingernails removed, two teeth pulled out and various punch bruises and bite marks across her body, her will finally broke.

Sobbing and unable to stand it anymore she answered each question they threw at her. Even a slight hesitation to answer incurred instant pain, so her words just flowed.

Finally, they pulled the gag back in place, climbed off the bed and put down their tools of torture, confident she had nothing else to give. Apart from her body.

Deciding it was better to leave in the morning, they began unbuttoning their clothes to have some fun, and her nightmare continued.

Chapter 30

Thursday morning and Deacon was sat having breakfast with Terri-Anne in the main building. The snowstorm had passed and the sky was clear and bright but almost two foot of snow had fallen. The wind had pushed some into deeper drifts. The temperature was still around 15°F., but the wind had dropped. He was just eating some toast when he felt the hairs on the back of his neck begin to bristle. Glancing around he saw some of his fellow diners grab their plates and move away. Looking up at Terri-Anne he saw her eyes widen at something behind him. Turning he saw four M4 rifle barrels pointed at him.

Noah Turner, Wade Horton, Travis McCabe and Dwight Emery were all holding weapons aimed directly at him.

"Morning boys. You going hunting?"

"Shut your motherfucking mouth, you motherfucking spy. Don't you move a motherfucking muscle," Dwight Emery said.

"I see your elocution lessons have been working."

"I said shut your motherfucking mouth, you motherfucker."

"I rest my case," Deacon said with a smile, "So, boys, are you joining us for breakfast?"

"You make a move, we'll kill ya," Horton said, "Now get up and put your hands behind your back."

Keeping his hands in full view Deacon said, "What's it to be, boys? Do I keep still or do I get up?"

"Put your hands behind your back. NOW!" Horton shouted.

Putting both hands behind his back, Deacon turned his head slightly. He could see three of the four weapons were still trained on him while Wade Horton had put his down on another table. Horton was holding a set of looped cable ties and approached Deacon from the side, while the others moved away to keep their weapons aimed at him.

Assessing the situation, he realized he could easily grab Horton and disarm at least one of them before seizing a weapon and shooting them, but with Terri-Anne sitting opposite, there was too high a risk she would get caught in any crossfire.

Meekly sitting there he felt the cable ties pass over his hands before being pulled tight around his wrists.

"Can't I even finish breakfast?" he said.

Next moment a rifle butt was smacked into his side, and he groaned and stumbled. Twice more it was jammed into his stomach until he was bent double and retching. As he vomited his breakfast back up, he heard Terri-Anne screaming, "Leave him alone. Why are you doing this?"

"Orders, Terri-Anne. Direct from the General. Now you go about your work," Noah Turner said.

"No, this little bitch is coming with me. I'll show you a real man," McCabe said, grabbing Terri-Anne's arm and dragging her away.

"You hurt her, and I'll kill you--," Deacon shouted before another rifle butt came crashing down on his skull and the world went black.

Groggily coming to Deacon could feel his head throbbing. He was lying on the cold floor of the same cell he'd spent the first day in when he'd arrived. Sitting up he could feel his hands were still tied behind his back. The same wooden bench was there along with the same dirty pillow, mattress and thin blankets. Gingerly, he tried to stand, but the dizziness made him sit quickly on the bench.

In the movies, people often get knocked unconscious then wake up and run around as normal. Not so in real life. Any head trauma brings on concussion. It just depends on how much. Light concussion is just some dizziness and a headache, severe would include vomiting, confusion and an inability to stand. It can also lead to actual brain damage or even death.

With his head finally clearing a little, Deacon stood and kicked at the door, shouting, "Hey, where's my coat," but never received an answer.

Accepting he would likely be there for a while in the sub-zero temperature without the slight added warmth of the blankets, he knew he had to break the cable ties. He was wearing a thick undershirt under a woolen long-sleeve check top shirt, but without his thick Parka, he was losing body heat fast. He needed to get his arms in front of him so he could squeeze down into as small a shape as possible, wrap the blankets around himself and conserve body heat. He was also losing the feeling in his fingers due to the tightness of the plastic ties that were cutting off the blood supply to his hands. Breaking the ties with your arms in front of you is possible by fully flexing your arm muscles and yanking your arms apart quickly. They don't always break the first time, usually cutting harshly into the skin, but they will snap under continued pressure. However, with your arms behind your back, the power of your muscles is hindered, and it makes this trick impossible to perform. Flexing his arms as much as possible and biting back the pain as the nylon strands cut deeply into his wrists, he managed to force his hands down over his backside and down the rear of his legs. Sat on the ground he managed to push his legs down enough to slip his wrists over, although this was made more awkward as the cable ties kept jamming on his boots.

With his hands now in front of him, he breathed deeply, ignoring the pain and the blood running down his wrists. Taking a deep breath and pumping his arm muscles rigid, he jumped up and yanked his wrists as far apart as possible as he landed. The extra downward force snapped the strands, and he was finally free. Rubbing life back into his numb hands he sat on the bench, pulled the blankets tight around himself and began to think.

Fuller Simpson and Boyd Lucas boarded their flight from San Francisco to Butte at 11:42. They had planned to drive back but what they'd uncovered the night before was too urgent to wait. They'd left the Jeep in the long-term parking and would send someone down to retrieve it at a later time. The flight was via Salt Lake City and would take a total of five hours, but they would be back at the compound by 7:30.

Washed and clean from the previous evening activities they only had overnight holdalls as hand luggage, although Boyd Lucas's overnight bag contained a small addition.

By 11:00 Deacon was cold. Almost as cold as at 'Hell Week' he'd attended all those years ago when joining the SEALs. The idea of that week is to try every possible way to make the SEAL volunteer candidates give up. Short of actual torture, the instructors do everything possible to the candidates including large amounts of sleep deprivation and tasks everyone else would find impossible. Added to that are regular swims in the cold Pacific, fully clothed. Some candidates give up. For some, it's just a step too far; the straw that breaks the camel's back. But others dig deep, deeper than they thought humanly possible and they find that extra bit of drive, that extra bit of effort. That extra bit of something that earns them the right to wear the golden Trident.

Today was that sort of day. Slowing his breathing until his heart rate dropped to less than 40 beats a minute he moved body and mind into a trance-like state. With his body slowed it used less energy for the ordinary matters such as breathing, so allowing more to be used towards keeping warm. He curled his body as tightly together into the fetal position as possible and wrapped the blankets and mattress tightly around himself. Closing his eyes, to anyone looking he seemed asleep, but his inner warmth began to spread outwards to his cold arms and legs. Keeping all movement to a minimum, he would wiggle his toes and fingers every five minutes or so, these being the body parts most prone to frostbite.

In this trance-like state, he no longer felt pain or cold. In fact, he felt nothing at all. All external feelings were effectively blocked as his body went into semi-hibernation. But not his brain. That started working overtime.

Chapter 31

In his numbed state, Deacon thought back to his last mission that had finished in Florida in July. He already had leave approved to attend the re-marriage of his ex-SEAL buddies widow, Alex Schaefer, in San Diego. He was excited to be giving her away. Her husband, Bryant, had been a close friend of Deacon's but had died in a roadside IED bombing some years previously. Before the wedding, he'd been called in by his commanding officer, and he had the situation explained to him. The initial hearing raised by reporter Lynda Anderson in Washington had found a case to answer, but an initial military investigation by the Naval Criminal Investigative Service (NCIS) had not agreed. However, due to the public interest raised by Anderson, there would be a military trial, conducted by the Judge Advocate General (JAG), but he would be found not guilty, and nothing detrimental would be placed on his record.

On his return from leave, while awaiting confirmation to re-join his team overseas, he'd received orders from Admiral Carter, the Chief of Naval Operations, to attend the Pentagon. Catching an overnight Navy cargo flight out of Halsey Field, he arrived early the following morning.

Admiral Carter had greeted him warmly, having got to know him well while working closely with him on his previous mission, while Deacon's close friend, Lieutenant Mitchel Stringer, had bear-hugged him.

Also present at the meeting were Lt. Gen. Warwick Dreiberg - Director of National Intelligence to the President, Simon Clark - Director of the FBI, and Dwight Morgan - Secretary of the Department of Homeland Security.

There was lots of backslapping and handshakes congratulating him on the success of his last mission before they got down to new business.

Simon Clark, the Director of the FBI, started the discussion.

"Lieutenant," he'd said, "There are currently somewhere between 500 and 550 Militia groups within the borders of the USA. We believe there are an additional 120 plus residing in the wilds of Canada. Also, there are tens of thousands of 'Preppers' - people, or groups of people banded together, who believe a catastrophic disaster or emergency is likely to occur and they make active preparations for it. This includes stockpiling food and weapons for when the 'system' breaks down, and it becomes every man for himself. What all these groups have in common is the willingness to take the law into their own hands. Following so far?"

"Yes sir, no problem."

"Good. Well, some of these groups are just casual, but some are violent and dangerous. We try to keep tabs on all of them and have infiltrated many, but we know there are more groups out there. One of the most dangerous ones we could identify is the Brethren of Christian Values headed by the millionaire Boyd Lucas. Many of the groups have little money, but not his. He funds his own private army, and his group or following are based up in the wilds of Montana. To make matters worse, there are whispers that they are planning on taking devastating action against the US soon."

Pausing a moment to drink, he sipped his coffee before continuing, "Now this group is a typical white supremacist neo-Nazi militia group. They, like most of the others, are for an all-white America and are willing to fight for their views. Democrats are usually more pro-immigration and pro-equal rights, while Republicans are less so. That's why the numbers of these groups rise when we have a Democratic government and fall when we have a Republican one and as you know, we are in an election year. But all the signals are pointing to another Democratic government when this current presidency ends next January, so the groups are on the rise again. Now we've tried to get our people into this particular group. We carried out a joint operation with Homeland last year, and one of Secretary Morgan's finest agents managed to infiltrate the group. She was in there a few months, then completely disappeared. No more contact. Nothing. Then a couple of months ago we sent in one of our own. A young, experienced field agent from Buffalo, New York. Married guy with two young kids. He'd already spent a year undercover in a drugs ring down south so was very experienced in this sort of role. He made contact once but then he also disappeared. We believe this Boyd Lucas somehow has access to our secure information. We don't know who or how, but we've lost two good agents and got nowhere."

"But if you suspect this group and have had two agents go missing, can't you just raid their place?" Deacon asked.

"If only it were that simple, Lieutenant. Unfortunately, the group are registered as a church, and their land is registered as church land. We need solid evidence to obtain a search warrant, and even then, many judges wouldn't sign it. After the disaster of Waco back in '93 ... well, let's just say we're still suffering from the major snafu's that occurred back then."

"How much evidence is needed? I mean, you've lost two agents ..."

"Correct Lieutenant, but in this age of political correctness judges are being even more careful. Although this group is supposedly Christian, the next might be Muslim. Any attack on a Mosque would be tantamount to declaring war on Muslims and no judge wants to be the instigator of that. So one rule has to fit all. But it doesn't make our job any easier. To make matters worse, the Brethren of Christian Values has spent a lot of money in the local area. They are well liked by the locals and even paid for a new police vehicle. They have a lot of local support, and we don't know how far up the line this goes or how many pockets might have been lined. When our agent disappeared, we had lots of keen words from the local police there and from the county judge, but he wouldn't issue any form of a search warrant."

"So how does this involve me?"

"Have you heard of the Posse Comitatus Act?"

"Vaguely. Isn't it something to do with the US Military can't be used by the government to enforce state laws?"

"Correct, Lieutenant," Admiral Carter said, "It was signed in 1878 and limits using the US military to enforce domestic policy. It's a safeguard ruling. The only military not included are the National Guard and the Coast Guard."

"Still not clear how this involves me, sir?" Deacon said.

Putting down his coffee, Simon Clark looked Deacon straight in the eyes and said, "Lieutenant. You have shown abilities to think on your feet and get things done. You have seen through ruses and proved beyond any doubt that you are capable. Now I am sure many of your fellow SEALs also exhibit these qualities. In fact, many of your colleagues in other special forces will also have these qualities. That's part of the 'special' that makes up our special forces. But we know you. We, that's myself, Admiral Carter, General Dreiberg and Secretary Morgan," Clark said, sweeping his hand around, "would like you to take on a special mission for us. For the President actually. We'd like you to infiltrate the Brethren of Christian Values, find out what these bastards are planning, if anything, and bring the bastards down."

"Here on US soil?"

"Correct, Lieutenant."

"What would be my backup?"

"You'd be on your own, Lieutenant."

"And when you say 'bring them down' ...?"

"Stop them from doing what they plan to do, whatever that is. Using your own judgment."

"And if I need to use force?" Deacon asked.

"You use whatever force is necessary to complete the mission."

"But surely that would contravene this Posse Comitatus Act?"

"Yes, Lieutenant, it would. And that's the problem."

"Sirs. With respect, we're going round in circles. You'd like me to do this but under our Constitution, I can't. Correct, sir?"

"Correct, Lieutenant. The only way you could take this on is if you were no longer a SEAL and in the Navy. Not an active serviceman."

Beginning to get angry, Deacon's voice raised slightly, and he said, "So you want me to resign my commission, everything I've worked for and a job I love doing, just to go after some wacko who runs around in the forest shooting at trees and chanting kumbaya?"

"Not quite, Lieutenant. Let me explain," Simon Clark said before discussing his idea in more detail.

"We don't know who or how secret information is getting to Lucas Boyd. Someone is passing him information, and we've been trying to find out who for the last twelve months. We don't even know if they are male or female. All we know is they have access to some of the very highly classified information at the FBI and at Homeland. Anyone we put in that is already in our records is liable to be discovered, and we've lost two already. You're not in our records. You're a Navy SEAL. As a Navy SEAL, you will have skills and training that Boyd Lucas will wet himself over in trying to get you to join him. With you on board his chances of success of anything planned will go up ten-fold and--"

"Even if I did resign, why would he trust me? One moment I'd be a SEAL fighting for freedom and doing what the government and president asked of me, and the next I'd be a renegade freedom fighter wanting to bring down that same government? It wouldn't work. They'd see straight through it," Deacon said.

"Told you he was quick," Admiral Carter said to no one in particular, with a smile on his face. Turning to Deacon, he continued, "Lieutenant, you're correct. He'd likely see straight through it and why wouldn't he? Nothing would have happened to change your view about the U.S. Government. But what if you were a disgraced former SEAL, angry at the government and wanting vengeance? He might be swayed to accept you, based on what you could offer him and his team. And the more disgraced and angry, the more attractive to him you'd be."

"What's your plan, Admiral?" Deacon asked.

"First, let me tell you, the President's on board. This impending court case. You're found guilty and thrown out of the Navy. You're angry and hurt and want revenge. Join their merry band and find out what's going on and then put a stop to it. Then re-instated back in the Navy - all a mistake. Record is wiped clean and back in the SEALs. I have here a signed letter from the President stating you will be fully reinstated back in the SEALs with no loss of service, benefits or pay."

"Same rank?"

"No Lieutenant. Whether you choose to partake in this mission or not you are being promoted to Lieutenant

Commander. Congratulations, Lieutenant Commander Deacon. You've earned it."

"When do I need to decide?"

"Take a few days, Lieutenant Commander. There are some other points you need to consider. First, you've been selected partly because of your history and background, but also because you are not in the Homeland or the FBI data base. We don't know who this mole or source is and we don't know what access he or she has to information. Because of that, this has to be kept top secret. Only the six of us in this room know about this, along with the President. Even his Chief of Staff hasn't been brought into this. Your contact has to be someone you trust fully; therefore it will be Mitch. He will only discuss this with me, Director Clark, Secretary Morgan, or Lt. General Dreiberg."

"Is there anything else I need to consider, sir?"

"Lieutenant Commander," Dreiberg said, speaking for the first time, "The press and media will vilify you both during and after the trial. This Lynda Anderson is trying to make a name for herself and will take every opportunity to condemn you. When you are found guilty she is, I believe, the sort of person who will use that to her advantage. The vilification won't stop at that point. Worse, your father is a decorated ex-Navy Captain. He and your mother, and possibly your sisters may receive negative press, even abuse. You need to consider this before you make any decision. I've asked the Admiral to extend your leave by five days to give you time to consider and perhaps to speak with your parents. You also need to think about your relationship with your young lady. I suggest you only tell them the absolute minimum. The less they know, the less they can accidentally disclose."

"Thank you, sir."

"Finally, Lieutenant Commander, let me say whichever you choose is entirely your choice. Should you choose not to partake, this conversation will never show on your record, and nothing about this conversation will be held against you. However, I would ask that you inform the Admiral of your decision within the next five days."

Chapter 32

The following morning Deacon arrived at his parents'
home in Smithfield, Virginia. Their house was a turn of
the century wood built two-story property with a half-
acre of land. The views across rolling countryside led
down towards the Pagan River. Painted in a cream color
with darker window surrounds it matched in beautifully
with the other Norfolk dwellings.

Parking his rental on the driveway, he walked towards
the porch steps when the front door was pulled open, a
welcoming smell of fresh baked cookies wafted over him,
and his mother embraced him as if she hadn't seen him in
years. In reality, it had only been a few months. He did
speak with them regularly, but both his parents and his
other family members knew the risks he took being a
SEAL.

With tears of joy in her eyes, she hustled him inside
holding him tightly before leading him to his father.

"Honey, he's here," she called as they walked into the
main lounge.

"Dad, don't get up," Deacon said to the grey-haired
man struggling to rise from the leather wing chair.
Instead, Deacon thrust a hand forward and gripped his
father's outstretched hand warmly.

Over a lunch of ham, cheese and salad washed down
with a chilled Pinot Gris, the three of them discussed all

the normal family matters. What they each had been doing, how they were all keeping, his niece and nephews' school reports, and his parent's age-related ailments.

Eventually, after his mother had brought coffee and cleared the table, Deacon senior turned to his son and said, "John, as always it's a pleasure to see you, but you're here for a reason. I could tell in your voice on the phone last night you're concerned over something. Do you want to talk about it?"

Helping his father stand due to rheumatism, they both walked slowly toward his father's study. Settling down into two comfy leather chairs after pouring them both a whiskey, John turned to his father and said, "Somethings come up, and I want to discuss it with you."

"Dangerous?"

"No, not particularly. Certainly not as dangerous as the other stuff I usually do ..."

His father just sat there listening. He knew his son, and he knew John would eventually come out with it.

"As a member of the SEALs I know I'm following orders, but these orders come from Central Command. Whether I've liked the order or not has never been questioned. I've always accepted them and carried them out. I've now been asked to take on a particular task and I'm concerned I may have to follow orders which I'm less happy about. There's an unwritten line in the sand between good and bad, and I'm worried I may be asked to cross that line at times, and I'm concerned whether I can and, if I do, whether I can cross back. In the Navy it's clear what's right or wrong, what's black or white, but now I may have to do something that's grey. And if I do and it becomes public, it could come back to haunt you and the rest of the family."

Sitting there in the quiet study the only sound was the reassuring gentle deep tick once per second from the grandfather clock in the hallway. Deacon junior sipped his whiskey as his father sat there deep in thought.

After a few minutes of silence Deacon senior took a sip of whiskey, handed his glass to his son and said, "Son, fill these up and push the door."

As he placed the filled tumblers back on their coasters and sat down, his father said, "John. What I'm about to tell you must never leave this room. I thought I'd take this with me to the grave. Now, unfortunately, you'll also have this burden ..." and he went on to explain.

"What you mean, son, isn't whether you can cross that line, it's whether you should. Life isn't black or white sometimes. As a serving officer all you can do is follow orders. Even if those orders take you across the line, you need to have the moral compass to know where that line is and to be able to cross back over it.

As you know, I was in the Navy my entire working life. I started as a Lieutenant Junior Grade and rose through the ranks to Captain in charge of a destroyer. After a few years in that role I requested to transfer to subs. Although I maintained the rank of Captain I was stationed aboard the USS Sunfish as XO, a Sturgeon-class nuclear attack sub. Bear in mind the CO, or commanding officer is senior and overall in charge of the vessel, but the executive officer takes charge in the absence of the CO. I was XO for a couple of years before becoming its CO for the rest of my career. I joined the Sunfish just after her major overhaul in '73. She had training and weapons systems testing through late '73 and was to be deployed to be part of the Mediterranean Sixth Fleet. However, we received orders to temporarily join the North Atlantic Fleet for a while so early in the New Year of '74 we deployed up towards the Barents Sea far north of Norway. You've got to remember we were at the height of the Cold War. It was constantly tense but there were periods that were critical. The most critical time was in the early sixties at the height of the Cuban missile crisis. We really were on the brink of all-out war. It was terrifying. I was engaged to your mother then and never knew from one day to the next whether we'd ever see each other again. Luckily that period passed, and by the late sixties it had calmed a little and détente had started. By '73, we were nearing the end of 'Nam and already pulling troops out and the Middle East oil crisis had started and prices were skyrocketing. The Soviet Union, as it was then, along with a number of other eastern-bloc countries, was beginning to stagnate, and it became more a Cold War of spies and intelligence rather than just saber-rattling, but it was still deadly. Both sides were constantly probing each other to try and gain an advantage. The Sunfish was equipped with some of the very latest sonar and monitoring equipment and, being nuclear, we could take our time just cruising. The Soviets had recently started launching their Delta-class nuclear subs. These were a game-changer for the West. They had long-range ballistic missiles on board and could reach a large number of US cities from just sitting there floating in the Barents Sea. The Brits had a couple of their 'O' class diesel-electrics up around there monitoring and keeping an eye on things. Boy, those Brit subs were quiet. Fast, silent and really hard to detect even with the latest gear. But being diesel, they only had a limited time before having to resurface, and the Soviets had the airspace pretty well covered to detect a snorkeling sub. So the Brits got clever. We already had SOSUS up and running. Do you know what SOSUS is?"

Rolling the cut crystal whiskey tumbler between his palms, Deacon junior looked at his father and said, "SOSUS? No, not really."

"Well, it stand for Sound Surveillance Systems," Deacon senior continued. "It began back in '49 and has been working ever since. Much better now than then, but basically it's an underwater early warning system located at various choke points around the globe. It uses very sensitive underwater microphones, called hydrophones, and listens in to the noise of ships and subs. Every vessel has an acoustic signature, some louder than others, but if we can detect the signature and then triangulate where it's coming from, we know exactly where each vessel is located. Russian crafted propellers were not very efficient in those days and therefore were quite noisy compared to British and American ones. Unfortunately, with the advent of computers the newer Russian models are now almost as good as ours, but then it was quite different. Ships are quite easy to find being on the surface and detectable by other ships, aircraft and satellites, but subs are a real problem. In those days, SOSUS was mainly operating across the seabed between Greenland to Iceland and to the UK, which was known as the GIUK gap and was used to monitor all Soviet vessels sailing down into the Atlantic. Then they'd be followed by our Atlantic fleet and in the event of war, sunk before they could fire their missiles. It was all cat and mouse. We'd track their subs and they'd try to track ours. But with those Deltas staying up in the Barents Sea we had no idea of where they were. We obviously could keep some of our subs up there monitoring theirs, and we did, but that tied up resources best used elsewhere.

Now the British fisheries trawlers were regularly up towards the Barents Sea in their usual fishing role. A couple of think-tank egg-heads had decided that if they put monitoring kit on board some of those fishing vessels, they could spy on the Soviets while going about their regular business. Great idea and worked well for a couple of years. The Soviets had already been monitoring our fleet exercises with their so-called fishing trawlers. Theirs were pretty obvious though. Masts and antennas everywhere and they'd come in close, maybe to within a mile or so of our ships on exercise. We even had to shoo them away at times. Anyway, the thought was why don't we do the same to them but with a little more finesse. There would be the regular fishing crew on board, but there would also be two or three Royal Navy technicians on board operating their equipment recording and monitoring anything they could detect. Personally, I always thought we had the better job being beneath the sea. The Barents Sea in winter is not a nice place. Incredible storms, extremely cold, ice everywhere and massive seas, but these fishermen were really experienced and entirely used to conditions like this. We were even cold in the Sunfish, mind you. The cold of the sea just crept through into everything, so I hate to think what it was like on the surface. Anyway, January '74 the British fishing trawler Gaul was sent up to the Barents Sea on its usual fishing run. The Gaul was a 220-foot long, 1800 tons large fishing ship. She was designed for not only catching fish but also to allow filleting and freezing. She was a complete factory ship - very sturdy and had been designed specifically for the sort of conditions experienced up around there. She had a regular crew of 36. Only this voyage she had two extras on board, but they were never recorded officially. Both were lieutenants in the British Navy, and both were sonar specialists.

The Gaul was also fitted out with the very latest sonar and listening devices from Plessey, the British electronics and defense manufacturer. It was identical to that being fitted in the latest ships and submarines in their Navy and was equally as good as anything we had. This was absolutely top secret. Only the CO and I knew of the Gaul's involvement. The crew just thought we were on regular listening patrol. So the journey started and the Gaul was out fishing. We were just moseying around trying to detect anything Soviet. On the second of February we heard what we thought might possibly be a Delta. Just once. It was a way off, but we marked it as a possible and slowly approached. This is real cat and mouse stuff, mind you. Either side is listening for the faintest noise above the background noises of the sea and then trying to identify it through all the background mush. So we are on the seaward side of a trajectory line and the Gaul is staying slightly closer inshore, fishing. The hope is we will get whatever is making the noise in a sandwich, and we will get two or more recordings of it. The Brit Navy is hanging around as well, but far enough away not to be a nuisance to the Soviets. Anyway, this carried on for a couple of days, and by the seventh we knew we had something definite to track but still couldn't be sure of what it was. We were in contact through surface radio to HQ and were ordered to proceed with utmost caution. The last thing anyone wanted was a 'trigger-happy' firing by them or us, or a collision of vessels.

The Gaul stayed with us although she was about fifty miles away. The weather worsened and on the eighth other trawlers in the area were claiming it was a Force 10 with waves of almost thirty feet. They all stopped fishing and just battened down to ride the storm out. Early on the ninth we detected a number of ships steaming at flank speed, or as fast as they could in those conditions, from Severomorsk, Murmansk, the home of the Soviet Northern Fleet. We tracked them heading directly towards the Gaul. The Gaul was in international waters but closer to the Soviet waters than we were. The Brits were even further out. Within a couple of hours it became apparent the Soviets were planning to intercept the Gaul and stop it from monitoring. They had an Ilyushin Il-38 reconnaissance aircraft almost overhead jamming radio signals to and from the Gaul, so all communication to her was blocked. It looked like the Soviets were going to blockade the Gaul and we were worried they might try and sink it. Then the penny dropped. They didn't want to damage the Gaul, they wanted to capture it. The repercussions for them in capturing the latest sonar equipment would have been enormous. It would have been highly embarrassing for the Brits if it ever got out and the technological lead the West had over the Soviets would be removed in a flash. We were the only 'friendly' craft in the region but apart from saber-rattling, there was nothing we could do. Even if we'd surfaced close-by, we couldn't defend the Gaul without threatening to sink one of the Soviets. The Soviets would say the Gaul was in danger of sinking and they were saving it. We were on the horn to Command when we received the message, *'Take all and any measures against the fishing vessel Gaul to ensure she does not fall into Soviets hands. Do not, repeat, not engage Soviets unless fired on first.'* We even had to confirm back to Command we understood what the orders meant. We closed to within 8,000 yards and fired a Mark 37 torpedo at her. We wanted to aim at the Soviets but any aggression like that would have started a full-blown war. I was in command at that time, and my CO made me issue the order. We listened for what seemed a lifetime before hearing the explosion. We blew a massive hole in her bow. I had tears in my eyes as I knew I'd murdered 38 innocent men. She went down in seconds. The Soviets knew what we'd done and turned and chased us but we had the advantage and it was easy to outmaneuver them."

Looking at his father, he could see tears running down his face. He'd never seen his father cry before and felt his own tears well up. Feeling immense sorrow towards his parent he managed to ask, "What happened?"

Wiping his eyes and then taking a large swig from his glass, Deacon senior continued, "The following day the UK fishing fleet started to get worried. They hadn't heard from the Gaul, and so raised the alarm, but the British Government didn't want anything found. They knew what had happened and deliberately delayed any search. They couldn't afford the publicity if it ever came out that they had sanctioned the murder of 38 of their countrymen to save their top-secret kit falling into Soviet hands.

The Soviets knew they would be seen as the bad guys and also kept quiet about it as they knew we could turn it around and make it look like they'd sunk her. But they also knew they could hold this over the Brits and us, and they leveraged that knowledge to get sanctions lifted. We could hardly announce that we have been instrumental in the murder of 38 of our closest allies, could we?

So the crew of the Sunfish were sworn to secrecy. We all had to sign additional security documents so this story would never come out. The Brits did what they are so good at doing. They lied and covered it up. The UK doesn't have the same freedom of information rules as we have here. They just bury it forever. They are past masters at hiding secrets so as not to cause any embarrassment to any of their officials. They will often bury details for at least a hundred years to make sure they protect their own. They're quite corrupt in covering their asses at times."

The two of them sat in silence for a few minutes with the realization that his father had caused the deaths of 38 innocent people slowly sinking in. Topping up their empty glasses, Deacon junior passed one to his father and asked, "But if the Gaul was so secret and there were other trawlers out there at the same time, how did the Soviets know to pick her?"

"Don't forget son, this was at the height of the Cold War. We had spies in Russia, and they had theirs over here and in the UK. Where the leak actually occurred has never been disclosed, even if the Brits know. They never told us who in their services knew about the Gaul, but someone somewhere tipped off the Ruskies. So I've lived with the knowledge and horror that I murdered 38 men that day, of which 36 were just innocent fishermen trying to earn a living. If that wasn't crossing a line, I don't know what is. But sometimes we have to do what is right for the bigger picture.

Son, you do what you have to do. Follow orders. But follow them with loyalty and honor and don't worry the press or anyone else hounding us. We can cope. Just remember in your heart you're a Deacon. You'll know where the line is so you'll know when you've crossed it. More importantly, you'll know when you've crossed back."

Chapter 33

Deacon had checked the cell, but there was no escape. The walls were over two inches thick and were solid wood, possibly oak or something equally as hard. There were a few small gaps between some of the thick planking but not enough to even get a finger between. However, the gaps let in a little daylight as well as the icy blasts of wind. The door was equally as solid and opened inwards with the hinges outside. There were three bars on the door at head height allowing the guard to see in, but thick Plexiglas, or similar, prevented anything being pushed through. The fixed wooden bench was directly opposite the door, and there was nowhere to hide.

The cell had not been built for comfort, and there was no heating. In his semi-dreamlike state Deacon slept and conserved as much body heat as possible as the wind picked up again and found entry through every minute gap in the walls.

At 8:30pm that evening the door was suddenly thrown open, and four men all carrying automatic rifles entered and ushered him out. Normally he'd have been able to fight, but the cold had robbed him of the ability to move quickly. His muscles were cold, and every movement was a strain. They half dragged, half carried him out into the corridor and cable tied his hands behind him. Two of his captors had long poles with rope loops at the end. Deacon recognized them as the sort animal catchers use to hold wild dogs as the loops were slipped over his head and tightened. As the five of them moved out, with his hands tied and strung between the two poles, Deacon had little choice but to obey.

McCabe was one of his captors and pushed his face in close to Deacon's.

"Not so brave now, sailor boy, are you?" he sneered as he spat in his face.

The weak winter sun had set hours before, and as they dragged him across the dark courtyard towards Lucas's hut, Deacon saw Terri-Anne standing outside in the loom of light coming from one of the windows. Even in the pale yellow light, he could make out the bruises on her face and her swollen lips. Locking his feet solid he stopped, his muscles already beginning to warm and the power within them returning. He stood firm against the pulls of the poles and looked at her.

"Who did this to you?"

McCabe smashed the butt of his rifle into Deacon back, making him gasp and partly fall.

"Few of us just showed her how to satisfy a real man, that's all," McCabe laughed.

Turning and thrusting towards McCabe, neck tight against the ropes, Deacon gasped, "You bastard. She's just a kid. I'll kill y--" as something heavy was swung with force at the backs of his legs and he collapsed on the icy ground.

Held by the arms and ropes around his neck, he was dragged in through the doorway before being forced to kneel in front to Boyd Lucas.

Three others were there including Fuller Simpson.

Unholstering his handgun, Lucas placed the barrel tip against Deacon's forehead.

"The court has charged you, tried you, and found you guilty. The sentence chosen is death. As commander of the court and General of the Brethren of Christian Values I will be carrying out the sentence."

"What am I charged with, asshole?"

"You're a traitor. You work for the FBI."

"Wrong, asshole. I'm not working for anybody."

"Is that right? Well, we have evidence contrary to that. We have a statement from a witness."

"You're full of shit. No one knows I'm here."

"Would you like to know where we've been? Brother Simpson and I have had a nice trip to San Francisco where we met a friend of yours."

Feeling an icy chill come over him, Deacon fought back the urge to ask the question.

"We met your girlfriend. Miss Rachel Sanchez. She thinks differently."

"You're lying. She wouldn't have told you anything."

"She didn't at first. Not before we ... shall we say *persuaded* her. Then she wouldn't shut up. She said you're working on a secret mission and that you'll be re-joining the SEALs after," Lucas said with a smile on his face as he dropped a photo on the floor.

Looking down Deacon could see it was the photo of them both. He'd last seen it on Rachel's bedside table.

With a lunge, he tried to get up but couldn't against the restraints. Twisting his face back up towards Lucas, he shouted, "You bastard! I'll kill you if you've harmed her."

"Harmed her? I'm afraid we killed her. Well Brother Simpson did actually. By his own fair hands. Put up quite a fight too. But before she died we showed her how to satisfy real men. Twice, in fact. Never mind. you'll be joining her soon. Still, we have a souvenir for you. Something to remember her by," as he pulled a small plastic box from his pocket.

"Shall I open it for you?" Lucas laughed, slowly lifting the lid and showing it to him.

With a roar Deacon struggled to get up and managed to kick one guard away. As one pole dropped free, he tugged violently at the other guard and started to move towards Lucas, but with his hands still tied behind him, there was little he could do. He heard the swish of air as Simpson struck him below the ear with his rifle butt and as he collapsed down towards unconsciousness, the last things he saw were Rachel's nipples spilling out of the plastic box.

Chapter 34

An icy blast of wind slowly made him come to. He was being half dragged, half carried along by his shoulders, his boots leaving twin trails in the snow. His neck throbbed from the attack with the rifle butt but the cold wind quickly revived him. Not wanting to make it easy for them he played unconscious until they finally got him near the main gate and dropped him in the snow.

"Get up FBI pig," Lucas shouted over the wind, "Today you're gonna join your tramp of a girlfriend. You tell her the General and Brother Simpson say 'Hello'. She'll remember us," he shouted, making obscene hand gestures.

Struggling to get to his feet, Deacon looked directly at Boyd Lucas.

"You better kill me right now 'cus otherwise I'm gonna kill you and that sick fuck Simpson," he said just loud enough for Lucas to hear.

Pulling his sidearm out Lucas aimed it directly at Deacon's face and spat, "Die, you motherfucking pig," and pulled the trigger.

Deacon was staring straight into Lucas's eyes as the hammer clicked and fell on an empty chamber.

"See! See he's so tough he don't even blink when we're gonna shoot him," Lucas squealed, his voice almost as high and shrill as a girls. "No, we ain't gonna kill you this way -- far too quick and easy for one of you tough SEALs. Brother Simpson, what do these tough SEALs claim to be as tough as? Is it five or six normal soldiers?"

"Only SEALs I ever met are pussies," Simpson replied, spitting on the ground.

"Well, let's have some fun. How about one so-called tough SEAL against ten of my men. You, Mister SEAL, can go free. We'll give you an hour start. Then we'll hunt you down like the goddam FBI traitor you are. Ten against one. You wanna take your chance against them odds, Mister tough SEAL?" he said, giggling and looking at Deacon.

"You're on pal. But you better get your spare men digging holes. Ten of 'em," Deacon said.

Calling for the gates to be opened and for the poles to be removed from around his neck, Lucas said, "You've got an hour. Then the hunt begins, and you'll be joining your little slut before daybreak."

Stumbling towards the gate, Deacon turned and said, "What about my hands and my coat?"

Lucas spat on the ground and said, "You're resourceful. Maybe you'll freeze to death before we find you," and turned and walked away.

As the gates closed behind him and he slipped and stumbled along the icy snow covered track, the wind blew another icy blast, and the snow flurries half blinded him. His legs and arms already felt icy and he'd lost the feeling in his hands. Deacon's brain went into overdrive, and he began to dig deep. He knew he'd need to use all his skills and training along with a fair bit of cunning if he was going to win this one.

Chapter 35

As soon as he was out of the loom of the powerful arc lamps positioned to either side of the gate he stopped stumbling and picked up speed. The first thing he needed to do was to remove the cable ties and free his hands. Each of the wooden posts along the access track had numerous nails and clips in them securing the fence wire. Running his hands down the posts trying to find a nail or clip sticking out wasn't the easiest of tasks with his hands tied behind him, and twice he fell over, but the third post bore fruit. Twisting his wrists around he managed to snag the plastic tie over the head of a nail. He then put more and more pressure downwards whilst twisting his hands further. Three times the plastic tie slipped off the nail head, but on the fourth attempt it finally parted. The ties were still around his wrists but no longer joined together. With a smile, he started rubbing some life back into his cold limbs.

Climbing over the fence into the woods provided a number of benefits. First, anyone on the open track would be easy prey for people or dogs. His footprints were clear in the snow, and unless a very heavy snow dump happened within the next half hour, his tracks would be easy to follow. In the woods there were no proper tracks or paths to follow. Also, the tree canopy was heavy with snow, but little was down at ground level making tracking more awkward. Thirdly, although still bitterly cold, the trees very effectively stopped the wind and finally, Deacon knew in amongst the trees and vegetation he would come into his own.

The forest was a mixture of trees and rough vegetation. There were some small pathways that had either been created by man or by animals, but even these were badly overgrown. There was a light dusting of snow and the ground was frozen, but Deacon made good headway. Even in the pitch dark, Deacon's eyes became adjusted enough that he could make out the dark shapes of tree trunks as he rushed past them. Only twice did he stumble into brambles that snagged on his clothes, the spikes tearing at his flesh. He could feel rivulets of blood running down his arms and legs, but he just gritted his teeth and ran on.

He knew Lucas would be bringing his best hunters to track him down. But hunting in a forest is awkward. It's easy to lose your bearings when you can only see a few feet in any direction. Also, the trees muffle sounds and often distort the direction they're heard from. When hunted, most animals move away from man and only turn to attack when cornered. They also usually have very keen sense of smell meaning you have to approach from downwind.

Hunting a man is a little different. Deacon had no intention of just running and being caught. He ran for almost forty minutes but instead on trying to keep to a straight line like most people escaping would, he moved in a large arc. Warmer now, he stopped to make his first trap. Knowing Lucas was a coward he expected more than ten chasers. He was also sure Lucas would set his dogs after him first to bring him down, so he planned his traps accordingly. He also knew Lucas couldn't be trusted and would send the chasers earlier than the hour he'd been given. Soon after he'd stopped, he heard the sound of a distant hunting horn.

Although he didn't have any man-made weapons to hand, not even a knife, he knew the forest was full of weapons if you looked for them. He'd been careful not to leave any footprints in the thin snow dusting, choosing invisibility over distance. Looking around the forest floor and feeling with his hands he found a number of thick logs and fallen branches. He also found heaps of pine needles. Twice he found small streams frozen solid, but he eventually found one with ice covering it but water flowing underneath. Using one of the logs to break the ice, he felt around until he found a rock of suitable size and shape. This one was a little larger than a baseball and slightly pointed at one end.

By now his legs from the knees down and his hands and fingers were numb from the freezing water. Grabbing handfuls of fallen pine needles he began rubbing them furiously over his body and arms to bring some circulation to the surface before jamming his hands deep into his armpits. As the feelings slowly returned to his fingers, he used the pine needles to rub between his palms and fingers to raise friction. This, in turn, warmed his hands faster than through body heat alone.

Warmer now and with normal flexibility slowly returning to his fingers and thumbs, he rested one thin fallen branch about three-foot in length against a tree trunk, while using the rock to crush and scrape its end into a rough point.

He now had his crude arsenal of weapons as he moved away from the stream. The faint noise of a hunting horn was clearer now. Still a while away, but closer than before.

The dogs would be able to follow his faint scent, but anything stronger would help, so he kicked and brushed the dead leaves away until he reached the frozen dirt underneath. Then he unbuttoned his fly and smiled as he relieved himself, the warm stream of urine melting the icy ground. Rubbing his fingers into the warmed soil, he scooped up a handful and rubbed it over his face and neck, providing a simple camouflage paint. He spent a few minutes collecting as many short but thick twigs and sticks as he could find before stripping off his shirt. Wrapping the sticks within the shirt around his left forearm gave him reinforced padding from his fingers to his elbow. In his right hand he hefted the sharpened stick. By his feet he placed the rock and the heaviest, thickest fallen branch of about six foot long that he could hold. Then he leant against a tree and waited.

He sensed them before he could hear or see them. He guessed they were almost a half mile away. There was no distinguishable sound, but it was almost as if he could feel their footsteps through the earth. He knew the dogs would be first. Sensing the direction they'd come from, he knelt on the ground facing them.

<><><>

The smell of the urine had done the trick. From a few hundred yards away the scent had attracted the dogs, and they'd approached it. Once closer, the scent of Deacon overpowered the urine soaked mud on him, and Satan and Lucifer had accelerated, jaws open and growling softly in anticipation.

Deacon stared in the dim forest light in the direction he heard growling. Suddenly out of the undergrowth he could see a pair of yellowy eyes heading towards him with another pair slightly further behind. Although dogs may hunt in packs, there is always an alpha dog or leader. He would always attack first with the others close behind. Satan was the alpha.

With a louder growl, Satan lunged at Deacon.

Chapter 36

Extending his left forearm forward, Deacon braced his knees for the impact. He knew if he fell backwards and they overpowered him, he'd be dead.

The Rottweiler reared up and leapt at Deacon, his jaws clamping down with all the force it could muster on Deacon's outstretched arm. Like most attack dogs, it had been trained to go for the arms first to drag its victim down before going for the softer tissue. As its teeth clamped, it began to shake its head from side to side, usually being more than enough to pull a full grown person to the floor. But Deacon just knelt there letting his arm be pulled and pushed.

With Satan busy, Lucifer reared ready to attack. As it leapt Deacon thrust the sharpened stick into its underbelly. The crude point jammed between the dog's ribs and Deacon thrust it as far home as he could. With a yelp, Lucifer fell, but with hatred in his eyes, he still clamored to attack. The stick and injury, however, slowed Lucifer down considerably. Focusing on Satan, Deacon twisted his left arm so the first dog's head was turned slightly sideways. With the side of the dog's head exposed, Deacon gave one more thrust of the sharpened stick into Lucifer then let it go and picked up the rock.

Turning it in his hand until the rounded part fitted his palm and the pointed end was downward, he raised his arm and slammed the rock down repeatedly as hard as he could into Satan's jaw clamped on his arm. With a crunch of teeth and splintered bones, the rock did its deadly work. Deacon could feel the jaws loosen, but still he slammed the rock home. On the sixth and largest of the poundings, the jaws finally opened and the pulped head of the dead Rottweiler dropped loosely down towards its paws, brain matter dripping from its open wounds.

Scrambling back out of reach from Lucifer, Deacon stood and picked up the other thick branch. Swinging it high over his head it still took two enormous swings before he'd broken its back.

Sweating, even in the cold, Deacon finally breathed out, not realizing he'd held his breath since the first attack.

Grabbing the thick branch and the rock he quickly disappeared back into the forest.

Ten minutes later Boyd Lucas came upon the bodies of his hunting dogs. With a cry, he fell and touched them gently. Satan's head was still slowly leaking brains, and Lucifer's back was broken, with his breathing labored and blood escaping with every breath. Eyes filled with rage he held them for almost a minute before suddenly standing and kicking both dogs viciously. Satan was already dead, but Lucifer yelped weakly as his boot crushed down on broken ribs.

"Useless fuckers. Kill 'em," he instructed before turning and moving further into the trees. "Deacon, you're so fucking dead," he screamed towards the trees as two blasts of a shotgun rang out as one dog joined the other.

"Spread out, he can't be far. A thousand dollar bonus to the first of you to shoot him. But I kill him. Understood? I KILL HIM," he screamed, white spittle forming at his mouth edges as the guards began to split up.

<><><>

Deacon could faintly hear the cries and threats coming from Lucas but wasn't worried. The thickness of the trees hid him, and he was still moving further and further away. He'd unwrapped his shirt from his forearm and checked for damage.

Only the shirt.

The wooden sticks and twigs had been thick enough to stop the teeth penetrating. Luckily they'd also been strong enough not to snap under the enormous pressure from the dog's jaw.

Slipping his shirt back on for the little extra warmth it offered, he knew the next step was to gain a proper weapon.

<><><>

In typical cat-and-mouse fashion, they spread out and began the chase, slowly moving in the general direction of where they thought Deacon was hiding. Keeping only a few feet apart, one man could always see at least two colleagues either side of him. They continued for the next hour slowly moving through the forest, the looms from their torches highlighting their limited progress.

Unfortunately for them, Deacon had moved faster and quieter than they thought possible and was already almost a mile further away, giving him time to prepare the next trap.

<><><>

Lucas and Simpson urged the men on. As expected, Lucas had brought a party of fifteen men, including himself and Simpson, all armed with shotguns or rifles, handguns, knives, and torches. Gradually the line of people extended and they all slowly moved further apart until there were often fifteen or twenty feet and a number of tree trunks between each man in the line.

Deacon had found a shallow hollow directly behind one large trunk. He'd quickly collected handfuls of pine needles and now lay in the hollow with almost an inch of needles covering his entire body, with another inch or so under him keeping him warm.

By now the line of men was almost three hundred feet wide, and he heard them slowly approaching. They were quiet, but their footsteps could be felt through the ground and as they brushed vegetation aside the sounds they made carried softly and their movements stirred the air, if you knew what to listen and feel for.

Animals had these fine-tuned senses by instinct. As a Navy SEAL, so did Deacon. The main difference was that any animal being hunted would have moved away ages ago. Deacon hadn't. There was a faint possibility that one of the chasers could stumble on Deacon accidentally, but he knew the odds were against that happening.

Laying perfectly still and with his breathing reduced to minimize chest movements, even the sharpest trained eyes would have difficulty locating the body lying in the hollow. He sensed the man's approach. The loom of the torch lit up the trees but never landed directly on him. He could hear the man's breathing and could even hear both the inward and outward breaths. He sensed him stop and could visualize him looking around. Had Deacon left part of his body exposed? Were there marks in the soil? The light suddenly turned off. The footsteps shuffled around slightly, and Deacon was just deciding whether he'd been found and should tackle the guy and escape before his colleagues got close enough, when he heard the faint sound of trickling water.

Trying hard not to move or crack a smile he thought to himself that of all the tens of thousands of trees in the forest, his chaser had to pick his to relieve himself against, as the mild smell of warm urine drifted his way.

Moments later, he could hear his hunter readjust his clothing, mutter something incoherent and stumble away to catch up with the others.

Deacon stayed precisely where he was for a slow count of one thousand. It's often good practice when hunting someone to leave a person behind in case the hunted is hiding. Many times a hunted person has been missed in the initial search but has left his lair too quickly and stumbled into someone quietly waiting. But it takes skill and dedication to wait quietly. Ninety-nine percent of the population would stand and wait five minutes, maybe ten, but then they usually get impatient. They fidget or move around. Not much, but enough to be detected. Deacon couldn't risk it so waited for the full slow count of one thousand, taking almost thirty minutes, his senses straining to hear or feel something.

Confident they had all passed him by, Deacon slowly got to his feet and brushed the pine needles off. They'd provided good insulation, and he was the warmest he'd been since sleeping with Terri-Anne over twelve hours before. He was also pretty happy that he was now in the right position. He was reasonably warm, a little rested, but more importantly he was behind them, and they didn't know it.

The hunted was now the hunter.

Chapter 37

Moving quietly through the forest Deacon edged towards the rear of the men who thought they still were tracking him. Even when they are keeping quiet, fifteen men make noise and it was simple for Deacon to track them. Added to that, some were using torches, the looms lighting the trees and reflecting off the snow-whitened canopies. It's human nature to expect the edge guys or last in line guys to be picked off first. That's the way they do it in the films. Poor old tail-end Charlie gets it, then the next in line. Not so in real life. Taking someone from close to the center of the group affects those remaining far more.

No advancing group keeps a perfectly straight line. Especially when trying to push through undergrowth and get around trees. Jake and Hank were having a very quiet whispered conversation just a few feet apart as they slowly moved forward. Hank had just finished saying he wanted to stop for a few minutes to have a drink when Jake didn't respond.

"Jake? Jake! Stop fucking around Jake?"

But poor old Jake wasn't answering Hank anymore. In fact, he wasn't going to answer anyone ever again. Deacon had crept up behind and partly to the side of him and clamped his left hand over his mouth. His right hand was still hefting the pointed rock and traveling towards his left hand with all the force he could muster.

The human head is quite hard with bones protecting the vital organ of the brain. In fact, the forehead bone plate is the hardest in the body, being curved to withstand even more shock. However, the bones at the back of the head are nowhere near as strong. Certainly not strong enough to withstand the pointed end of a hand-sized rock being slammed against it under heavy force. The pointed rock split the bones and penetrated the brain easier than when it had been used on Satan, and Jake was brain dead within a tenth of a second after feeling the hand cover his mouth. The crunch of the rock splitting his skull was no louder than a twig breaking under a heavy footstep.

Quickly laying the still twitching body down, Deacon grabbed Jake's shotgun, handgun and hunting knife. He left the torch, having no need for it and silently slipped away.

It was another four minutes before Hank raised the alarm and some of them found Jake's body. By then Deacon was over three hundred yards away and completely invisible.

<><><>

It took Lucas and Simpson almost ten minutes to settle the others down. The fact that somehow Deacon had taken out a person near the middle of the widely spread group without a sound frightened them. Even worse, he'd done it after silently killing two vicious attack dogs when he'd been unarmed. Now he had guns, and a knife. A couple of them started questioning why they were chasing him instead of letting him go and heading back to camp.

By now Lucas was getting desperate. Realizing that his control and hold over the others depended on his ability to catch and kill Deacon, his only option was to threaten them into continuing.

"The first man to turn his back and walk away will be shot down like a dog," he screamed at them. "God has sent me his message and the Lord God Almighty wants this sonofabitch flayed and burnt at the stake," he seethed, eyes bulging and spittle spraying everywhere. "He's a traitor and our mission's too important to stop. We're gonna kill him. Now get out there and get him," he ranted, as he fired a warning shot into the air.

One or two of his followers looked worried, but they could see Fuller Simpson eyeing them all. If Lucas didn't shoot them first, it looked like he might.

Deacon had skirted around to the right and sat hunched down watching Boyd Lucas slowly losing his sanity. He took no pleasure in killing but had no problem doing it when needed. He hoped that the nerve of those chasing him would break soon, but while they were still after him he really had no choice ...

Moving away, he approached and caught up with the far left end of the new line of men that had formed to hunt him. Silently moving up behind the last man in the line, he crept round a large fir tree trunk just as the hunter came round the other side. Before the guy could say anything, Deacon sprang at him and jammed the blade of the hunting knife up under the man's chin. The nine-inch blade pierced the soft skin under the chin and continued up through the membranes of the tongue and on through the roof of the mouth, punching up behind the eyes and into the lower portion of the brain.

Just to make sure, Deacon twisted the knife ninety degrees sideways. As the body began to sag, he gently lifted the assault rifle from the guy's dead hands. He rolled the body over and stripped the thick Parka jacket from it. Surprisingly, it had little blood on it. Slipping it on he found the guy had been an inch or two shorter than him, but otherwise, it was a reasonable fit. Within seconds he had taken up the dead hunter's place and to anyone watching the hunter had merely walked behind a thick tree trunk and come out the other side.

To add to the disguise, Deacon also slipped the dead guy's hat on as he continued walking with the others.

After another ten minutes or so, the message passed down the line of hunters to stop for five and regroup on the General. Each hunter received the message and passed it on to the guy to his left. Being the last in the line, Deacon was the last person the message would be passed to. The hunter nearest him half whispered and half shouted the message to him before turning and moving towards the central group. Deacon grunted a reply, stopped, propped his stolen rifle against a tree, pulled his knife free and crept up on him. Snaking his left hand around the guards head and clamping it firmly over his mouth, at the same time his right reached around the body and thrust upwards. The tip of the knife entered the guard's chest at the top of the stomach just under the rib cage and headed upwards into the chest cavity, the razor sharp blade slicing apart everything in its way. The point of the blade sliced the heart in two and the guard was dead before his brain had registered the pain of the blade or the blood gushing from his chest. Quietly lowering this one, Deacon wiped his blood-soaked hands and knife on the dead guy's jacket, frisked him and found a Colt Python revolver. An old favorite of Deacon's, this was the 8-inch barrel version designed for hunting. It only had 6-cylinders but packed an almighty punch. It was also incredibly loud. Silently moving up on the next guard thirty foot away, Deacon recognized him as Noah Turner, Lucas's right-hand man. Raising the weapon, he closed his eyes tightly and fired once. From the distance of less than six feet, Turner's head almost shattered. The muzzle flash of the weapon discharging illuminated the scene momentarily and temporarily destroyed some of the remaining guards night vision, while the deafening sound of it discharging froze people in their tracks. Deacon opened his eyes, ducked and ran back the way he'd come, grabbing his assault rifle before a mass of random firing peppered the area and the prone bodies of the dead guards.

Chapter 38

"Four dead, Lucas, and you're next!" he shouted through the trees, but the only response was more continued rifle fire, all of it hitting the trees. The nearest any of it got to him was from ricochets and flying splinters of wood. Armies don't like fighting in thick woods because of the lack of visibility and the abundance of hiding places. But Deacon knew he could use that to his advantage. Nine hunters remained, urged on by Simpson and Lucas, but Simpson was the one to be reckoned with.

US Army trained and combat experienced, Simpson had fought and survived tough situations before. He also had, Deacon knew, total disregard for the others and would happily let them walk into a trap. However, that could also be used against him.

Moving back the way he'd come, he skirted the next two hunters and hid. They were now moving in pairs hoping it gave them more protection. Waiting for two of them to be away from the remainder of the group took a little while, but eventually, there was a good seventy or eighty feet separating them.

As expected by now, when one person screamed for help, the others were reluctant to rush over, fearful of a trap.

Taking careful aim, he shot the first of the two in the leg. With a scream, the guy fell down, his voice echoing out through the trees. The second hunter didn't know where the shot had come from and searched around, eyes wide in panic. Not finding a target, he bent to check on his fallen colleague just as Deacon stepped out of the shadows.

Any movement at that exact time would have made the hunter jump. Having a six-foot-tall stranger, face blackened with just the eyes showing step out, holding a pistol aimed at him in one hand and a fearsome looking hunting knife in the other was too much. Dropping his rifle, he whimpered, "Please don't kill me. I've got a wife ..."

Without a word Deacon motioned the guy to move away from his fallen rifle. Picking it up he released the magazine and threw it away into the darkness and then threw the body of the rifle elsewhere. Keeping his pistol aimed at the whimpering guy, he said quietly, "Do the same," and pointed with the knife at the weapons the first guy had dropped.

"You've a choice to make," Deacon said, "Helping your colleague back to the compound and then staying there is the right one."

"Wha ... what is the other one?"

Deacon looked him straight in the eye and said, "Take option one."

As the wounded hunter was helped slowly to his feet and they both began moving away, Deacon smiled to himself and thought he'd let the others suffer a bit more before he tried anything else. None of the others had come to assist these two. Moving almost a mile away and well out of earshot, he searched for and found two long straight saplings. Trimming small leaves and branches off with his blade soon turned them into potential spears. He then sat down and started sharpening the ends.

Simpson and Lucas called the others together.

"Brothers, Brother Simpson and I need to put the next stage of the plan into operation. There's seven of you. I need you to capture that bastard dead or alive. I'll send up more guards to support you, but I want him caught. Do you understand? DO YOU UNDERSTAND?"

Getting nods of agreement, Lucas and Simpson checked their weapons and headed back towards the compound leaving the remaining seven of them a little more worried than before.

Deacon had slowly gained on them but was out of earshot for Lucas's message until Lucas had shouted part of it again. Seeing some movement between the tree trunks, he crouched down. The sky was beginning to lighten, and shadows and shapes were just becoming discernible, even in the darkened forest. He saw Lucas and Simpson move off, eyes alert and scanning around them. Not sure whether this was a trap, he took the safer option and moved away a hundred yards or so. He could hear the others moving away and could have gone after the two leaders but realized he needed to finish things properly first.

By now they'd been hunting Deacon for a little over six hours and were getting tired and hungry. For the last hour or so they hadn't heard anything and didn't know their missing colleagues had merely been wounded and were still alive, so a mixture of apprehension and terror had set in. Suddenly, Deacon's voice boomed out close to them.

"There were fifteen of you. Now there's seven. This isn't your fight. Leave now, and you'll all be safe. If you stay, I'll kill you all."

Their response, as Deacon had expected, was a mass of gunfire in the general direction they assumed him to be. Waiting until it lulled, he again tried, "My argument isn't with yo--" but again the firing continued.

Within the hour two more were dead. Deacon shot one with his rifle as the guard traveled across a clearing. Deacon just rose up out of the scrub and shot him from 250 feet, straight through the head, before dropping down again and disappearing. The second was up close and personal. Deacon leapt from behind a tree and stabbed the sapling spear straight through the guard's chest. It penetrated entirely through and stuck out his back. As he staggered back, his fingers closed on the trigger and the boom of his shotgun echoed through the forest.

With a total of eight of their colleagues either dead or missing and the two leaders having left, the will of the remaining five collapsed, and Deacon heard them crashing through the forest as they ran back towards the compound. Unfortunately, they ran directly into a party of another ten, led by Travis McCabe, who'd been sent up to support them. A fierce firefight ensued killing or wounding a total of seven from both groups. Eventually, those remaining began carrying and ferrying the wounded back to the compound.

Chapter 39

Deacon stayed in the forest most of the day. He went back and checked the bodies and took snack bars, water and binoculars off some of them. He also took and disabled the remaining weapons, having already reloaded his. By lunchtime, he hadn't heard or seen any movement, so carefully made his way back down close to the compound. He heard vehicles moving regularly along the track, but the forest was too thick to see precisely what was happening. Creeping even closer in the late afternoon he eventually got to an area of trees where he could see sections of the compound with little risk of being discovered himself. Even he was surprised by what he saw.

The compound looked almost deserted. The main gates were open, and at first glance, there was no one to be seen.

Suspecting a trap, he sat there for almost an hour. In that time he only saw three people wandering around, one of which was Terri-Anne. He heard, rather than saw, the approaching minibus. It came in through the open gates, turned facing outwards again and stopped. The driver hit the horn three times, and suddenly almost twenty people appeared from various cabins and the main building all carrying luggage. Within five minutes they'd loaded the minibus, clambered on board and it had exited heading back up the track, swaying ominously from being heavily overloaded.

Skirting the edge of the forest but with his weapon ready, it took him almost fifteen minutes to get back near the main gate. Climbing over the fence, he walked in towards the compound. There were discarded items lying about, from clothes to books and tools. The place looked deserted.

Walking around one particular corner, eyes scanning for any sense of a trap and his rifle ready for instant action, he almost bumped into Travis McCabe coming out of a doorway.

"You!" McCabe gasped. "I thought you were dead!"

"Yup, me. And still alive, asshole."

McCabe went for his pistol, but Deacon was quicker. His left hand smacked down on McCabe's right just as he reached his holster and lifted his weapon. The pistol, knocked from McCabe's grip, spun away to land in the snow as Deacon's right hand came round in a fast and wide open-palmed smack to the side of McCabe's face.

The force almost knocked him over and as he shook his head and turned back to Deacon he was slammed with a left, right, left and finally a thunderbolt right to the stomach.

Bent double and gasping for breath, Deacon pulled his head up by the hair, looked him in the eyes and said, "So you like to beat up on women, do you? You like your sex rough? Find it fun to beat and hurt Terri-Anne? Well, every step you take in future will remind you why," before he hit him once more, very hard.

As McCabe slipped unconscious to the floor, Deacon picked up his fallen rifle, held it by the barrel and slammed the stock down hard, once, twice, to each of McCabe's ankles. Hearing the small bones snap and fracture he knew that McCabe would heal and be able to walk again but every step would be painful. Painful enough to remind him of what he'd done to Terri-Anne and possibly other women before her.

Moving on, he headed to the main building. Chairs were overturned and the place was deserted. He checked various rooms before heading back outside towards his and Terri-Anne's cabin. Five people were heading towards the main gate, all carrying suitcases or holdalls.

"Hey, what are you doing? Where are you going?" he shouted.

"We're leaving, Brother Deacon. Troy's driving the minibus and dropping people off in Westerton. He'll be back for us soon."

Walking into his cabin, he found Terri-Anne sitting on the edge of the bed, crying. As soon as she saw him, she burst into tears, rushed towards him and held him close.

"I thought you were dead," she sobbed, "They said you'd been killed. We could hear loads of gunfire."

"Me dead? Nah! They couldn't even hit a tree in a forest. They shot at everything that moved and some things that didn't, but look ... not even a scratch."

"But we saw bodies being carried down. Someone said one was you."

"Well as you can see, it wasn't! Look, this place is being deserted. You need to pack all your stuff and get the minibus into town."

"But where will I go? And what about you?"

"You need to head off to be with friends or maybe to southern Cali to find your parents."

"But what about you, John. Where are you going? Won't you come with me?"

"Terri, we've both got lives to live, but not together. And my work here isn't finished yet. Go on packing. I'll be back in fifteen," he said, before picking up his rifle and heading out.

Sprinting and slipping in the snow, he headed for the vehicle shed. On the way, he saw one of the hunters from last night, the one he'd allowed to live. Expecting trouble, Deacon raised his weapon, but the guy was busy filling a bag. When he saw Deacon, he put his hands up and blurted: "I don't want any trouble. I'm not armed. I'm trying to leave."

Deacon looked at him for a few seconds, then replied, "Keep thinking that way and get lost. If I see you again, you're dead," before sprinting on.

When he reached the vehicle shed he found the door closed, but not locked. Sliding the door open carefully, he entered with his pistol at the ready, but the place was deserted. All the vehicles except the old backhoe digger and one of the tractors were gone.

Heading back, he ducked into the explosives shed. The door was open, and it was empty.

Cursing, he turned and ran back to Terri-Anne.

Walking in, he found her just finishing packing. He went to her and they hugged. She was still an innocent young girl, and she'd had to suffer things nobody deserves to. She'd stopped crying now, relieved to know

Deacon was alive. Sitting her down again on the bed, he asked her, "The panel van I was working on the other day and the Jeeps. They're gone. Do you know where?"

"They all left at lunchtime, John. They were busy after the General and Brother Simpson came down from the woods this morning, saying you were dead. They left just before lunch."

"Who was driving and where've they gone?"

"Brother Emery was driving the van and Brother Horton was driving one of the Jeeps. I'm not sure but I think Brother Walters was driving the other but the windows were covered in frost and I couldn't see clearly."

"Were they alone?"

"No, there were three other passengers in each Jeep."

"What about Lucas? The General, I mean. And Simpson. Did you see them?"

"Yeah, they went off after. Once Emery, Horton and the other Jeep left, Brother Simpson went and got the BMW and parked it outside the General's office. They were in there quite a while, then came out with suitcases and a suit carrier. The General was carrying his special briefcase, and he was being real gentle with it, like. Anyway, they put everything in the trunk and headed out."

Taking her arm and carrying her other cases, Deacon helped her to the open gates. The lights of the approaching minibus were reflecting off the snow lying on the track, and the smaller crowd moved apart as the minibus pulled up.

Grabbing the driver by the collar, Deacon half-pulled, half-led him away to the rear of the vehicle. "You know Terri-Anne, right?" he said to the worried man.

"When you get to Westerton you wait with her until she gets on the bus to Butte. You understand? If the bus is late, you wait. Am I clear? You know who I am. If you do what I'm telling you, you'll never need to see me again. Right?"

Receiving urgent nods from the driver, he let him go and finish loading the vehicle. Pulling what little money he had in his pocket, he gave it all to Terri-Anne before cupping her pretty face in his hands.

"Terri, you're a beautiful young woman. You're smart, quick-thinking and kind-hearted. Go and find the life you deserve and forget about this place."

He then gave her a long lingering kiss and a tight hug before gently nudging her onto the bus.

He watched it drive away before he turned and walked back to where he'd left Travis McCabe.

Chapter 40

Finding him crawling back across the snow towards his cabin, Deacon walked up behind him before putting a booted foot against his side and pushing him over.

"Brother McCabe, going somewhere?"

"Fuck you."

"Now that's not very polite, seeing I let you live. You just answer a couple of my questions, and you can crawl away."

"I ain't telling you anythi-- Agggggggh," he screamed as Deacon slowly put his booted foot down on McCabe's left ankle.

"Brother McCabe, or can I call you Travis? It's quite simple. I have some questions, and you're going to answer them. The only choice you have to make is when. You can answer them now or after I hurt you more."

"You've already fucking hurt me. You can't hurt me any worse."

"Do you really want to put that to the test, Travis? Your ankles will heal. In time. They might be a bit painful for the rest of your miserable life, but you will be able to walk. But if I smash them again you might be in a wheelchair for the rest of your shitty life. That's before I get to your knees. Then your wrists and elbows. Can you imagine sitting in a wheelchair having to have a helper feed and clothe you? Even wipe your ass for you? Maybe

I'll finish with your neck. Break it just enough so you just sit there dribbling all day, not able to speak or move and unable to put yourself out of your misery. So, Travis, bearing in mind this little escapade is over, and everyone is leaving, it's now time for you to decide. Hmmm?" he said, very gently increasing the pressure on McCabe's ankle just a fraction.

"OK, OK, what the fuck do you wanna know?"

"That's better. See, we can be friends. For starters, I want to know where the truck Emery is driving has gone?"

"To fuck your Mama."

"Oh dear! Just when we were beginning to get on so well," Deacon said suddenly stamping hard on McCabe's ankle.

Waiting until his screams died down and he'd wiped away the tears in his eyes and snot running from his nose, Deacon tried again.

"The truck?"

"Fuck y-- Argggghhhhhhh."

"That was a loud scream. I actually heard it echo off the surrounding hills," Deacon said, with a smile, balancing all his weight through his foot on McCabe's ankle and beginning to bounce.

It took another twenty minutes until Travis McCabe was totally broken and blubbing. Deacon found out that the panel van loaded with ten containers of ANFO was heading to Denver, but McCabe didn't know exactly where. He also found out that the Jeep with Horton driving had three others on board, as did the second one driven by Abe Walters. Both Jeeps were heading over to North Dakota loaded with some C4 and dynamite to attack the two pipeline pumping stations. As to Boyd Lucas and Simpson, they were headed somewhere else with the last Claymore mine on board. McCabe said he heard them talking and the General had mentioned something about Sunday morning and that interest rates would suddenly drop and Simpson had laughed and replied that interest rates weren't the only thing that would drop Sunday. Deacon had also asked about the panel van loaded with ANFO that Lucas and Simpson had taken out a few days ago. All McCabe knew was that San Francisco had been mentioned and that Sunday at 22:00 they'd be rid of those 'Animals of Satan' as Lucas called them, forever. Finally, Deacon asked where the information about him had come from. McCabe swore he didn't know exactly where. He knew Simpson had a source somewhere within the government and that's where they got the information on Deacon from and about the other agents a while back, but he swore on his life he didn't know who or where they were.

Leaving a sobbing McCabe to gather his senses and crawl to a cabin, Deacon headed over to Lucas's private rooms.

Inside was a mess. Papers were strewn all over, and the desk drawers had been left open. The filing cabinet was also unlocked. It was apparent the occupant had left in a hurry. The only noticeable thing missing, Deacon noticed, was Lucas's reptile skin briefcase.

Walking over to the control room door, he could see it was still padlocked but unguarded for a change. It took three blows with the rifle butt to break the padlock and Deacon was surprised when he went in. So much for being cut-off up in the boonies, he thought. Four high spec computers were running with some sort of satellite link providing ultra-fast connections to the internet. There was also a bank of monitors showing images from hidden cameras around the compound, as well as from cameras mounted on the light towers and access track. The control panel on the desk allowed easy switching between the hidden cameras and standard TV broadcasts, including all the mainstream news channels. We might be out in the middle of nowhere, Deacon thought, but Lucas had better signal access than you get in New York. There was also a couple of landlines and a collection of cell phones. Against the far wall were multiple digital recorders that could record off-air broadcasts or from the internal cameras.

Switching through the internal monitors, he recognized the images of the central canteen area, the rest area and the expected outside views including the vehicle shed, explosives shed, watermill generator and main gates. He also could see pictures of what he guessed to be the women's shower block and bedrooms of the married cabins as well as the spare sleeping quarters. The sick fucks liked to watch the women having sex, he thought.

The door to a small safe swung open under his touch. What it had contained could only be guessed at.

He sat down behind the computer with the largest screen which he assumed to be for Lucas alone. Scrolling through the internet history, he found most entries had been erased. There was a Denver news item mentioning this coming weekend was expected to be one of the busiest for shopping, being the last complete weekend before Christmas and also adverts showing forthcoming January sales.

On the desk were various pieces of paper and folders. In one he found a map of Vegas with enlarged aerial photos of the central area, along with multiple photos from different angles of the Beldorf Palace. Access and exit routes were highlighted. There was also reference to Carl Hobbs and his bodywork shop.

Looking through the computer files, he found one called 'Keystone'. Clicking on it opened a series of maps and graphical images of parts of the Keystone pipeline. These were very high-resolution images of the entire pipeline project in both North and South Dakota. Looking further he found satellite images and Google Earth prints of the Turtle Mountain Reservation area, the chosen site where the explosives had been planted. He zoomed in on the satellite images and followed the small twin-track road they'd followed. There were a number of bridges and turns, but it only took moments for Deacon to recognize the small bridge with the road sharply turning back on itself. From there he tracked eastwards until he saw the pipeline before zooming in further to see the exact concrete structures where they had set the explosives. Along the bottom of the screen were the exact latitude and longitude coordinates of the cursor. Deacon placed them over the pipeline and picked up the telephone.

Chapter 41

The telephone was answered on the second ring.

"Mitch, Deacon. How're you doing, pal?"

"Holy fuck, John, where are you?"

"Still at the compound, but most have left. It's going down tomorrow. Get with the others and call me back in an hour," he said, reciting the phone number written on the handset, "I'll email you some stuff," he continued, before hanging up.

Typing and sending three emails took moments before he stood and walked out of the building. Heading back through the darkening skies he went back to the cabin he'd shared with Terri-Anne. Stripping off his dirty clothes, he jumped into the shower, turned it to hot, just stood there under the cascading water and began to think.

The plan had come together well. After meeting his father Deacon had confirmed his willingness to participate to the Admiral. Then the planning had started. The first part was the dummy court case. It had to stand up to scrutiny and look genuine. It would be handed over to the Judge Advocate General department and would continue like any other case. Deacon would be assigned defending counsel, and there would be prosecuting counsel as standard. The trial itself would be carried out as usual. No one knew it was slanted and it would only be when the verdict was handed down that certain members of JAG would be brought into the picture.

Next was setting Deacon up as a failure. This would be through him leaving town, getting into bar fights and generally getting a bad name for himself.

Convincing the Brethren to take him in was a challenge. Although Deacon was sanctioned at the highest level to find out what was going on and stop it, he was still constrained by the laws of the land. Anyone innocent had to be protected, but it had to appear that he had gone rogue. Sat chatting that evening, Mitch and Deacon had come up with the shooting of the Montana State Troopers. It had to be convincing, but he obviously couldn't actually harm them. Simon Clark of the FBI had agreed on the plan and arranged it. Two troopers would be 'killed' and kept dead for the duration of the mission. Both troopers chosen for the ruse were single and heavy background checks were performed on them to make sure they were totally clean. The younger one, Larry Merit, was hoping on getting engaged in a few months and the elder, Chuck Gibbons, had completed a fairly messy divorce. To ensure they weren't seen and the ruse exposed, they would both be re-assigned for the duration of the mission for extended interview techniques training at FBI HQ, Quantico, expenses paid by the FBI. The problem of how to kill them was easily solved using Hollywood-type stunt tricks. They would be shot with blanks, but it had to be in public and look realistic. The best way was using one of the officer's own weapons. They would stop Deacon in his truck, he would resist arrest, grab the officer's gun and shoot him. Then he'd turn the gun on the other officer and shoot him as well. However, there had to be blood to make it appear real. That's where Hollywood and its special effects came in. Each officer would be wearing explosive blood sacks as used in films and on TV.

237

The question of guaranteeing it was Deacon stopped and not anyone else and of also ensuring the officer still had a loaded weapon while on duty - a legal requirement for officers within the State of Montana - was solved by Deacon. The officer would carry a standard full live load, except for rounds two and five, which would be blanks. When stopped, before any action took place, Deacon would ask 'two and five' and the officer would respond and answer the same. If either party failed the test, no action would commence. This way the officer still had four live rounds out of the six in his Colt Python pistol - enough to keep within Montana's rule.

Deacon would grab the gun and discharge the first live round, then shoot Officer Gibbons with the blank second, before firing two more live ones and then the next blank at Officer Merit.

The concern, however, was only a very few senior staff in the Montana State Police knew this was a setup. When the hunt for Deacon commenced, every police officer nationwide would be genuinely trying to apprehend Deacon, dead or alive, for killing two of their own.

Finishing his shower, he thought of how well it had worked.

Changing into his own clean clothes, he grabbed his thick Parka that Terri-Anne had returned to his room from the breakfast area the day before. With his stomach rumbling, he headed over to the canteen to look for something to eat.

Everyone had left, but he just went into the main kitchen and checked out the fridge. Soon, five rashers of thick bacon were sizzling on the skillet while a three-egg Spanish style omelet was cooking on the adjacent ring. He also heated up some decent coffee before sitting back and enjoying the first proper meal in two days.

Back in the control room, Deacon picked up the phone on the first ring as the hour ticked off precisely.

"John, we're at the Fed HQ. I've got Lt. Gen. Dreiberg, Simon Clark, Secretary Morgan and the Admiral all here," Mitch said.

"Lieutenant, are we glad to hear from you. We were beginning to worry," the Admiral said.

"You and me both, Admiral. It got a bit hairy here. Don't know how, but they found me out. Been chased all over the countryside, so it's been a bit of a rough ride the last two days."

"Lieutenant, before we continue, I've got some awful news for you. There's been an attack, son. I'm afraid Rachel has been murdered."

"I know, sir. I also know it was bad. Really bad. One thing I need to know, sir, and please be honest. Was it quick or did she suffer?"

"Lieutenant," the Admiral said, his voice faltering a little after waiting a few seconds, "I'm so very sorry to tell you she suffered. She suffered a lot."

Deacon just stood there in silence. He'd loved her and her him. Their relationship had been slow to start, and she knew he lived a dangerous life, but the worry was always about him getting hurt or killed, not her. Her job was safe. She was a gentle, caring, highly intelligent person studying earthquakes and volcanoes. She'd always joked that the most dangerous aspect of her daily life was using the stapler at work. And these bastards had killed her. Not just killed her, but tortured her for information and

239

then raped her for their own sordid, twisted pleasures. Finally, they had defiled her body in the sickest way possible and removed parts of it for Lucas or Simpson to keep as a souvenir. Silently vowing to catch these two and make them suffer in the same manner, he just stood there, tears streaming down his face.

After a minute of silence with no one knowing what to say, Deacon pulled himself out of it.

"Thank you, sir, for your honesty," he said, voice faltering a little, but gaining in strength. "I know who did it - the bastards gloated about it. All I can say is they're dead men walking, however long it takes. But now I need to make you aware of what's happening."

Sat at the computer screen, he opened various documents before continuing.

"I believe Lucas has planned a total of four attacks. I was too late on board to get involved in the Vegas one. I didn't even know about it until after it had happened. What's the final count on casualties?"

Simon Clark cleared his throat and said, "We are now at two-hundred and eighty-eight confirmed dead and almost four hundred and fifty injured, many seriously. But these bastards were good. We've been over everything multiple times, but there isn't a single piece of evidence tying it to this group. Had you not told Lieutenant Stringer we'd still be kicking our heels and wasting time looking. So what about the other three? What's planned and when?"

"Well, there's plenty of evidence here. As you know from when I met Mitch, the Keystone pipeline is the next target. Since then, we've been back and planted the charges on the pipeline itself. Lucas brought it forward due to the bad weather that came through in the last three days. In the email I've sent you are the exact coordinates of the three structures we strapped up. There's C4 around the base, C4 on the top mounts and two or three sticks of dynamite taped to the pipe near each mount."

"Holy shit, Lieutenant. And you've left it live? When the fuck's it due to detonate?" Secretary Morgan said.

"Don't panic, sirs. It's quite safe. Yes it is all in place and wired together, and the timers are set for tomorrow at twelve noon, and all the explosives are genuine, but all the detonators are dummies. I wanted to delay laying these charges, but Lucas insisted due to the bad weather, so if I'd have refused it would have likely blown my cover, so I did the next best thing. Having planned and shown everyone everything working, I crept back to the explosive shed that evening and doctored all the blasting caps. None of them at the pipeline will work."

"They didn't keep everything locked up or guarded?" the Admiral asked with disbelief.

"That they did, sir. But one of the tricks Coronado teach is how to pick a lock in the dark with nothing more than a paperclip or a bit of stiff wire. It took me less than a minute."

Breathing a sigh of relief, the Admiral said, "I'll remember that if ever I lock myself out of my house. What exactly did you do, Lieutenant?"

"I don't know if you all know how blasting cap type detonators work, but they're pretty basic. There is usually a thin aluminum tube filled with black powder. At one end is a thin wire element and two wires. You push the other end of the cap into the bigger explosive charge, and connect the wires to some form of electrical trigger. With a timer, the timer activates and passes electrical current through the wires. The element glows red hot, instantly igniting the black powder, which explodes. This small explosion triggers the larger charge, dynamite, C4 or whatever, and the whole lot goes up. All I did was uncrimp the end of each cap and empty out the black powder. But Simpson would easily have detected that because of the weight change, so I filled them with sand instead and recrimped them. Look and feel exactly as normal and even pass a continuity test, but no black powder means no bang."

"But surely the C4 and dynamite is still deadly?" Secretary Dreiberg said.

"It is, but it needs to be triggered. This pipeline is in the middle of nowhere, and it's very cold there. Chances are no one would ever find it, and dynamite only becomes unstable when hot. All you need to do is send in a bomb disposal team to remove it all, and I've already emailed you the exact location."

"Since Mitch brought back the approximate area I've had a drone circling a ten-mile radius keeping check. I'll get the bomb squad on it right away," Simon Clark said, "What else?"

"They also plan to blow two pumping stations and place explosives on the inspection PIGs that travel in the pipe itself. The other coordinates I've sent you are the two pump sites in North Dakota they plan to attack. There's eight of them traveling in two dark blue Jeeps, one to each pump site. They'll be carrying C4 and dynamite and automatic weapons. Their blasting caps are also dummies. Get SWAT at both sites. The attack time is shortly before noon tomorrow."

"I don't know exactly where the third and fourth attacks will take place. There's a white panel van loaded with ANFO and dynamite heading to Denver and another has been left in San Francisco. They're each loaded with half the amount used in Vegas."

"Ye gods," the Admiral said, "How the hell do we evacuate either in time?"

"Sirs, the van in Frisco is already there. Lucas and Simpson took it there before the bastards killed Rachel. The blasting caps there are live. They headed out before I could doctor them. I've been told it's due to detonate at 22:00 Sunday night. My 'source' doesn't know where it's located but said Lucas had told him he'd be rid of those 'Animals of Satan' at that time."

"What 'source' do you mean, Lieutenant? Who is it and how reliable is he or she?"

"It's a 'he', sir. I don't want to go into details, but I can guarantee he's telling me the truth."

"What does 'Animals of Satan' refer to, Lieutenant?" Secretary Morgan asked.

"Boyd Lucas is a religious fanatic, sir. He regularly gave sermons and would always highlight his hatred of abortions, amongst many other things. I think it's likely planned to attack an abortion clinic in Frisco late on Sunday evening."

"Leave that with us, Lieutenant," Lt. Gen. Dreiberg said, "I'll get the President call the mayor and I'll call the

SF Chief of Police as I know him. We'll put them on high search alert."

"Sirs, as to the panel van heading towards Denver. The caps in that van are safe, but the explosives aren't. ANFO is very unstable, but the van only left today so is still en route. I've found a map on Lucas's desk, and the 16th Street Shopping Mall is circled. This fits in with his other sermons and, according to reports, tomorrow is expected to be one of the busiest shopping days, being only a week before and the last Saturday before Christmas. That would give him maximum effect and casualties. It also fits in with his tirades about people missing the real reason for Christmas and just using it for personal greed."

"We'll put blocks on all access roads. They won't get through," Clarke said, "Lieutenant, first light tomorrow I'm sending in a team of twenty agents to take control of the compound and close it down. Anyone still there will be arrested and questioned. In the meantime, we'll put Denver and Wyoming Police on high alert. There's a chopper on its way to pick you up and take you to our Denver HQ. It'll be there in twenty minutes. We're using the Gulfstream and will see you in four hours."

With that, the phone went dead.

Deacon had a last search around the control room. In one drawer he found over a dozen cell phones. Powering them on he found two had three-quarters to full charge, so he put both of them in a pocket before heading back to his cabin and grabbing his few possessions.

The clatter of the approaching UH-60M Black Hawk helicopter increased rapidly as it circled once above the compound. A bright spotlight beam suddenly illuminated

Deacon, blinding him temporarily before the chopper landed in the area out front of Lucas's cabin.

As his eyesight returned, Deacon sprinted towards it and waved at the guard as the door was slid open.

"Lieutenant Commander Deacon?" the guard confirmed.

"Affirmative."

Within seconds of climbing aboard, the helicopter rapidly ascended before making one more full circle over the compound. It had been on the ground less than ten seconds. Climbing further, it headed in an easterly direction.

Deacon leaned back into his seat, fastened his seatbelt, closed his eyes and slept.

Chapter 42

The Black Hawk flew directly to Denver Airport and landed close to the East Terminal. Deacon had slept the entire way, only waking as the rotor pitch changed for landing. As the rotors wound down, a black Yukon SUV arrived, and the driver opened the rear passenger door for Deacon. Climbing in, the driver carried his luggage to the rear, got back in the driver's seat and the vehicle sped away. Accustomed to having to carry his own luggage and open his own doors, Deacon smiled and thought how he could get used to luxury.

As they pulled up at the FBI building, the receptionist already had a pass organized.

He waited while his photograph was taken and printed onto his pass before being taken upstairs. He was shown to a conference room, asked if he wanted refreshments, and then left alone.

Less than two hours later the others from Washington arrived, and Lieutenant Mitchel Stringer was the first to bear hug Deacon.

"John, good to see you and I'm glad you're still in one piece."

"Me too pal, me too, although it did get a bit worrying at fifteen to one, but I offered to let them go get more men," he said smiling.

The others then walked in, and it was congratulations all around.

"Too soon sirs," Deacon protested. "We need to stop the truck from getting here, find and disable the bomb in San Francisco, and Lucas and Simpson have disappeared somewhere with a live Claymore."

"How was your cover blown?" the Admiral asked.

"I don't know, sir. They got hold of my complete military record. That's pretty secure shit. I still don't know how they traced Rachel from that."

Turning to Simon Clark, he continued, "How deep a cover did you set for me?"

"We did a good job, Lieutenant. We cleaned your background and completely erased any friends and colleagues. We left the military side to the Admiral, but we deleted Rachel from everything and anything connected to you, as you requested."

"Well, you didn't do it fucking well enough, did you?" Deacon said, his voice growing angry, "cus if you had they'd have never found Rachel, and she'd still be alive," he said, prodding Clark in the chest.

"Lieutenant Commander," barked Admiral Carter, "Stand down." He softened his voice slightly before continuing, "Director Clark offered Rachel protection, but as you know, she refused. She said she didn't want to be nursemaided by anyone. I'm deeply sorry she's gone, son, she was a lovely girl, but we need to focus our energy on finding and defusing those bombs, then finding out how they knew about her. You sure it was Lucas and Simpson?"

"Sorry, sir. You're right. And yes, I am sure it was them, they boasted about it. And I will get them."

"God help them when you do," the Admiral said quietly to himself.

They spent the remainder of the evening going over everything that had happened in great detail. Simon Clark contacted the squad leader who would be arriving at the compound at first light and instructed him to collect all papers and any documents and to get the computers over to Quantico as rapidly as possible. He also contacted Melissa Rogers, his most trusted and most capable computer expert back at base and advised her of the computers' arrival. He instructed her to work alone on this, treat it as the highest priority, and find out who and where the mole was.

Pulling up a large-scale map, they looked at which route the van would take to Denver. There were really only two routes. East along the I-90 then south down the I-25 through Casper and through Cheyenne, or south down the I-15 to Ogden then east on the I-80 and then through Cheyenne.

Clark spent almost thirty minutes on the line with both Idaho and Wyoming police forces. They agreed to monitor the roads and stop and search any suspect vehicles. As the suspect vehicle was thought to be containing high explosives, they would only apprehend when it was out of town.

<><><>

At six-ten on Saturday morning, two FBI helicopters flew up the valley low. The thunderous roar of their rotors disturbing wildlife for miles around while the rotor wash flung the fallen snow off the top branches. Circling twice, their spotlights glaring down, anybody still in the compound couldn't have missed them. As one began to descend, the red, white and blue flashing lights of five large GMC Suburban station wagons reflected off the forest trees as they came down the track at speed.

Four of them sped through the open gates and slewed to a stop in the snow outside the main building while the fifth blocked the exit route.

Ten FBI agents wearing full body armor, helmets, night scopes, flashlights and automatic weapons rappelled down from the circling helicopters. Some took up guard positions while the others ventured out into standard search patterns. Another ten agents just wearing bullet-proof vests and carrying handguns climbed out of the vehicles and stayed close.

Everyone waited until the searching groups radioed back 'all clear' statuses before moving out.

The FBI quickly detained the thirty or so people still staying in the compound. None put up any form of resistance, and they were taken away to be questioned. In the days to come, most would be released without charge.

The office of Boyd Lucas was carefully searched, and four large black bags of paperwork were carried to one of the vehicles. Inside the control room, the screens and recorders were all removed, along with any recorded discs and were placed in two of the GMC's. The computer systems were loaded onto the second helicopter and was rapidly airlifted to Bert Mooney Airport, Butte, where a US Navy aircraft was waiting to take them to back east.

Before leaving, two agents powered up the backhoe digger and demolished the explosives storage area. They then moved earth over it in order to make safe any remnants of explosives.

Chapter 43

At seven the next morning while having breakfast in the Four Seasons hotel with the others, Director Clark was on his phone being updated on the success at the compound when an urgent call came in. Putting the original caller on hold, he checked his messages. With a smile on his face, he turned to the others and said, "It looks like the truck has been spotted. A suspect vehicle with two men on board was just seen driving through Casper, heading south. We've got a couple of unmarked following at a safe distance, and Wyoming SWAT has been alerted. The road is fairly quiet this early, and they plan on intercepting as soon as everyone is in place."

<><><>

Marty Robbins was driving this morning. They'd left the compound yesterday around lunchtime with Dwight Emery driving and had made good speed. All the major roads had been cleared of snow. They'd kept to the speed limits and had done nothing to draw attention to themselves.

They stopped overnight in a motel in the town of Buffalo, and had kept to themselves before leaving early the next morning. Now driving through Casper, Robbins felt the hairs on the back of his neck bristle. Nothing discernible had changed, but he felt uneasy as he kept looking in the mirror.

"I think we've just been made."

"What? Who?" Dwight Emery said looking around.

"Two guys in a tan colored sedan the other side of the road. They seemed to show a lot of interest and eye-balled us. Can see in the mirror they've just turned around and are following. Another darker sedan has just joined them as well. Also got two guys in it."

Turning around in his seat and looking, Emery said, "They're just cars."

Waiting a few seconds and keeping his eyes on the mirror as he slowly accelerated, Robbins said, "That's why it's suspicious. Everyone else around here is in trucks or pickups. Two sedans. Both with two up front. And they both sped up a little when we did and slowed back down again now. I'm telling you, we've been made."

"Fuck, what're we gonna do?"

"If they know what we got on board, they ain't gonna get into a shooting match, 'specially if there are others around. But they ain't gonna let us get to Denver either. Not after what you guys did in Vegas. We should surrender now with no harm done. Might get a bit of jail time but we ain't done anything yet."

"You ain't done anything yet, but I was with Simpson in Vegas. I'll be seen as much guilty as him. No, we gotta get through this and on towards Denver. They won't try and stop us if we're near others. Catch up with that Greyhound bus in front."

Seeing a bus a few hundred yards in front, Robbins put his foot down, and the van surged forward.

Over the next few minutes, they slowly gained on the Greyhound bus.

The bus driver was on the last leg of his journey. This route was from Seattle, through Spokane, Butte, Billings, Buffalo, Casper, Cheyenne, Denver, Kansas City and finally arriving at St Louis. His current leg was Billings to Cheyenne, and he'd be finished well before lunchtime. Looking in his mirror, he noticed a dirty white van slowly gaining and then holding a position about twenty feet back. Glancing in the mirror, he thought to himself *'All these miles of open road and this jackass has to sit right on my ass.'*

Five miles ahead the Wyoming SWAT team was ready. Two vans blocked the two-lane highway, and six officers were waiting. The land here was very flat and open. In the distance, the shape of a bus appeared heading towards them. The dirty-white van was close in behind and couldn't easily be seen.

The bus driver could see the road blocked ahead and the flashing red and blue lights. Taking his foot off the accelerator, the vehicle began to slow. Behind, Robbins and Emery could also see the blockage and moved in even closer to the bus.

Both vehicles slowed to a crawl with the passengers looking scared. The senior SWAT officer picked up a bullhorn and shouted, "Stop your vehicles."

As the bus finally stopped, Robbins pulled in close behind, and Emery climbed into the dark rear.

"You in the vehicle. Switch off your engine and show me your hands," the bullhorn voice shouted.

"Fuck you! You let us through, or we'll detonate it now. Everyone'll be killed. If anyone gets off the bus we'll detonate it," Emery shouted.

"What the fuck, man? We gotta give up. They'll shoot us otherwise. I don't wanna die," Robbins said. Turning towards Emery, he found himself staring straight down the end of an automatic rifle.

Ordering the Greyhound driver to keep the doors closed, the senior SWAT officer cursed and picked up his phone.

Director Clark took the call in the main meeting room at the glass-fronted local FBI headquarters at East 36th Ave, Denver. Cursing, he passed the details on to the rest of the team. Although the driver was in sight and could easily be shot, they couldn't risk firing into the rear of the van and had no idea where the other person was hiding. Deacon turned to him and said, "Get me out there in a chopper with a sniper on board."

Instructing the SWAT officer to wait fifteen minutes, then let both vehicles continue, he ordered a fast car to take Deacon to the airport where the same helicopter from the previous night was waiting.

Rushing downstairs, Deacon ran across the entrance and dived into a waiting Yukon. Tires squealing and lights flashing, it raced towards the airport.

The rotors were already spinning as the Yukon skidded to a stop and Deacon ran across the last fifteen feet of tarmac. Before he was even strapped in, the sliding door was slammed shut, the whine of the engine increased rapidly, and the Black Hawk lifted quickly off the ground.

Swinging around onto a northerly course, the pilot dipped the aircrafts' nose and pushed the throttle to the maximum. With its engine screaming, it was at its maximum speed of one-hundred-and-eighty-three miles an hour within seconds.

Forty minutes later, it closed on the column heading in its direction. Two black vehicles were leading, clearing the way, then the Greyhound bus followed very closely behind by the van. A few hundred yards behind that were two more SWAT vehicles.

Pressing his microphone switch, Deacon spoke to the pilot.

"Can you call up the bus driver on the radio?" he said.

"We can now, sir. Since 9/11 and the increased risk of terrorist activity, all buses, trains and emergency services in the US have independent operating channels but also monitor one common encrypted channel. Let me try contacting him," the pilot replied.

Within seconds the pilot was talking to the bus driver. He nodded to Deacon who switched to the same channel.

"This is Lieutenant Commander John Deacon of the United States Navy. Who am I talking with?"

"I am Miguel Lopez. I am the bus driver."

"Mister Lopez. First, please relax. You and your passengers have done nothing wrong. It is the van behind you that we are interested in. We believe it contains a bomb and they are keeping close to you so we can't intercept it. If we try to stop it, they will likely explode the bomb and you and your passengers might get hurt."

"Madre de dios! What can we do?"

"Mister Lopez. Miguel. Just do as I say, and everyone will get out of this alive. You just keep driving. Unless I tell you differently, just keep going and don't stop for anyone. Tell your passengers to get down on the floor and as far forward as they can, away from the windows. OK?"

"Si, Si," and he switched the internal Tannoy system on and started advising passengers.

In the meantime, Deacon changed frequencies and radioed the senior SWAT officer and outlined his plan.

Listening to Deacon, Captain Scott Lawson interrupted him and told him to stand down. This was a Wyoming SWAT matter now and they would deal with it. Thanks, but no thanks for your continued involvement. Knowing time was running out, and he had no intention of getting into a pissing contest, Deacon called up the others in FBI HQ in Denver and briefly explained the situation as well as his plan.

Monitoring the open SWAT channel, even Deacon was surprised to hear the booming voice of Admiral Carter on the radio a few moments later.

"Is this Captain Lawson? It is? Now listen here, you jumped up little prick. I'm Admiral Douglas Eugene Carter, Chief of Naval Operations at the Pentagon. On the line with me is Lieutenant General Warwick Dreiberg, the Director of National Intelligence to the President. Also present is Simon Clark, the Director of the FBI, and Secretary Harold Morgan, the Secretary of the Department of Homeland Security. In that helicopter circling above you is Lieutenant Commander John Deacon, US Navy SEAL. He's done more brave things to save this country than you've had hot dinners, so when he tells you his plan and asks for your help, you little pissant, you say Yessir, three bags bloody full sir. Do you understand? Or I'll make one phone call and you'll be spending the rest of your career directing traffic in Buttfuck, Iowa. DO I MAKE MYSELF CLEAR, SON?"

A suitably chastened Captain Lawson came back on the radio and asked Deacon to restate his plan before offering him every assistance.

Chapter 44

Marty Robbins was still driving down I-25 and keeping in close behind the Greyhound.

"See, I told you they'd let us through," Emery said, his weapon still pointing in the general direction of his colleague.

"You're mad. They won't let us get to Denver. They know we got explosives on board. They won't let what happened in Vegas happen again. They'll stop us and shoot us."

"They can't. They can see you but don't know where I am. I could set this lot off anytime and it would blow up the bus as well. They can't chance that."

"They won't let us get there. Not now. They'll sacrifice the bus passengers and us if need be. We need to give ourselves up. It's our only chance," Robbins said, easing his foot off the accelerator.

"You fucking speed up or I'll kill you now, you motherfucker," Emery screamed, aiming his weapon at Robbins' head. "I swear I'll fucking kill you. SPEED UP!"

Pushing his foot hard down, Robbins quickly wiped a tear away from his face. He hadn't signed up for this. Not cold-blooded murder. He'd been sickened when he'd learned of what they'd done in Vegas. He'd just joined the group to get away from the rush of his standard day-to-day life for a while. He liked the idea of living off the land with a group of like-minded people. He wasn't religious but didn't mind the daily praying. He didn't even know what exactly this trip was about until Emery had told him this morning after they'd left Buffalo. He knew they were carrying explosives but didn't know they planned to leave the van in a shopping center. He thought they were going to blow up the pipeline. He didn't mind that too much. That was radical and a fight against the way the country was headed. Spilling a little oil was one thing, but blowing up a shopping center full of innocent men, women and kids was something completely different.

Keeping his right foot hard down on the accelerator, he very gently pressed the brake with his left. Not hard enough to slow the vehicle, but just enough to move the pedal and make contact with the brake light switch. He didn't know Morse Code but knew the three dots, three dashes, three dots of SOS. Keeping this up was awkward and a little sporadic, but with the rifle pointing at his head from less than four feet away, he really didn't know what else to do.

Deacon had explained his plan. All he could think of was either blocking the road completely and shooting the driver when the van stopped and bringing in a negotiator to try to get the other occupant to give up; or to wait until the van was passing a gully or ditch and shooting the front tire out hoping the van would swerve that way before the explosives could be triggered. Neither option was guaranteed to work and both put the lives of innocents at risk. He planned to have the helicopter drop in front of the van and the sniper lined up on the driver. If the other passenger could be seen, he'd be terminated first, as it would be unlikely a second trigger switch would be with the driver. Although not the best scenario, he'd been given authority to stop the van at all costs and not allow it to get to Cheyenne or beyond.

The driver in the first black FBI Yukon following the bus was watching the rear of the Jeep when he noticed the braking lights were blinking. Ignoring it first, thinking it must be a faulty connection, he didn't notice the repetitive pattern. Gradually, however, the constantly flashing rear lights made him look again and he began to read them. Recognizing the message they were flashing, he called Captain Lawson on the radio.

"Captain, I think the driver's sending an SOS message using his braking lights."

Deacon heard the message before Lawson passed it on to him and instructed the chopper to circle once behind the van. Sure enough, the lights were still flashing the SOS message.

Realizing this was a significant game changer, he called up the Admiral and altered his plan.

About ten miles south of Chugwater the road straightened for almost eight miles. This was where Deacon would execute his plan.

The helicopter swung out wide until it was at ninety degrees to the traveling van. Using a thermal targeting scope Deacon was hoping the heat signature of the occupant sat in the rear would show. Unfortunately, the image wasn't clear, and the sniper in the helicopter couldn't guarantee a clean shot. The obvious worry was either the shot would miss altogether, it would wound but not incapacitate, or it would hit the explosives and trigger a detonation.

He realized his only option was to get in close, so Deacon committed to plan B.

He spoke with the pilot before fitting a harness and taking the sniper's handgun. The pilot carefully maneuvered the helicopter with the wheels at approximately twelve feet above the road and flew in fast from the left. The noise inside the van as the helicopter flew barely inches above its roof was deafening. The downdraft rocked the van on its springs as the chopper flew across it and over to the right-hand side.

Turning quickly, it carried out the same maneuver in reverse.

Twice more it did the same. But the fifth fly-past was different.

Inside the van was turmoil. Dwight Emery had kept his rifle pointing at Robbins continuously for almost thirty minutes. Twice more he'd had to threaten Robbins he'd shoot him or blow the van up right now just to make Robbins keep up speed.

"Look man, I don't want to die for a cause I don't even believe in," Robbins said.

"The General believes in it. We need to rid the country of non-believers. Get back to the old days when people respected each other. Too selfish now. That's why we gotta show them."

"Who? Who's got to show them? The General? Where the fuck is he? Why isn't he here? Why are we gonna die for his cause?" Robbins said, pleading.

"You're messing with my head, man. Shut the fuck up and just drive before I shoot you. What the fuc––?"

The deafening noise increased rapidly in volume, and as the shadow of the Black Hawk crossed over the van it rocked violently on its springs. Trying to see what was happening, Emery stretched forward to look out the passenger window, but the helicopter was already swinging away.

Three more times the helicopter buzzed them right to left or left to right. Each time Emery couldn't see clearly what was happening as they traveled at over sixty miles an hour down I-25.

On the fifth fly-past the noise was as deafening as before but didn't let up. The shadow stayed over the van, and the downdraft rocked them and kicked up loose snow all around, almost to the stage where Robbins had trouble seeing the road.

With a loud bang something slapped against the rear doors, and instinctively Emery looked towards where the noise came from.

Determined to take as many with him as possible, with the bus just yards away and the helicopter merely feet above, Emery grabbed the timer from his lap, twisted the dial to zero and smiled as the timer electronics triggered and sent a voltage spike down its wires.

Chapter 45

On the fifth pass Deacon was already outside the Black Hawk and hanging by the harness. Both hands were tightly gripping onto the left landing wheel that held him steady. As the helicopter hovered above the fast-moving van, Deacon yelled 'Forward' into his mouthpiece, and the pilot surged the heavy aircraft ahead.

As Deacon slammed into the rear of the van, his feet were almost touching the ground. He yanked at the double doors, missing the handle the first time. As he tried again, he managed to grab the handle and yank the left door open. The startled face staring straight back at him was Dwight Emery. Emery's voice was whisked away by the rotor noise and wind but Deacon saw the look of surprise on his face as he said the word 'You!' as he turned a button.

The timer did its job correctly. Nine volts of DC were sent down the two wires. Only three volts were actually needed. The heater wire stuck firmly inside the blasting cap glowed red hot in an instant, but there was no black powder to ignite and explode. Instead, the sand just warmed around the heater wire until it burnt itself out five seconds later.

Realizing something had gone wrong, Emery jiggled the timer again but still no explosion. Reaching for his rifle, he swung the barrel towards Deacon who was holding onto the van door frame by his left hand as his right came up holding a pistol. Emery's finger pulled on the trigger just as Deacon pulled on his. The retort of both weapons seemed to happen as one. Emery's automatic rifle discharged three rounds. The first one missed entirely while the next two hit Deacon firmly in the chest. Deacon's pistol discharged one round that hit Emery center face.

The force of the rounds hitting Deacon pushed him back out of the van as he swung on the harness like a pendulum, before the forward motion of the helicopter swung him back into the van.

Crashing partly on top of Emery's body Deacon gasped, "Stop" but his voice was masked by the noise of the rotors.

Marty Robbins had seen the shadow of the Black Hawk stay over the van and knew something was happening. He didn't hear the crash of Deacon hitting the rear, but the sounds of Emery's rifle firing in the enclosed space was loud enough to penetrate. Expecting a bullet in the head any second, Robbins glanced around and saw a person dressed in black Nomex, wearing goggles and a helmet, half lying, half sprawled across the bloodied body of Dwight Emery.

While Deacon's hand frantically tried to find and press the harness 'quick release' button, Robbins raised his hands off the steering wheel, jammed his foot on the footbrake and screamed, "DON'T SHOOT. I SURRENDER. DON'T SHOOT."

Deacon's harness clicked open a fraction of a second before the Black Hawk overshot the rapidly slowing van. The harness forcibly yanked back out of the rear of the vehicle, catching and shredding itself apart on the door frame.

Looking up, Deacon said mostly to himself, "Thank fuck that worked."

The two chase vehicles had already stopped, and SWAT members were handcuffing Marty Robbins as Deacon climbed shakily out the van. His bullet-proof vest had stopped the worst damage but he knew he'd cracked one rib at least from the impact of the first round and would have heavy bruising from the effects of the second for weeks to come.

Deacon heard Mitch's voice in his ears, "Holy shit, man, that was incredible."

It was only then he remembered the helmet had a built-in camera and communications and it had been streaming back live to the FBI HQ in Denver.

"Yeah, well, never a dull day, you know," was all he could think to reply.

<><><>

Ninety minutes later he walked stiffly into the conference room back at East 36th Ave.

"You know, some days I think I'm too old for this shit," he said, as first the Admiral, and then everyone else shook his hand.

Sitting down, he was brought a coffee when Simon Clark joined him.

"Your plan for the pipeline seems to have worked well. Bomb disposal has been at the pipeline itself since first light. They've defused and removed the explosives you planted. You did a good job, as always. Almost too good. The team leader spoke to me and said if you hadn't supplied the exact coordinates, they'd have had trouble finding the right structures 'cus the blankets covered it so well and blended in."

"The problem was, I could have fooled the others, but Simpson is ex-Army. He might have been fooled, but he was already suspicious, so anything I did had to stand up to his examination. What about the pump stations? Are they secure?"

Gathering around the large TV monitor, Mitch pressed 'Play' on the digital recorder. All members of the SWAT team had been wearing headcams, and the images had been relayed live back to FBI HQ and recorded.

Deacon watched as the various SWAT members moved to strategic positions around both pump sites. The monitor was split into left and right. Left was a live feed of the pump site at Burtsville, the right was at Hesper. In the top corner of both halves were live aerial views taken from FBI drones now circling each area. Deacon could see there were ten team members at each site.

The attackers at Hesper arrived first. The pump station was unmanned, and the Jeep drove up to the gate. Three figures got out, and one used bolt-cutters to open the chain that was locking the gates together. As the gate opened a little, one person headed towards the generator building, took aim and shot out the camera covering the main compound before planting something the size of a rucksack next to the door. He twisted something in his hand before darting away. In the meantime, the driver who'd stayed in the vehicle drove in and stopped directly outside the main building.

A few seconds later it was obvious that something had gone wrong and the parcel against the door hadn't exploded. As the attacker moved back to check it, a SWAT member edged around the corner into view and challenged him. At the same time, more headcams showed other SWAT team members lining up the other attackers in their sights and challenging them. Three threw down their weapons, but one raised his. Deacon and his colleagues could see four puffs of dirt fly off that attackers jacket as two of the SWAT team opened fire. The body fell, and a SWAT member ran over to it. The other three attackers were by now kneeling down with their hands behind their heads as two SWAT members kept their weapons on them while others secured them.

Movement on the other half of the screen drew their eyes towards it. This group wasn't even allowed to break into the pump station grounds. SWAT was located on the empty approach road and stopped the vehicle in classic style. Two team members, lying in ditches either side of the road shot the Jeep's tires out while six others, three in front, three behind covered the vehicle from all directions. The team leader shouted instructions through a bullhorn and after almost twenty seconds, the windows opened, and the attackers dropped their weapons out onto the snow-covered road. Closely following orders being shouted to them, they opened the vehicle doors before exiting one-by-one, moving to the rear and away from the vehicle and lying face down on the road. Within a few minutes, all four were knelt in the snow, hands tied behind them, while other SWAT members disarmed the explosives.

Deacon heard Admiral Carter say, "Lieutenant, let me introduce some people to you."

Turning, Deacon was surprised to see two people stood in front of him.

Chapter 46

Extending a hand, Montana State Trooper Officer Chuck Gibbons shook Deacon's hand warmly.

"Two and five, Lieutenant?" he said.

"Not this time, officer," Deacon replied, with a smile on his face. Shaking hands with his colleague, Officer Larry Merit, Deacon continued, "Officer Merit. We've not met, but I killed you. Center chest, if I remember?"

"You're correct sir. But no hard feelings - we hadn't been formally introduced."

Officer Gibbons pulled his notepad out of his pocket and continued, "There's a little matter of you having an open can of alcohol in your driving cab when we met last. That's a driving citation and a five-hundred dollar fine under Montana State law. I can either arrest you now, or we could go to a bar and you could buy my colleague and me a beer to say sorry."

"I owe you that, gentlemen, but I'm afraid I'll have to take a rain check. We've still got a live explosive device somewhere in San Francisco, and I can't celebrate until I know it's safe."

"We understand, sir. We're heading back up to Helena. Director Clark arranged for us to stop here and just say howdy. We've got a 'plane to catch. Now we're going to go surprise the shit out of our colleagues. The ghosts of Merit and Gibbons return! Ha! Can't wait to see their faces. See you around, Lieutenant. Drop in next time you're in God's own country," Gibbons said, as they shook hands before heading towards the door.

That afternoon and evening were taken up with re-examining of the contents of the bags removed from the Brethren compound. There were BOLOs (Be On the Look Out) for Simpson and Lucas, and all ports and airports were on alert for them. The overall assumption was they were now hiding somewhere in Canada, being so close to the Canadian border. Although no one matching their descriptions had been seen crossing any of the many border crossing points, it was well known the border was fairly porous to those living close to it.

The computer systems from the compound had arrived in Quantico and were now in the tender care of Melissa Rogers. Once one of the best hackers around, she'd been caught and faced eight years in prison. Simon Clark's wife, a high-school teacher, had known Melissa since fifth grade. She'd always been highly intelligent and well above average in mathematics and science. Unfortunately, schools are designed for the masses, not the individuals, and Melissa's interests had wandered. When she'd heard of Melissa's arrest, she'd mentioned her to him and he'd arranged to meet her. After thoroughly vetting her, he'd offered her a chance to work at the FBI in return for putting her sentence on the back-burner. With a proper focus for her amazing talent, she'd blossomed and quickly proved her worth. There wasn't a computer system she hadn't managed to crack when she put her mind to it.

In San Francisco, SFPD were combing the entire Bay area looking for the other vehicle. They'd already been around the main banking commercial district and hadn't found it. They'd widened their search area to include shopping malls but again to no avail. All parking lots were being examined, and the bomb squad was on full standby. All abortion clinics had been checked, many of which were on regular police check routes anyway, but nothing had been found. However, three young college girls against abortions were shocked when twelve armed police surrounded them, weapons drawn, while they were daubing red paint over a window of one clinic. They were even more shocked when one of them was tasered, and all three were forced roughly to the ground, handcuffed, questioned and kept in isolation cells for ten hours.

Early evening, Mitch, the Admiral, Director Clark, Lt. Gen. Dreiberg and Secretary Morgan had all taken the FBI Gulfstream back to D.C. while Deacon decided to stay the night in the hotel before heading down to Phoenix to visit Rachel's distraught parents and help plan her funeral.

He stayed in a local bar most of the evening trying to relax, but his mind was still active. Heading to bed later that night, he couldn't settle. His mind was going round and round with the same information, but it wasn't getting him anywhere. He kept thinking of the sermons Boyd Lucas had given and how his rants had always centered around the same few things. Banks and bankers, people being commercialized and always buying and wanting more, gambling being the root of all evil, the triple evils of homosexuality, prostitution and lust. And of how his actions and messages to the people would make them change.

Eventually, sleep overcame him and he finally drifted off into a pitiful slumber.

Tossing and turning, images kept leaping into his dreams. Barrels and barrels of ANFO, detonators, Det cord, Chief Petty Officer Martock, Laura and Michelle Williams, Masoud Saadi, Boyd Lucas, Terri-Anne, Claymore mines, Fuller Simpson, Noah Turner, packets of C4 explosives, Lucas's paper-strewn desk, a moving clock face like a Disney cartoon striking 22:00, a suit carrier, a briefcase, the pipeline not exploding but Lucas laughing about it, more barrels of ANFO, Lucas's paper-strewn desk ...

Jolted awake, he sat up, sweat dripping from his face. What was it? What was his subconscious trying to show him? The van was missing somewhere, but maybe it had never even gone to San Francisco. The police had checked everywhere.

Glancing at the bedside clock, it was 04:15. The police still had almost eighteen hours to find the van. No, that wasn't what woke him.

Running through things one more time he re-examined the facts as he knew them. He was sure all the ANFO had been accounted for except that which might be in San Francisco. Likewise, all the doctored detonators had been found, but the ones being used in Frisco would be genuine. Lucas and Simpson had gathered all their stuff and headed out, likely to Canada or even possibly south to Mexico. They'd last been seen with cases. Suitcases and the alligator briefcase. Why? What was special about that briefcase? And where was the missing Claymore? And what was it with the paperwork on his desk?

Coming more fully awake now, the briefcase image was the one strongest in his mind.

'Shit!' he thought as it finally dawned on him that the Claymore had to be inside the briefcase. But why take that to Mexico or Canada? It didn't make sense.

Rubbing his face with his hands, he said to himself, 'Think John, think.'

Then it happened. His thoughts finally cleared and began falling into place. Boyd Lucas had originally said there would be four acts. Deacon had counted Vegas as the first, the pipeline second, the third the pumping stations, and the fourth as somewhere in San Francisco.

That's where he'd been wrong; adding up.

The first two were correct, but the third wasn't the pumping stations - that was all part and parcel of the second attack on the pipeline. The third was San Francisco, and the fourth was unknown.

Or ...

The fourth was San Francisco, meaning the third was very soon and presently unknown.

The image of Lucas' desk kept coming into view. Wooden and almost five-feet long it was no bigger than many he'd seen before, so why did he keep seeing it? Or was it something on it?

Wracking his brain he tried to remember what had been left on the desk. Closing his eyes he remembered papers, but nothing stood out at him. The stuff about Vegas was old now. The only other thing had been a calendar. Was something marked? Was there a particular date?

He knew his subconscious was trying to tell him something, but he didn't know what.

Deciding to go for a walk to clear his mind, he dressed, grabbed his Parka and went downstairs. As he was walking through the hotel lobby, he saw a bank of computers against the wall set up for hotel guests to use. Walking over, he sat down and connected to the internet. It was early on the morning of the 18th December, so he opened Google and searched to see what events were planned locally for the next few days.

The normal pre-Christmas events were displayed. Santa would be visiting certain stores today and every day until the 24th. There were carols being sung today by City Hall. The Salvation Army was playing at an event in the afternoon, and so on.

Deacon realized Lucas had gone completely mad but still didn't think he meant to hurt churchgoers or children. That wouldn't fit with any of his preaching or sermons. He was against people who didn't worship, not those who did.

He spent a few more minutes looking and was just about to turn off the computer when he noticed a flyer referring to the Aspen Conference Centre under the screen stand.

He picked it up and opened it. He remembered he'd seen it before. There was an identical flyer under some other paperwork on Lucas's desk. The main photo showed a three-story building in a beautiful location. Additional images were of the inside rooms and views and were equally as impressive.

Just out of curiosity, he opened a new browser page and typed in the website address.

Scanning the pages nothing looked out of the ordinary.

Then he clicked on the calendar page ...

And suddenly everything made sense.

Chapter 47

Racing over to reception he grabbed the night manager.

"I need a car or truck, but I need it now. It's an emergency."

"Calm down, mister. What do you mean you need a car? It's four-thirty in the morning, man. Nothing's open yet."

"Look, I have to get to Aspen. It's a matter of life or death."

"Mister, if you don't calm down I'll have to call security."

"Call your fucking security then, but get me a damn car. NOW!"

A heavily built black security guy came ambling over. Looking pretty mean, he said, "Now gents, what's going on?" although his eyes and body language were directed towards Deacon.

"Look, I'm a US Navy SEAL. I was here earlier with senior people from Washington. I need to get to Aspen urgently. There's a bomb due to go off in a few hours. I need a car."

The night manager picked up the phone and said, "I'm going to call the police."

The security guard leaned over the counter, put his big hand on the phone cradle, and said, "No, Tony. You gonna give this dude the keys to your wagon."

Seeing the startled look on the night manager's face, the security guard continued, "You watch the news? This dude stopped a van of explosives today. It was heading for the 16th Street Shopping Mall. Some radical bastards were gonna blow it up at midday today. My Sherri-Lee was down there with our two little ones to see Santa. Give the man your goddam keys now."

Passing the keys over, the guard pointed to Deacon which vehicle it was, and said, "I've only got a Toyota, it might get stuck in the snow. His wagon'll see you through. Thanks for what you did earlier, mister."

Running over to the Chevrolet Tahoe, he leaped in, started it and wheel-spun through the slush out of the parking lot.

He only saw one other car as he accelerated out of town towards the I-70. He pushed the Tahoe as fast as he dared in the icy conditions. The road had been cleared of snow but flakes were still falling and settling and the temperature was now extremely cold and into single digits Fahrenheit. There were roadworks in various places causing him to slow down. Grabbing one of the cell phones from his pocket that he'd retrieved from the compound he powered it up and waited for the system to connect. After what seemed an age, the display showed five bars of signal. Dialing a number from memory, he swung the Tahoe onto the I-70.

"Mitch? Mitch. Wake up, man."

"Wwhaaaat, John, its six-forty in the morning. I didn't get home until two, whatthefuckchawant?"

"Mitch, Lucas is going to bomb the bankers today in Aspen. That's why he's got a Claymore."

"What? Start again and slower. Go on."

"I couldn't sleep. Things weren't balanced right. I couldn't understand why Lucas and Simpson would run away after what they'd done and with a Claymore as well. They'd know the pipeline hasn't been destroyed and my rescue here in Denver is all over the news so they'd know about that as well. But they were still up to something. All of their attacks have been against something he's preached about. Vegas was for the gamblers and prostitutes, the pipeline was to bring everyone back into simpler times and not travel, stay as a family more. The Denver shopping center was against commercialization of Christmas and people just buying things instead of turning to God."

"OK, that all makes sense, but why bankers and why Aspen?"

"His other rants were about bankers and money lenders. Called them the root of all evil. Every year on the last complete weekend before Christmas, they hold the Western States Annual Bankers Conference. It's this weekend. Yesterday and today. The Saturday is fun on the ski slopes and then a big gala evening meal and drinks. The Sunday is the conference. It starts at 09:00 through 13:00. People are then free to stay longer and ski or head back home. That's what he's going to hit."

"Well, I guess it makes some sense, but how sure are you?" Mitch asked.

"It was the briefcase and the suit carrier that clinched it. If he was just running, why the suit carrier? He's rich. He could buy clothes anywhere. And why was the briefcase being carried carefully? 'Cos the Claymore's inside it. But why? What sort of meeting would you need to wear a suit for and carry an expensive briefcase? A bankers meeting, that's what!"

"OK, so what is this meeting?"

"Think of it as a small Davos - that's where all the World Economic Forum leaders meet in Switzerland every January. Monetary decisions are made there that affect the remainder of the world. This is similar but on a smaller scale. Senior bank executives and managers from all the western states of the US gather in Aspen for a conference weekend. Most fly their private jets in on Friday, and it's a big party atmosphere being just before Christmas. Helps them meet their colleagues and decide how to set interest rates for the next twelve months. Senior members of the Federal Reserve from Washington will also be present. Decisions made over this weekend will affect almost every single American."

"And it's held in Aspen every year? I've never heard of it."

"Makes sense, because it's nothing like Davos, which is seen as positive. This is mainly just banks involved in the rates people pay for mortgages and loans, and most people wouldn't support it, especially when you look at what's on the menu. Talk about excessive corporate greed. So it's not advertised. I saw it by accident. It's held at the Aspen Conference Centre and Hotel. The brochure shows this place as a three-story building located on a steep slope with fantastic views out over the town and the mountains. The middle floor is a 360-degree restaurant, and the upper floor is a massive conference room again with all-around views. A Claymore set off in the middle of that room would be devastating."

Losing the cell signal for a few minutes as he raced through the countryside, he finally saw signal bars on his phone again and redialed Mitch.

"John, where have you been?"

"Just poor signal, man. It's back now, but I'm up in the hills headed for Aspen. Call Clark and the Admiral. Get them to roust the troops. Tell them what I've told you."

Engine racing, Deacon slewed the Tahoe along as fast as he could. Snow had started falling again, and it was already pitching. The snow ploughs would be out later, but this early on a Sunday morning he had the roads to himself. However, the heavy tread tires gripped well. Keeping up a constant speed of almost ninety miles-an-hour, it took him just two hours to get to Glenwood Springs.

Other road users were out now, keen to hit the slopes, but he just overtook them all, headlights blazing and horn blaring. Twice he almost lost control after hitting an ice patch or a particularly deep snowdrift, but he made good progress.

Turning onto CO-82, the traffic thickened and his speed slowed. It was still a two-lane each direction road, but with a long incline and a heavy snow covering, his overall speed dropped to less than forty. Eventually, just outside Carbondale, a police cruiser was waiting to escort him. With the cruiser's roof lights glaring and siren wailing, ground speed quickly increased again and by eight-twenty, the 'Welcome to Aspen' sign came into view.

Heading towards the Conference Centre, Deacon was eventually waved down by three other police cruisers.

Captain David Piper shook Deacon's hand and introduced himself. "Lieutenant, I've been in touch with Denver PD. What can we do to help? Do you want the conference center evacuated?"

"No sir, not at this time. I don't know where the bomb is set or how it's triggered. If it's already in place and triggered remotely, any form of evacuation might force them to detonate it early. Let me head in quietly and see if I can find them."

Deacon jumped back into the Tahoe and drove the last mile before swinging the heavy vehicle in through the car park and stopping.

Chapter 48

At 08:37, Boyd Lucas and Fuller Simpson arrived at the center. Lucas was wearing an aircrew pilot Captain's jacket and hat and was carrying the alligator skin briefcase. Simpson was dressed in a similar fashion, but with one less shoulder chevron.

Walking over to reception, Lucas said, "Hi, I'm the pilot for Randolph Jackson, CEO of Bank of Middle America. This is his attaché case. He left it on his aircraft yesterday and called me this morning. He needs it for his presentation. He said he's up in the conference room now and I need to get this to him."

Glancing at his uniform, the receptionist replied, "Well, you shouldn't really, but I'm sure it's not a problem. Please go to the third floor," and she signaled to the two heavyset guards by the elevators to let them through.

As the minute hand on his watch moved to 08:45, Deacon drove into the car park and stopped, tires slipping in the snow. Rushing up the steps towards reception he was pleased to see two police officers standing guard duty outside the main doors. Half walking, half running, he realized he still looked unkempt. He'd shaved his beard off in the Four Seasons but hadn't yet had his haircut. Now, with an overnight stubble showing, wild looking hair and wearing scruffy jeans and a Parka coat, he realized he didn't look like the clientele the conference center was expecting today.

Both officers were working the weekend shift at the center as overtime and had come on duty both yesterday and that morning directly from home. Neither had had chance to check the latest reports and duty roster at their office. Glancing at Deacon as he rushed up the steps and into the center, something about Deacon triggered something in Officer Todd Stanhope's memory. Sliding a hand automatically and subconsciously to the grip of his pistol, he loosened the weapon, turned and followed Deacon in. His partner, Billy Collins, sensing trouble, followed suit.

Deacon rushed over to reception and asked what the agenda was for today. Startled, the receptionist backed away, looking towards the two security men for assistance.

Raising his voice, Deacon said, "The conference. When does it start and where exactly is it? Come on, answer, I need to know!"

By now both guards from the elevator had walked the few paces over, and one of them said, "Excuse me, sir, what appears to be the trouble here?"

"Look, I'm trying to find one or two people who might be trying to get into the conference. Has anyone unexpected turned up this morning?"

"Unexpected like you, sir? I think you'd better leave. This is a private event today, and no one without a pass is allowed in," the guard said, putting a hand on Deacon's shoulder.

"Well there was the pilot and co-pilot that went up just now," the receptionist interrupted.

"Were they carrying anything? A briefcase? Anything?"

"As a matter of fact the pilot was. A very attractive briefcase if I remember. Crocodile or Alligator, I think," she said.

"When? How long ago? Quickly!"

"Five, ten minutes ago maxi--"

"You need to let me up there now."

"I'm sorry, sir. That's impossible. As I told y--" the guard started to say.

"Look, I'm Lieutenant John Deacon, and I think there's a bomb a--"

"FREEZE ASSHOLE. Get on the ground and put your hands behind your head. NOW, ASSHOLE!" Officer Stanhope's voice echoed throughout the reception area.

Turning his head, Deacon could see both police officers moving towards him, weapons drawn and aimed at him.

"I knew I recognized you from the BOLO. You're that motherfucking cop killer. Just give me an excuse, boy. GET ON THE GROUND NOW!"

As the two guards let go of him and moved away, he turned fully and saw both officers were stood a little over ten feet away from him at forty-five-degree angles. Both had raised weapons pointing at him and at that distance, neither could miss.

"Officers, you're making a mistake. I'm working with your Captain Piper," Deacon said, raising his hands.

"One more word, motherfucker, and I'll blow your fucking head clean off. Now get on the ground. NOW!"

As Deacon began to lie down, he glanced sideways and saw the rear shapes of Simpson and Lucas, hands empty, exit the elevator and move towards the exit.

"That's them. You need to sto--" Deacon started to say as a booted foot slammed down on his back.

Spinning on his hands like a break-dancer and flipping over onto his back, Deacon grabbed the boot and twisted as Todd Stanhope stepped back. With one foot held and unbalanced on the other, Deacon's legs swept around and knocked him clean off his other leg.

Landing awkwardly on his back, Todd Stanhope gasped as the wind was knocked out of him a fraction of a second before Deacon partly pulled him on top, one hand freeing Stanhope's weapon and using him as a shield.

Billy Collins had seen what had happened but was too slow to react. Deacon was now hauling Stanhope to his feet and was shielded completely behind him. To make matters worse, Stanhope had his own stolen Glock pressed tightly into his throat.

"Drop your weapon or your colleague dies," Deacon said to Collins, "Drop it."

With Stanhope red-faced and gasping, partly from surprise and partly from having the barrel of his own weapon thrust firmly into the folds of his neck, Collins carefully laid his weapon down, saying "Look, nobody needs to get hurt. We can forget anything has happened," as Deacon suddenly thrust the weight of Stanhope at him.

As the two officers staggered back, Deacon rabbit-punched Stanhope's neck and he went down, out of the fight. Collins moved in to tackle him. Deacon hit him once, hard, with his right elbow just below his ear. People will often try to punch, but a swinging elbow with all the weight and force of a shoulder behind it is more than enough to put a person down.

Grabbing one of the fallen weapons while kicking the other under the desk, he said sorry to the two semi-conscious officers, saying he would have to explain later, as he ran towards the stairs.

Although Simpson and Lucas were gone, they'd come back down without the briefcase. Reaching the conference room doors, he glanced through the windows down into the carpark and saw both of them getting into a dark colored BMW.

Gatecrashing into the room, it was crowded. Most people were sat facing the stage, but a number were stood near the food-laden side tables. Running up to the stage he brandished the weapon and shouted, "Two men in uniform were just here. Where did they leave their briefcase?"

Many of the faces looked on blankly while a couple of the guests made their way towards Deacon, urging him to leave. Then a shout went up that he had a gun and the room turned into an uproar.

Realizing he only had one option left, Deacon fired twice into the ceiling and ordered, "Stop!"

In the ensuing silence, he tried again.

"Two men in uniform were just here. They had a bomb in their briefcase. Where is it?" he shouted.

Some began to panic and tried to run, but a few pointed towards the food table and said they'd been standing there.

Leaping down from the stage Deacon grabbed the material covering the table and yanked it off, plates and food cascading everywhere.

Just underneath but far enough under not to be detected was the alligator skin briefcase, stood on its back. Carefully sliding it out and picking it up, he began to run gently towards the doors when Officer Collins rushed in, weapon pointed at him.

Someone shouted, "He's got a bomb!" and Deacon stopped and yelled at Collins, "He's right. This is a bomb. But I didn't bring it. You've got about ten seconds to either shoot me and we all die or let me get this out of here."

Stunned, Collins just looked on as Deacon rushed past.

Running towards one of the other large picture windows, Deacon pulled Stanhope's weapon from his waistband, aimed and fired five rapid shots at the glass. As the window exploded into fragments and people started screaming and shouting, Deacon skidded to a stop and spun like an Olympic hammer thrower before letting go of the briefcase handle and watching it sail out through the shattered window into the gently falling snow.

As it fell end over end and away from the conference center, it dropped lower and lower before it landed midway down the steep slope. There it began a small avalanche and started to slide further down the hillside.

A groggy Officer Stanhope, Billy Collins, and the two guards were now on Deacon. He was punched hard in the stomach and doubled up. Out of the corner of his eye, he could see Collins was about to club him with his pistol.

The enormous explosion and shock wave hit them through the broken window before the sound of the blast registered. The force knocked them over with snow being blasted everywhere. Rolling over on the floor Deacon tried to put his hands over his head to offer some protection from some of the loose glass fragments blown in with the blast, but both arms were grabbed and savagely forced behind him and handcuffed.

The business crowd which had exited the conference room started clapping and cheering as he was pulled to his feet. Todd Stanhope looked pleased with himself until he realized the crowd was cheering Deacon. Dragged downstairs at gunpoint and still handcuffed, he was forced into the rear of their waiting cruiser as four other police cruisers arrived.

Minutes later, Captain David Piper arrived and said, "Stanhope, let him go. He's a hero."

"Sir, he's that motherfucking cop killer up in Montana."

"No, Todd. That was all a mistake. You should read your daily briefings. Now let him go."

"But what about what he's done today? He attacked Billy and me."

"What he's done today, Todd, is save over two hundred lives after having saved countless others yesterday. Now please let Lieutenant Deacon go."

<>

Thirty minutes later in a small conference room Deacon sat with Captain David Piper and looked at the teleconferencing screen currently set up in three-party call mode. As the screen flickered and burst into life, Deacon could see Admiral Carter and Mitch at the Pentagon on one half of the screen, and Simon Clark at FBI headquarters in Washington on the other.

Deacon introduced Captain Piper before giving a quick overview of what had happened. After listening carefully, Simon Clark asked, "So, Lieutenant, do you know where Lucas and Simpson are now?"

"No sir. I saw them getting away, but I had no ability to chase them. I knew they'd left the explosives somewhere and obviously that was my priority."

"And yet again, Lieutenant, you made the right choice. So what made you guess this convention?"

"It was just too neat. In his sermons Lucas kept going on about money lenders and bankers being the root of all evil. Something Terri-Anne had said about the two of them leaving with suit carriers and the briefcase. She said Lucas was carrying it carefully. I put two and two together about the Claymore - it would easily fit in a briefcase - but that still didn't answer the where or when. It kept niggling in the back of my mind. Then something McCabe had said when I interrogated him. Lucas had mentioned that interest rates would drop Sunday morning. Then everything began to click together and here we are."

"Well, you've just saved the lives of over 180 bankers. Some people will love you for doing that, others will hate you, but I'll bet you'll never have a problem getting a loan again," Mitch interrupted.

After the laughter had died down Deacon said, "My main concern now is the last truckload of ANFO. The detonators are live, and it has the power to flatten a city block. Are we sure SFPD have checked everywhere?"

"They've confirmed all abortion sites are under extra police guard and shopping centers and parking lots are being searched. The entire central business district for banking has been cordoned off with an excuse of a suspected gas leak plus we have additional security checks. We've even put extra guards around some of the government buildings including the police headquarters in Mission Bay and the FBI offices on Golden Gate Avenue. We've stepped up surveillance on vehicles using the Golden Gate and the Oakland Bay Bridges. We've locked the city down pretty tight. Any more and the public will notice, and that raises its own problems," the Director of the FBI said.

"I need to be there," Deacon said, "I don't know what I can do beyond what everyone else is doing, but I need to be there."

Agreeing to arrange transport as quickly as possible for Deacon to go back to Denver, the video call carried on as Captain Piper stood and left the room.

Five minutes later Captain Piper returned.

"Lieutenant, a car's waiting downstairs for you."

"Back to Denver?"

"No Lieutenant, just down the road to Aspen-Pitkin Airport. I just interrupted the conference. There's a lot of very grateful bankers in there. I said you needed to get to San Francisco urgently and you had eight offers of private jets before I even finished speaking. One's being refueled as we speak."

"I'll have Special-Agent-in-Charge Henry Cussack waiting for you at SFO. He's my liaison with Chief Bridges of SFPD," Clark said, "We have BOLO's out on Lucas and Simpson so it's only a matter of time ..."

Chapter 49

Deacon barely had time to leap into the rear of the waiting police cruiser before the driver accelerated hard out of the car park. Eight minutes later, sirens wailing, it screeched to a halt next to a 14-seat Dassault Falcon 900B Executive jet. The engines were already turning, and he was welcomed aboard by a pretty hostess who pressed the 'close door' button as he stepped into the cabin, shaking the snow off his shoulders. With a faint whine, the steps folded up and the door closed and latched as the pilot eased off the brakes and the Falcon rolled forward. By the time Deacon had fastened his seatbelt and the hostess had fastened hers, the pilot had announced they were taking off. With a sudden thrust that pushed Deacon firmly back into the plush leather seats, the small executive jet screamed down the runway before leaping clear of the ground.

Seconds later it soared through the thick cloud and burst out into brilliant sunshine and the rich blue of the sky above.

The voice of the pilot came over the intercom, "Lieutenant, I'm Captain Wilkes and we were instructed to get you to San Francisco with all haste. We have a priority cleared flight plan, courtesy of the FBI, and will be touching down in SFO in one hour forty-eight minutes.

I'm ex-Navy, and it will be a pleasure to push this bird the way I love to fly. Please sit back and enjoy the ride."

Having decided yet again that traveling by private jet and staying in expensive hotels was a habit he could get used to, Deacon enjoyed a large black coffee and ate a late breakfast, courtesy of the eager-to-please hostess.

Sure enough, one hour and forty-four minutes later, Captain Wilkes came back on the intercom stating they were on final approach.

Swinging off the main runway and over towards one of the many taxiways, Deacon could see a large black GMC Yukon was waiting for him. As the aircraft stopped and the door began to open, Deacon popped his head into the cockpit and thanked Captain Wilkes and his colleague for their urgency, saying he'd be happy to fly with them again anytime.

Walking down the steps, the hostess passed a folded napkin to him with her name and phone number, but he just smiled and put it in his pocket. The raw memory of Rachel was far too recent to even think of spending time with someone else yet.

A tall, bald-headed man exited the driver's seat of the Yukon.

"Lieutenant, I'm Henry Cussack, SAC here in San Francisco. Director Clark has fully briefed me about everything you've endured. Pleasure to meet you, sir. Chief Bridges is waiting to meet us at his HQ, and I'm to take you straight there."

Sliding into the vehicle, Cussack revved the engine, and they headed over to a private access gate to the airfield where a SFPD cruiser was waiting to escort them into town.

With the cruiser clearing the traffic ahead, they made quick time up route 101 and onto the 280 into Mission Bay and 3rd Street. Fifteen minutes later Deacon and Cussack were escorted into the plush offices of Chief Bridges.

"Hi Henry. Welcome to San Francisco, Lieutenant. Warwick Dreiberg is an old friend of mine. We were both in the Air Force for many years. He's fully briefed me on what we have here. You'll have the full support of the SFPD. We need to stop this bastard after what he did in Vegas. I'm also really sorry about what happened to your friend, Rachel Sanchez. Please accept my condolences. I've been told it was the same person who has masterminded this attack and the attack on Vegas?"

"Chief, a pleasure to meet you and thanks for your thoughts. The ringleader or mastermind is Boyd Lucas but calls himself 'The General'. As to Rachel, it was two of them that murdered her, Lucas and his second-in-command, Fuller Simpson, ex-Army. Both are currently in the wind after I almost caught them in Aspen trying to blow up the Conference Centre where they were hosting the Western States Annual Bankers Conference this morning. That's where I've just come from, courtesy of one of the banker's private jets. Top priority now is finding the truck if it's here."

"Since Warwick called me Friday evening, we've secured the central business district, all hospitals, all abortion clinics, the major hotels, and all shopping malls. All adjoining parking lots have been checked and all side roads up to three hundred yards. We also have a number

295

of boys-in-blue in situ, but nothing so far. We've put extra security monitoring traffic on the Oakland Bay and Golden Gate bridges and put a five-hundred-yard traffic exclusion zone around the tourist areas of Pier 39 and the adjacent waterfront. We've also tightened up security at the airport, but that's pretty tight anyway. We're sure if it's here it would've been found by now. Are you sure your information was correct?"

"I was, my contact was pretty certain. He specified 22:00 hours here tonight, but I'm beginning to wonder myself now."

"Well, while you're here, Lieutenant, why don't I introduce you to Harry Jablonski," Chief Bridges said while pressing a buzzer on his desk. "It's not something I'd do for a member of the public, but seeing your involvement ... He's Detective 3rd Grade and in charge of the investigation into the murder of Rachel Sanchez."

Moments later the door opened, and his secretary motioned for a tall, heavily built person to enter.

"Lieutenant Deacon, let me introduce Detective Harry Jablonski."

"Lieutenant, my pleasure. Please call me Harry or Ski –– all my friends do."

"My name's John, but everyone just calls me Deacon," he replied, a level of confidence growing that this detective was the sort of old-fashioned, tenacious type who wouldn't give up until the perpetrators had been found, arrested and charged.

"If you've got an hour or so I'd be happy to let you examine the crime scene if you want?" the detective added.

"That, Ski, would be very welcome," and the pair of them, along with Henry Cussack headed downstairs to the carpark.

Thirty minutes later they pulled up outside Rachel's home. Deacon knew the house well as he'd often visited Rachel there. Walking in past the 'Police - No Entry' tape surrounding the door was chilling. Various articles and ornaments had been dropped or thrown on the floor, but most things were in their correct place. Heading upstairs was another story. The walls of her bedroom were splashed with blood, and her clothes were in tatters on the floor. They'd been ripped or cut from her body and lay where they'd been dropped. There was fingerprint dust over almost every surface, and police photographic size markers were still lying next to ripped clothing and blood drops on the floor. Strands of white polypropylene rope were still tied to the head and feet of the bed, and the sheets were almost completely covered in blood.

"Do you want to know what forensics and the ME have determined?" Ski said.

Finding it hard to speak, Deacon just nodded.

"They entered through the main door and managed to disable the alarm. The victim arrived--, I'm sorry, Rachel arrived home, parked her car and came in as usual. There is evidence of a struggle downstairs, and she was brought up here. We think chloroform or something similar was used. She was tied and held on the bed and, we believe, questioned. Force was used ... we found evidence of toes being crushed and fingernails removed--"

Looking at Deacon, Ski could see he was white. Not with shock, as most people would be, but with rage. Pure rage. Struggling to remain as calm as possible, Deacon managed to say, "Go on."

"Two teeth were also removed. Not knocked out but deliberately pulled out with pliers."

"Dear God!"

"Then, I'm afraid, it got worse."

"Go on."

"She was raped and sodomized a number of times. She was forced to perform oral sex––"

"How do you know?"

"The medical examiner performed a full autopsy and found evidence of semen in her stomach. DNA has come back with two different sources of the semen. She received various bite marks to her body, particularly to her thighs and breasts, and finally, the sick bastards removed her nipples with a pair of nail scissors from the bathroom, but at least that was post-mortem. The actual cause of death was manual strangulation."

Deacon was rigid. He was a deathly pale color, and his muscles were locked solid. This was his Rachel they were talking about. His Rachel who'd laughed and smiled as they'd sailed back down from Catalina Island. His Rachel who he loved and cared for. His Rachel who worried every day about the job he had, worried he'd get hurt or injured. His Rachel who was actually pleased when he took this undercover role as she thought he'd be safer there than in war-torn Iraq, or Afghanistan, or where ever else he'd be sent.

"We're waiting on DNA and fingerprints to confirm, but I understand you know the perpetrators?" Ski continued.

"Yeah, Lucas Boyd and Fuller Simpson. Simpson's ex-Army," Deacon said.

"How sure are you?"

"It was those two. They boasted about it."

"Fuck. Well there's already a nationwide BOLO out for them," Ski said.

Deacon said quietly, "If they're caught first, fine, but if I get to them first, they're mine," before walking back downstairs and outside to get some fresh air. He planned to meet Rachel's parents in the next day or so to discuss the funeral arrangements, but he wouldn't tell them of her injuries. He'd never speak of that to anyone - ever!

"Let's go back to town and get an update on the van search," Deacon said.

Chapter 50

At eight o'clock Sunday evening they were in the main headquarters' control room. All traffic and surveillance cameras in the city fed back here. Ten police cruisers had completed additional drive-pasts of all identified prime targets and were again confirming no vans of any type were parked in the vicinity. Deacon had already been out with one of the police commanders and had surveilled all the potential targets. Officers and city engineers had examined the below road level bridge support structures of both the Golden Gate and Oakland Bay bridges, but nothing suspicious was found.

A large interactive map of the city was along one wall. Resource indicators showed where patrol officers were, along with police cruisers.

At seven minutes after eight, the alarm went up. A gray van had traversed the Embarcadero towards Pier 39 twice in the last ten minutes. Within moments, the police blocked the road in front and behind, and armed officers surrounded it. The driver, a white male in his early twenties, was pulled from the driver's seat and forced to the ground at gunpoint, while his female passenger just sat there transfixed with fright.

Within seconds of the alarm being raised, Deacon and Cussack raced downstairs to his waiting Yukon and were rushing to the scene.

With flashing red lights and sirens wailing, it took them less than seven minutes to cover the three-and-a-half miles, tires squealing on the damp road surface.

Leaping out before the car fully stopped, Deacon could see the female passenger had also been removed from the cab, both suspects were handcuffed and were under armed guard in separate police cruisers. At first glance, the van looked similar to the one they were hunting, but Deacon could see clearly this vehicle was a different style and model. The police had secured it and were waiting for the bomb squad to arrive, but he knew this wasn't the one they were after. Ignoring the local police sergeant, who demanded he keep his distance, Deacon walked up to it and opened the rear door.

There were empty food wrappers strewn about, along with at least three empty wine bottles. The metal floor of the van was covered in carpet with an old mattress covering most of it.

Slamming the door, he jogged over to the cruiser. One glance at the white-faced suspect confirmed all they'd caught was a pair of young lovers out for an evening's fun in their 'love truck'.

Cursing quietly, he joined Cussack before heading back to police headquarters.

By now it was almost five after nine as they walked in and took their seats. One of the senior officers was going over that evening's plan one more time and discussing where resources were best allocated. "We have all available officers patrolling with an extra ninety-six drafted in on overtime. So far all is quiet apart from a sidewalk scuffle on Haight at the LGBT rallies," the officer stated.

Henry Cussack partly raised a hand and asked, "LGBT rallies?"

"Yeah, this year there's two at the corners of Haight and Pierce."

Like a mist clearing, Deacon found himself staring straight at Chief Bridges. Realization clicked in both their eyes at the same time.

"Lieutenant, this 'General', were any of his sermons or rantings homophobic?" the Chief asked.

"Fuck. Damn right they were. 'Animals of Satan' - that's how he referred to gays. That's why we haven't found the van - we've been looking in the wrong goddam place!"

The Chief quickly issued an urgent radio call instructing twelve cruisers in the vicinity to drive around and examine all roads and parking in and around the Castro and Haight Street areas, with particular emphasis on Haight and Pierce. Deacon and Cussack were already racing back downstairs. Leaping into the vehicle, they wheel spun away, the tires shrieking, still hot from their last use.

By the time they approached the Castro district, the police radio in the Yukon was already awash with chatter. A panel van matching the description had been sighted parked less than one hundred feet from both party venue bars by two of the officers on foot patrol. The van was old and dirty. And without trying the doors, the officers had looked in through the front windows. Whatever was in the rear was covered with tarpaulins of some form but, when asked, the officers confirmed that the van looked full and was low down on its springs. As a precaution, the bomb squad had already been called and was on their way.

Even with red and blue lights flashing, progress was slow. The streets around the area had been closed and cordoned off since ten o'clock that morning in preparation for the rallies. There were almost six thousand people milling around, some in the actual bars hosting the parties, but most had spilled out into the traffic-free roads.

By the time Deacon and Cussack arrived, over a dozen other police officers were on the scene. Trying to manhandle drunken members of the public was failing, especially those who then decided the police were just trying to stop them from having fun. Many of them even joined arms to act as a barrier to stop the police moving them on.

After what seemed an eternity, but in reality was only a few minutes, Deacon managed to get close to the van. The rear doors were locked and didn't have windows, so all examination had to be carried out from the front. Peering in through the dirty windshield Deacon could see the same tarpaulin covered shape the officers had reported. By now the partygoers had begun to spill out closer to the van and Deacon was afraid someone might shake the vehicle. Not only were the roads getting crowded but the revelers were singing and dancing, happy to be in a party mood.

Ten minutes later a green Army Humvee came roaring down the main road followed by a large truck with Bomb

Squad stamped in big black letters on its sides. Some of the partygoers moved away a few feet, drunkenly thinking they were now far enough away to be safe, while others staggered outside to watch.

It took almost a half-hour to close the parties down and move everyone away to a safe distance. During that time, the bomb squad had examined the van using a remote buggy. They carefully planted a small amount of explosives on the rear door and detonated it, causing the lock to disintegrate and one of the rear doors to gently swing open. Looking in, it was clear there were at least a dozen barrels strapped down, and the inside walls of the van were covered with adhesive tape holding nuts, bolts and nails. Using the buggy, its claw gripped part of the tarpaulin and pulled. As the tarp fell away, the operator could see sixteen barrels arranged in a four-by-four pattern. The four corner barrels had two sticks of dynamite taped to each barrel with wires feeding back to a central unit with an amber light flashing. Maneuvering the control arm and extending it further into the rear of the van, the onboard camera showed the timer on the central unit was still running and counting down. The display showed seven minutes and twelve seconds.

One member of the bomb squad, a captain, heavily protected with Kevlar plates and a bomb suit walked as quickly as he could in his bulky gear towards the van. He was carrying a range of tools in a side holster. Carefully checking the other rear door wasn't wired to trigger anything, he gently opened it and slowly climbed inside. He was in contact with the squad commander by low-power radio and explained what he could see.

"There are 16 containers filled with a substance that smells like ANFO. There are eight dynamite sticks as triggers centrally wired with a blue wire, a green wire, and a yellow. There doesn't appear to be any form of vibration sensor, which makes sense being located here where anybody could bump into it, but there is an anti-tamper mechanism. It looks to be active. It's a standard continuity sensor, so I will check for residual current," he said.

Connecting a milliamp detector across the connecting wires showed a very low current flow. Speaking again, with urgency in his voice, the captain said, "The yellow is the current sense. If any wire's cut, the control unit will detect the change in current flow and trigger the remaining detonators. I need eight current dump switches. NOW!"

Some of the crowd had begun to move nearer the police cordon. The police commander raised his megaphone and shouted instructions, urging the public to stay back, while quietly counting down the minutes in his head.

Six minutes, eighteen seconds.

A bomb squad sergeant climbed out of the squad truck with eight of the switches. Deacon rushed over to him, grabbed half and together they ran to the bomb. The bulk of the protective suit the captain was wearing would slow him down too much in the confined space, so as the sergeant climbed in the rear, Deacon smashed the glass of the driver's door with his gun butt, unlocked it and climbed in.

"Who the fuck are you?" the captain said.

305

"Navy SEAL. No time to argue. You two do those front five, and I'll do these three," he said, passing one switch over.

Pulling out his knife, he squeezed in behind the driver's seat, gently gripped one set of wires and shaved the razor sharp blade along a half-inch section of the plastic of the blue and green cables exposing the copper within, careful not to let them touch together. Then, placing the sensor dump switch on the floor, he gripped the two crocodile clips in his fingers and clipped them simultaneously to the exposed wires, and pressed the dump switch. The small LED glowed green, and he used his knife to cut the blue and green wires nearer the detonator.

He called out, "One," moments before he heard the others say "Two" and "Three".

The counter was down to four minutes and three seconds.

His second took slightly longer than the first, and the others had already called "Four" and "Five" before the LED glowed green on number six, and he cut the detonator free and called it clear.

One minute, thirteen seconds.

The bomb technicians, using tools designed for the purpose, worked quicker and thirty-five seconds later he heard the call of "Seven."

Twenty-eight seconds.

"Get out, I'm almost done," he shouted as the sergeant helped the bulkily dressed captain to climb down.

Deacon clipped both croc clips onto the last exposed wires and pressed the dump switch.

Nothing happened.

He jiggled the clips and the switch, but still, the LED refused to light.

He had a faulty current dump switch.

With the counter showing nine seconds, he knew he only had one choice left. Reaching for the blue, green and yellow wires, he cut all three.

The control unit detected a change in resistance and the anti-tamper safeguard operated exactly as it had been programmed to do. It instantly sent a flash current down all eight pairs of wires to the detonators to trigger immediate detonation.

The seven dump switches connected across the seven pairs of wires operated as planned by absorbing the large charge of the flash current. The exposed ends of the eighth pair of wires, still firmly clenched in Deacon's right fist, sparked, but the detonator had already been cut free.

Moments later he stepped out of the rear of the van with the central timer unit and three blasting cap detonators swinging from his hands, calling out, "Safe."

Other team members then sprayed the inside of the panel van with a foaming chemical agent which would reduce the chance of a secondary ANFO explosion before the vehicle was carefully lifted onto a waiting police trailer to be driven away safely and examined.

Chapter 51

It was three days after the failed attack in San Francisco and everyone was getting prepared for Christmas. Late on the Wednesday afternoon, amid gently falling snow, a dark colored 4-wheel drive pickup truck drove slowly down the access track to the compound, its headlights dancing across the smooth snow surface.

The entire area looked undisturbed and uninhabited. There were no tire tracks or footprints, and none of the buildings had lights showing or smoke rising from the chimneys. The FBI had finished their work and left long ago. By the time they had arrived, most followers had already left. The few remaining were still being held at the FBI Denver offices.

Coming gently to a stop the vehicle just stood there, exhaust gases slowly pumping out the rear. After a minute or two, when the occupants had been looking around through the darkened windows, the engine suddenly stopped and Boyd Lucas stepped down from the driver's side holding a pistol. As he climbed down, the passenger door opened and Fuller Simpson climbed out brandishing an automatic rifle in his hands. No words were spoken between them and they moved carefully towards the main building. The headlights were still on and illuminating their way as their feet left footprints in the otherwise virgin snow.

As they neared the building, four shots rang out, less than half a second apart. Both headlights of the car exploded, and then two shots hit the radiator grill and with a hiss steam began to escape. Both men froze momentarily, but Simpson, being ex-Army, recovered quickly. Diving for cover they clearly heard Deacon shout, "I knew you'd come back. Today's the day you pay for what you did to Rachel, you bastards."

Simpson pointed to Lucas to head to the right and he would go left. Daylight had left over an hour ago, but the snow-filled sky, along with the snow already on the ground, produced a gloomy illumination filled with shadows. As they headed around either side of the building, they expected to see Deacon somewhere between them. Instead, there were footprints leading away.

Ducking back behind limited shelter, Simpson shouted, "Your fucking slut of a girlfriend screamed and cried. She gave you up. She wasn't worth—" as two shots in quick succession rang out and echoed around the hillsides and the snow near his feet exploded.

"Shut it, Simpson. She was innocent and you know it. And I'm gonna kill you," Deacon's voice echoed around the buildings.

"She was a good fuck, I know tha--" as the sound of another shot split the air and his rifle was shot out of his hands, a bullet shattering the main stock.

"What if I tell you everything?" Simpson shouted, trying to gain time while pointing to Lucas to head up into the forest.

"It's all over, Simpson. None of the explosives went off. You and Lucas are wanted men, but you're never going to serve time in jail. You're both going to die here and your vermin-ridden bodies will be eaten by animals."

"What're gonna do? Shoot me, you pussy? Fucking SEAL pussy," he shouted back as he watched Lucas climb over the fence and disappear up into the forest.

"No! I'm gonna beat the living crap out of you first and then kill you," Deacon said quietly as he stepped back into the dusky light.

Tossing his rifle away and slipping out of his heavy Parka, Deacon slowly approached him. "Just you and me, pal. Army versus a SEAL. Let's see how tough you really are," Deacon said, taunting him.

Unzipping his jacket, Simpson slipped it off before suddenly lunging at Deacon, shouting, "Ha!" and then stopping short when Deacon didn't react.

"Ha yourself, asshole."

Facing each other and slowly circling, hands extended, palms down they both made a number of fake lunges at each other, both trying to gain an advantage, just testing. Simpson suddenly half jumped forward, swinging a massive right hook, but Deacon managed to sidestep just in time. Had it connected, it could well have been game over right then, but it was still close enough for Simpson's shirt cuff to touch Deacon's ear.

While Simpson was in close, Deacon managed two quick fierce jabs into his stomach and side, before he moved back out of reach, leaving Simpson partly winded.

Deacon feigned a blow right and managed to land a haymaker left to Simpson's stomach, before turning and kicking out his left leg and partly connecting with Simpson's left knee. With his knee going partly numb, Simpson lurched back out of range.

"She cried, you know. Like a baby. Like a pussy seal baby. Actually begged not to die. Then we fucked her. Over and over. Took turns. Good enough for a pussy SEAL, good enough for us. She cried and begged as I squeezed the life outa her. My face was the last thing your slut girl saw--" he taunted until Deacon suddenly charged him.

Feigning left, Deacon managed another hard punch to Simpson's stomach receiving only a poorly placed blow to his left cheek before he managed to grab the arm, twist it inwards and slam his other hand down on the reverse of the elbow. With a loud crack, followed by a louder scream, the elbow shattered before Deacon let go and moved back away. As Simpson turned slightly, trying to protect his broken and useless arm, Deacon again feigned left before driving his right knee high into Simpson's crotch.

With a gasp like a deflating balloon, Simpson staggered back head doubling down before Deacon spun and slammed his right elbow into his face, breaking his nose, then turned slightly and stomped with all his might with his right foot onto Simpson's exposed left knee.

With the full weight and force of Deacon behind it, Simpson's knee folded backward and, gasping for air and trying to scream at the same time, he collapsed back into the snow.

Retching and trying to breathe, with blood running down his nose and mouth, Simpson started to taunt him even more about Rachel, but Deacon had had enough.

Looking Simpson directly in the eyes, he said, "Who's the pussy now?" as he stomped once, very hard, on Simpson's throat.

With a crack loud enough to echo back from the trees, Simpson's neck snapped, he twitched twice and died.

Standing there, looking down and breathing hard, but with no more pity than if he'd squashed a bug, he murmured, "One down, Rachel, one to go."

Chapter 52

Shaking the snow off his fallen jacket, he slipped it back on and began to walk towards the fence. He left his rifle where he'd tossed it. Lucas had left clear footprints in his rush to escape. Following them over to the forest edge, he shouted, "Lucas! Simpson's dead and you're next. You've got an hour." before turning and walking towards the main buildings.

Looking around the kitchen, he found a discarded clean mug and some coffee. Minutes later the heady smell of brewing coffee began to drift slowly up the valley. He sat there in the cold and dark, drinking and thinking, before heading back over to Lucas's private room.

A few minutes later, he made his way over to the fence at the edge of the forest. It was now very dark, but the white of the fallen snow still gave some pale illumination. With the possibility that Lucas might be waiting just inside the tree line with his pistol aimed at where he'd climbed over, Deacon deliberately chose a different section to traverse.

As before, most of the snow had failed to land on the forest floor, being captured on the overlying canopy branches far above, so with a smile Deacon entered in.

Hunting in the dark is always more awkward than in daylight, but Deacon didn't need to use a torch. Years of training had helped him hone his sensory skills and the air within the forest was very still. The hour sitting in the dark had helped his eyes adjust to their maximum sensitivity, and although there appeared to be nothing to see, his peripheral vision could easily pick out shapes and objects as he moved slowly uphill. He had always marveled at how human eyes worked, how the center circle of the eye, or fovea, contained cones that respond to fine detail and color, but are not sensitive enough to work in low light. Outside the fovea, rods respond with less clarity but higher sensitivity. He'd discovered, as a boy, that looking directly at stars at night often make them disappear, but looking to the side of them make them reappear. That was called peripheral or edge vision.

With that in mind and by turning his head left and right slightly, he could quickly see the trees and objects in his way, and he pushed on up into the forest. After a few minutes, he sensed the air had moved, and he stopped and just relaxed. The air around him still had faint movement in it and the faintest hint of body smell. Not body odor, or aftershave, but maybe deodorant or something similar. It was recent, but not just. At least twenty minutes old, maybe thirty. But he was on the right track.

Stopping behind a tree, he pulled Lucas's hunting horn from his pocket and gave it a long, loud blast.

Boyd Lucas had moved away quickly to the fence by the forest on Simpson's urging. He was armed with a Sig-Sauer P226 automatic pistol in its 10 round, .357 variety.

He was also carrying a 10-inch hunting knife and a torch. Climbing over the fence he had watched Deacon and Simpson fight it out and he moved up into the trees when he saw Simpson was losing.

He was only two-hundred meters or so in when he heard Deacon's shout that he was next, but far enough away so that the loom of his torch wouldn't be seen. Clicking it on he raced as fast as he could deeper into the forest and uphill. He knew the torch would partly destroy his night vision, but distance was important.

Eventually coming to the clearing almost in the forest center, he found a fallen tree and waited. Suddenly, in the distance, he heard his hunting horn being blown. A shiver ran down his spine and he realized the effect the horn had on those he'd hunted and he just smiled. He knew Deacon had outfoxed him and none of the planned explosions, apart from the first glorious one in Vegas, had detonated. He didn't know how they'd failed but by now his madness had taken control, and he didn't really care. All he wanted to do was kill Deacon.

Balancing his torch on the fallen tree, he sat and waited.

Deacon moved slowly and carefully up through the trees. The disturbed air was stronger now - Lucas had passed within the previous ten to fifteen minutes. Suddenly, the tree line finished and he was on the edge of the clearing. Backing ten feet or so into the tree line, he put the horn to his lips again and blew.

The sudden loud blaring of the hunting horn so close to his hiding place made Lucas jump. He'd been keeping alert, hoping to see or hear something of Deacon's progress and the horn had startled him.

Closing his eyes to retain his night-vision, he clicked the torch on. Leaving it where it was he moved away into the trees before opening his eyes again, raising his pistol and slipping the safety catch off.

The glow of the torchlight would attract Deacon, and when he was illuminated, Lucas would be able to shoot him from his hiding place twenty foot away.

<><><>

Deacon saw the sudden brightness of the torch and heard Lucas move away towards the trees. Lucas wasn't noisy, but Deacon's senses were super-tuned and working flat-out, and even the tiniest of noises sounded loud tonight.

Very slowly skirting around the clearing, he stopped twice and felt the ground gently until he found a number of small broken branches just a few inches long. The smell of Lucas became stronger than ever as he closed to within ten feet of him.

Suddenly a new sound came to him. A gentle rustle of a bush here, a movement of some branches there. Then the smells came. Animal. Dog like. A couple of minutes later he heard a faint panting, and after very slowly and carefully moving his head slightly to peer around one of the trees, he could see the yellow eyes of a wolf looking back at him.

Slowly moving back so as not to startle the wolf, Deacon tossed one of the small branches overarm towards the light. It landed with a soft thud. A second one followed the first, and then the silence was split by the sound of four rapid gunshots.

Lucas surged forward towards the clearing and through the grey cloud of gun smoke, expecting to see Deacon mortally wounded or dead. Instead, he found nothing. Backlit now by the loom of his own torch he was suddenly hit by a flying branch as the voice of Deacon shouted, "Over here, asshole." Turning quickly, he fired two more shots that thudded harmlessly into the trees.

Moving back into hiding Lucas was beginning to panic. The hunting horn sounded again, so close and so loud. Nervously, he fired two more shots towards its sound and retreated further.

The bush to his side moved slightly and he turned and fired. Hearing a gasp and a groan, he fired again and again, the second pull of the trigger producing just a dull click.

"And that," Deacon said, walking into view from his right "makes ten shots fired."

Before he had a chance to release the magazine and insert a spare, Deacon was on him. Leaping at Lucas and screaming into his face had the desired effect of momentarily shocking him which was enough time for

Deacon to grasp the weapon in his hand, twist it until Lucas released it and toss it away.

Moving back a couple of feet, Deacon said, "That's better. Now we can talk. Who's your mole that found out about me?"

In answer, Lucas slid his hand towards his side and came out with a razor-sharp hunting knife.

Deacon casually sidestepped the knife lunge, grasped Lucas's outstretched right arm in his left hand and karate chopped hard down onto the elbow joint. Pushing Lucas away, Deacon bent and picked up the knife. He grabbed the front of Lucas's jacket, spun him around and pressed the sharp blade up against Lucas's throat, the sharpened edge of the blade already leaving a thin red line where it touched.

"Second chance. The mole?"

"Fuck you, Deacon. I am the General, and I answer to no one," he hissed, spittle forming at the corners of his mouth.

Punching him once hard in the mouth caused a number of his fine white teeth to be expelled. Smiling, Deacon said, "Fine, have it your way," before dragging Lucas over to the fallen tree.

Dragging Lucas up over the trunk, Deacon transferred the knife from his left to his right hand, raised it slightly and looked Lucas in the eyes. Suddenly, he thrust it down with all the force he could muster. The blade tip burst through the laces of Lucas's right boot before slicing open the skin and splitting apart the intermediate and lateral cuneiform bones of Lucas's right foot. The blade continued down through the muscles and membranes before penetrating through the toughened rubber sole of his walking boot and burying the first four inches of the blade into the solid wood of the fallen Western Larch.

Deacon stood back and waited for his screams to die down. Then he turned and said, "That's for Rachel. See you in hell."

Through tear-streaked eyes, Lucas gasped, "You can't leave me here all alone."

As he moved away, Deacon said, "You're not alone, pal. Look around!" pointing to the yellow eyes of wolves coming slowly through the trees towards them.

As he walked towards the compound he knew his father was right - he'd had to cross the line, but he knew when to cross back.

Chapter 53

On New Year's Eve, Laura Williams was the happiest she'd been in a long time. All summer she'd milked the publicity of her and her friends' kidnapping. She'd found fame and had a huge Facebook following, especially after the highly publicized court case.

She found plenty of new friends, both male and female, and loved being the center of attention.

Recently she'd met a new guy. He seemed nice, and they spent many evenings together coming up to Christmas. He drove a big, old Chevy Impala. Now on New Year's Eve he'd said they were going to a party.

She was all dressed up and raring to go. She'd even decided tonight could be 'the night'.

He'd picked her up on time, and they were heading out towards the countryside.

"Where are we going, honey?" she asked.

"Not too far. Just gonna pick up a couple of friends on the way. OK?"

"Oh, I s'pose," she said, rather disappointedly.

As he cruised down one of the less affluent roads, he suddenly pulled over and three male friends climbed into the car.

As he pulled away one of them turned to Laura, grabbed her by the hair and said, "So you're the bitch that likes to fuck A-rabs."

Chapter 54

Three weeks later, with Christmas and the New Year celebrations out of the way, Rachel Sanchez was buried with full honors. Her family and friends, Deacon's family and friends, Mitch and his wife Helen, and Admiral Carter, FBI Director Simon Clark and Secretary Harold Morgan were in attendance.

After the ceremony, Simon Clark and Mitch pulled Deacon aside.

"We've found the mole, or should I say Melissa Rogers found the mole. She is a distant cousin of Fuller Simpson. She was in our IT department in Dallas. She's been there for years. She passed all security and background checks. But her knowledge and position allowed her cross-departmental access into other databases way beyond her pay grade. She was also able to cover her tracks. What do you do when you have an IT security breach concern? You go to IT to investigate. She was in the perfect position to cover her ass. Anything she did she could cover up afterward. It's made us rethink our entire security set-up. Anyway, thanks to Melissa she's under arrest now. I'm just sorry she caused the deaths of two agents and Rachel," he said.

"We've also started finding bodies," he continued. "I've had a team there searching the forest with cadaver dogs and ground penetrating radar. The bodies of both agents have been discovered along with almost a dozen more. There is also the bodies of an older couple. Both had been shot close range in the back of the head. We're waiting on final DNA but from personal items left in your cabin, especially a toothbrush, I'm sorry, but we believe we have a familial match between this couple and your Terri-Anne Miles."

Admiral Carter and Harold Morgan joined them.

"Mitch, one thing that isn't clear to me," the Admiral said, "is how you found out the rough coordinates of where Deacon and his colleagues were going to attack the pipeline?"

"John called me three days before with a very brief message to meet up. He didn't know where exactly but knew the approximate area and said he'd get the details to me. I headed over and stayed local and the evening before I got a call from a young lady bar server with a brief message and a time. I had trouble making the last part of the journey due to the weather, but I was sitting in the Blue Skies Diner when John came in. We never acknowledged each other but I was sitting behind him, and he talked and passed me details before his colleagues came looking for him. That way, even if John couldn't get further details to me we had the rough coordinates to begin watching," Mitch said.

Then the Admiral turned back to Deacon and handed over an envelope.

"Lieutenant-Commander. I have here the signed order from the outgoing President to fully re-instate you back into SEAL Company Three, with your confirmed promotion to Lieutenant Commander, effective immediately, and with your court-martial wiped clean."

Saluting the Admiral, Deacon said, "Thank you, sir."

"Or," the Admiral said.

"Or what, sir?"

"Lieutenant Commander. The President-Elect has been made aware of everything you've done for this country over the past ten years. Not only are both the current President and President-Elect incredibly grateful for everything you've done, they're immensely proud of all their the armed services. However, there are times when it is useful for a President to have certain delicate problems resolved 'off-the-books' as they say, while being able to deny all knowledge. Something like that needs a small team of dedicated people ... and ..."

"And?" Deacon said after an embarrassing few seconds of silence.

"And, how do you fancy working directly for the President?"

Epilogue

In a small footnote published in the Los Angeles Times, it referred to a missing person.

'On New Year's Eve, Laura Williams, recently released from captivity in Iraq disappeared. Laura Williams, along with her sister, Michelle, and three friends, Cheryl Thomson, Emily Baker, and Debbie Morgan had been kidnapped by ISIS in Iraq in the summer of 2016 whilst providing humanitarian aid and support with the International Aid Committee and Rescue Charity, IACRC She was last seen standing on the corner of Lambeth and Stanton, waiting for a friend to pick her up on the evening of 31st December. Her parents Christine and Ronald Williams are distraught. Anybody with information should contact Detective Josh Butterman at the Santa Monica Police Department'.

Fact File

❖ The USA has the largest numbers of White Nationalist groups that advocate a racial definition of national identity for white people. These groups range in size from small to large and vary in their levels of extremism. Many cite violence as the only way forward.

❖ The Keystone Pipeline is 2,151 miles long and runs from Alberta, Canada, to Oklahoma. It pumps 590,000 barrels, or approximately 23 million gallons of crude oil daily from Canada to the USA. In November 2017, it was temporarily closed after leaking over 210,000 gallons of oil in South Dakota.

❖ The fishing vessel Gaul was a deep sea factory ship based in Hull, United Kingdom. She was built in 1972. She sank sometime on the night of 8-9 February 1974 in storm conditions in the Barents Sea, north of Norway. No distress signal was received and her loss was not realized until 10 February after she twice failed to report in. An extensive search operation was launched but no trace of the ship was found, apart from a lifebuoy recovered three months later. All thirty-six crew were lost.

The official explanation for the loss of the vessel was that the Gaul was capsized by a succession of huge waves and sank before the crew was able to issue a distress call. However, as the Gaul was modern (less than eighteen months old) and specifically designed to operate in the harsh waters of the Barents Sea, many people were skeptical of the official version of events. In the weeks and months after the loss of the Gaul, conspiracy theories – fueled by the fact this happened at the height of the Cold War – began to emerge. This was aided by the UK Government's reluctance to extend the search for her. Although the wreck has since been found, no conclusive explanation of her sinking has been released.

About the Author

I am the author of the John Deacon series of action adventure novels. I make my online home at www.mikeboshier.com. You can connect with me on Twitter at Twitter, on Facebook at Facebook and you can send me an email at mike@mikeboshier.com if the mood strikes you.

Currently living in New Zealand, the books I enjoy reading are from great authors such as Andy McNab, David Baldacci, Brad Thor, Vince Flynn, Chris Ryan, etc. to name just a few. I've tried to write my books in a similar style. If you like adventure/thriller novels, and you like the same authors as I do, then I hope you find mine do them justice.

If you liked reading this book, please leave feedback on whatever system you purchased this from.

www.mikeboshier.com

Books & Further Details

The Jaws of Revenge

The fate of America lies in the hands of one team of US SEALs. The US mainland is under threat as never before. Osama bin Laden is dead, and the world can relax. Or can they? Remaining leaders of Al-Qaeda want revenge, and they want it against the USA. When good fortune smiles on them and the opportunity presents itself to use stolen weapons of mass destruction, it's Game On!

Al-Qaeda leaders devise a plan so audacious if it succeeds it will destroy the USA for good. With help from Iran and from a US Navy traitor, it can't fail.

One team of US SEALs stand in their way. One team of US SEALs can save America and the West. However, time is running out. **Will they be too late?**

High Seas Hijack - Short Story

Follow newly promoted US Navy SEAL John Deacon as he leads his team on preventing pirates attacking and seizing ships in and around the Horn of Africa in 2010. When a tanker carrying explosive gases is hijacked even Deacon and his team are pushed to the limit.

Terror of the Innocent

As the Iraqi Forces build up for the liberation of Mosul, ISIS wants revenge.

The UK and USA are in their sights ...

In a daring rescue mission to release aid workers held hostage by ISIS, US Navy SEAL John Deacon stumbles across an ISIS revenge plot using deadly weapons stolen from Saddam's regime.

Masterminded by Deacon's old adversary, Saif the Palestinian, and too late to save the UK, Deacon and the world can only watch in horror as thousands suffer a terrible fate.

Determined to stop the same outcome in the US, it's a race against time.

Using all the resources he can muster including his friends in the Pentagon, Deacon must find and stop Saif before the lives of hundreds of thousands of Americans are ruined forever.

Check out my web page http://www.mikeboshier.com for details of latest books, offers and free stuff.

VIP Reader's Mailing List

To join our VIP Readers Mailing List and receive updates about new books and freebies, please go to my web page and join my mailing list.

www.mikeboshier.com

I value your trust. Your email address will stay safe and you will never receive spam from me. You can unsubscribe at any time.

Thank you.

Printed in Poland
by Amazon Fulfillment
Poland Sp. z o.o., Wrocław